"HOW CAN YOU DO THIS TO ME?"

Tess hesitated by the door to the Arctic Fancy Room. Never before had she heard Fern raise her voice. Fern was always so controlled. But at the moment she sounded almost unhinged, certainly frantic.

"You know I can't do that!" Fern cried. "No! It's out of the question!" Hearing no response to what Fern was saying, Tess deduced that she was on the telephone. She raised her hand to knock, then froze. Fern would be mortified if she knew Tess overheard her end of the conversation.

"What do you imagine that will gain you?" Fern was demanding. She had dropped her voice and now spoke slowly. But there was something about her tone that was almost too calm when she spoke again.

"I'm listening." There was a pause, and then, "Now you listen to me. I'll kill you before I let you do that."

The threat was issued in a deadly quiet voice. And that made it more frightening than if she had shouted it . . .

Blooming
MURDER

JEAN HAGER

*To Sharon
Best wishes,
Jean Hager*

AVON BOOKS ◆ NEW YORK

BLOOMING MURDER is an original publication of Avon Books. This work has never before appeared in book form. This work is a novel. Any similarity to actual persons or events is purely coincidental.

AVON BOOKS
A division of
The Hearst Corporation
1350 Avenue of the Americas
New York, New York 10019

Copyright © 1994 by Jean Hager
Published by arrangement with the author
Library of Congress Catalog Card Number: 93–90640
ISBN: 0–380–77209–4

First Avon Books Printing: June 1994

AVON TRADEMARK REG. U.S. PAT. OFF. AND IN OTHER COUNTRIES, MARCA REGISTRADA, HECHO EN CANADA

Printed in Canada

UNV 10 9 8 7 6 5 4 3 2

Author's Note

I am indebted to C. T. Thompson, M.D., and Richard A. Marshall, M.D., who shared their knowledge of potentially fatal genetic conditions, particularly those that met the requirements of my story.

I am additionally grateful to Jerry Rendon and Jim Rendon who spent several hours creating the blueprints for Iris House based on my specifications.

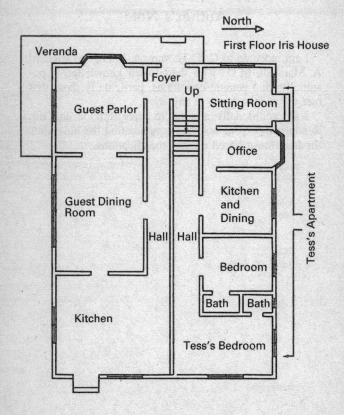

North →

First Floor Iris House

Veranda

Foyer

Up

Sitting Room

Guest Parlor

Office

Guest Dining
Room

Kitchen
and
Dining

Hall | Hall

Bedroom

Bath | Bath

Kitchen

Tess's Bedroom

Tess's Apartment

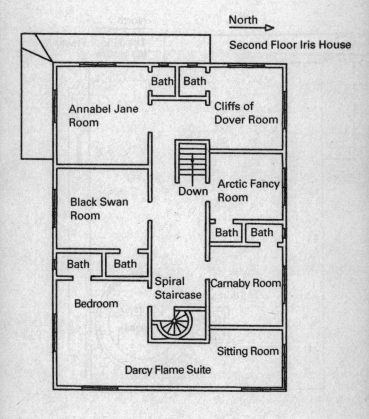

North →

Second Floor Iris House

Bath | Bath

Annabel Jane Room

Cliffs of Dover Room

Down

Arctic Fancy Room

Black Swan Room

Bath | Bath

Bath | Bath

Spiral Staircase

Carnaby Room

Bedroom

Sitting Room

Darcy Flame Suite

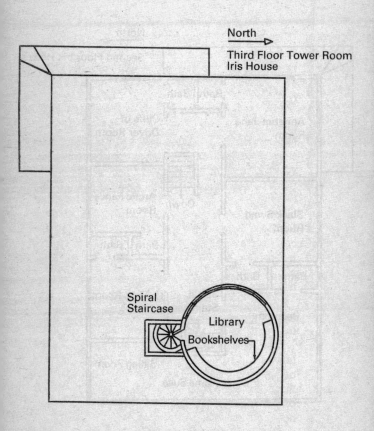

North

Third Floor Tower Room
Iris House

Spiral
Staircase

Library

Bookshelves

Chapter 1

A click as soft as a whisper broke the silence of the April night. Tess Darcy awoke abruptly, aware that a sound had roused her from the deep sleep of exhaustion.

She stared at the moonlight-washed wall opposite her brass bed, trying to get her bearings. Perhaps Primrose was having a restless night. She slid out of bed quietly, padded to the door, and switched on the hall light. No sign of the cat.

She moved down the hall and peered into the dim sitting room. The gray Persian was curled in her favorite chair, which featured a Renaissance Revival design with a medallion on top and a comfortably padded seat. Tess had given up trying to keep her out of it. At the moment, Primrose was dead to the world. Tess hesitated. What had awakened her?

Puzzled, she glanced at her watch, which read one-ten, and retraced her steps, turning off the hall light as she passed the switch.

She had grown accustomed to being in the house alone at night, so possibly she'd heard one of her guests moving about upstairs. All seven of them had checked in last evening for tomorrow's official opening day of Iris House, Tess's brand-new bed and breakfast.

She crawled back into bed, hoping she could fall asleep again quickly. She needed to be rested for what was certain to be a hectic day.

As she sighed and drew the bed sheet over her,

she caught the movement of a shadow on the moonlit wall of her bedroom. Alarmed, Tess shot to a sitting position. Was that a tree branch? But there was no wind, and besides, it didn't look like a branch.

As Tess stared, the ghostly figure of a woman in a long, flowing garment floated across the wall in the drenching moonlight. Whoever was casting the shadow was outside, behind the house.

Tess threw back the sheet, crept to a window, and drew aside the sheer curtain. A pale-clad form flitted across the yard away from the house. Light from a full moon turned the woman's gown and blonde hair a spectral white.

As Tess watched, the figure paused at the tall hedge which separated Tess's property from the adjoining backyard. Then, before Tess's eyes, the woman disappeared. She blinked and pressed closer to the window before it occurred to her that the woman had found an opening in the hedge wide enough to squeeze through. The hedge at that point hid a gate in the white wrought-iron fence that enclosed the back and side yards of Iris House.

Tess continued watching for several long minutes, but the woman did not reappear. Now that she was gone, Tess could almost believe she'd dreamed it. But no, she was wide awake and she didn't believe in ghosts.

The woman could only have come from Iris House. The sound that had awakened Tess must have been the back door closing. Furthermore, only one of Tess's guests had blonde hair. What on earth was Lana Morrison doing wandering around outside in the middle of the night in her nightgown?

Tess watched for a few minutes longer, chewing her bottom lip as she wondered what to do. If anything. Finally, she convinced herself it wasn't really any of her business if a guest wanted to take a stroll at one A.M.

In the end, she went back to bed. Still troubled by what she'd seen, however, she lay there for some time before she began to feel drowsy. Then, as she was about to drop off, a troublesome thought intruded. What if Lana was sleepwalking? She could have locked herself out of the house. She could even fall into a ditch or walk in front of a car.

Tess got up again and hastily put on her robe and house slippers, worried and castigating herself for waiting until now. She should have checked on Lana immediately. If something terrible happened to her, Tess would never forgive herself.

After turning on the hall light once more, she let herself out of her apartment, switched on the foyer light, and crossed the tile floor. Stepping into the dim parlor, she came face-to-face with Lana Morrison.

Lana yelped. "Good grief, Tess! You scared the living daylights out of me!"

Tess gasped and pressed a palm to her pounding heart. "I'm sorry. I thought someone was outside."

"You must have been dreaming, Tess. Or you heard me in the kitchen." Lana's wide-eyed look was guileless.

"Is your room too warm? Maybe I should turn on the air-conditioning."

Lana shook her head. "No, no. The temperature's fine. I couldn't sleep for thinking about the conference tomorrow. Nerves, I guess. I'm conducting a morning session."

"Oh."

Lana could conduct a gardening session off the top of her head. Why was she lying?

"And I was hungry," Lana went on. "I robbed your cookie jar. I hope you don't mind."

"Of course not."

"Good night, then." Lana swept past Tess, gauzy white negligee and platinum hair whirling, and mounted the stairs. Tess watched her with knitted brow until Lana melted into the shadows on the second-floor landing.

Something was going on but, for the life of her, Tess couldn't figure out what.

Chapter 2

Alexis Dinwitty spun slowly on one spike heel before the rose-etched vanity mirror in the Darcy Flame Suite. She was pleased with her image. Tickled pink, in fact. Admittedly, she was plump, always had been, but she had learned to emphasize her assets—slender ankles, a flawless ivory complexion, and thick blue-black hair. At fifty, one expected to find a few gray strands among the black, but a tint every four weeks took care of that.

She wore her crowning glory swept back from her smooth face and firm chin (the skillful handiwork of a St. Louis plastic surgeon) and done up behind in an intricate French knot. She had worn it that way for twenty-five years, since the day her husband told her it made her look exotic, "like a Japanese emperor's favorite geisha." In his younger days, Harley had been given to extravagant turns of phrase. That particular one had delighted Alexis so much that she had gone out and bought an Oriental-style dressing gown, a red satin kimono with a gold dragon undulating down one side. It had been unconscionably expensive, but Harley could afford it. All of her dressing gowns since that first one had had an Oriental flavor, each more expensive than the last. The current one, which was hanging in the closet of the Darcy Flame Suite, was emerald-green, lavishly spangled with fine gold braid and seed pearls.

This morning, however, there was nothing of the East in her attire, a turquoise silk dress with a full skirt, fitted waist, and a big organza collar that lay in soft ruffles on her magnificent bosom. The vamps of her black patent leather shoes had turquoise insets and the heels were three-inch spikes, which called attention to her trim ankles. Two-carat diamond teardrops glittered at her ears, a four-carat pendant nestled in the hollow of her throat. Not bad for a snot-nosed kid yanked up by the hair of her head in a tacky trailer park on the wrong side of Wichita, Kansas.

She frowned a little. Were the diamonds overdoing it a bit? Gauche, even? But no. As president of the Victoria Springs Garden Club, she would deliver the welcoming address at this morning's opening session of the Four-State Iris Growers Conference. She hummed a few bars of "Oh, What a Beautiful Mornin'," as she imagined herself standing at the podium in the Hilltop Hotel's ballroom, the focus of more than four hundred pairs of eyes, seventy-five percent of them envious female eyes. The reflected light from the chandeliers would flash, flamelike, from the diamonds with her every movement.

Whooeee! Wouldn't she dazzle the bloomers off those tight-assed old dames in their orthopedic shoes? Oh, this conference was going to be such fun!

She laughed in sheer delight and, turning from the vanity, she moved to the sitting room of the suite, which was separated from the sleeping alcove by a beautiful Chinese folding screen, coral and blue lilies hand-painted on black lacquered panels. She settled into a Victorian slipper chair and picked up the text of her speech. She already knew it by heart, but it wouldn't hurt to go over it one more time.

After she'd done that, she tucked the speech in a side pocket of her patent leather bag. With a deep sigh of satisfaction, she let her gaze sweep the suite—the Darcy Flame Suite, named for the bright-coral hybrid iris bred by old Iris Darcy herself ten years ago. The Darcy Flame had made quite a splash among iris lovers

at the time. It had won the blue ribbon in every show
in which it was entered that year.

A gilt-framed oil painting of the Darcy Flame hung
on the wall next to one of the suite's swag-draped windows. The pattern of the drapery fabric and the bed
canopy was a seemingly haphazard scattering of bright-
coral roses, the exact color of the Darcy Flame iris,
against an ivory background. The sofa was covered in
a quilted coral fabric, the two slipper chairs in ivory
ribbed in coral. The sofa and chairs were arranged on
either side of a low glass-topped table with heavy brass
legs in the shape of giant S's.

It was the only suite in Iris House and Alexis had
commandeered it for herself, as befitted the president of
the Garden Club, one of Victoria Springs's oldest and
most exclusive organizations. One simply had not arrived in Victoria Springs until one had received an engraved invitation to membership in The Club. That's
how people in Victoria Springs referred to it—The
Club—as if there could be no other.

Actually, it had been Lana Morrison's idea that the
officers of The Club stay at the bed and breakfast during the conference, rather than the hotel. "Much more
private and so cozy," Lana had said. And it would give
dear Tess Darcy's new bed and breakfast a fine send-
off, once word got around that the officers of The Club
had booked every room for Iris House's grand opening.

Alexis had instantly claimed the idea as her own and
reserved the suite before one of the other officers beat
her to it. Fortunately, Lana hadn't seemed to mind
Alexis's taking the credit. Lately, Lana had gone out of
her way to befriend Alexis. Occasionally, Alexis wondered what Lana was up to. Usually she banished that
nagging little doubt from her mind by concluding that
Lana, who'd gone through her third divorce last year,
was merely lonely. The poor creature certainly did have
trouble with her men.

At any rate, Alexis didn't want negative thoughts to

mar her pleasure in having been cunning enough to ensconce herself in the Darcy Flame Suite. It was her way of making a statement, which she was certain had not escaped the other officers.

All the rooms in Iris House were quite lovely and of generous proportions, but the suite was twice the size of the other guest accommodations. And cost twice as much. Tess Darcy's prices were at the top of the range for Victoria Springs's bed-and-breakfast establishments, but Alexis was sure Tess would have no trouble filling elegant Iris House for the entire tourist season, from mid-April to mid-December.

In Alexis's case, price had been no object. After all, she deserved the best. Lord knew, she'd earned it.

Alexis had spent her high-school years observing the girls from wealthy families. She copied their hairstyles and makeup. She learned to talk like them and walk like them. By the time she graduated and took a secretarial job, she had acquired an eye for clothes with style and flair. One good dress was far better than ten cheap ones, she'd learned. At eighteen, she had changed her name from Alice Mae to Alexis and made up her mind to marry a wealthy man. At twenty-three, she had achieved her goal.

When she married Harley, he'd just rung up his first million as the owner of a discount department store. In the twenty-seven years since, the store had become a corporate chain and had gone public. Harley was now the richest man in six states.

Unlike Victoria Springs's old-money crowd, Alexis saw no reason not to flaunt wealth if you were fortunate enough to have it. Maybe that was why people like the late Iris Darcy took one look at her and knew what kind of background she had sprung from. The snooty old bitch hadn't wanted Alexis admitted to the Garden Club, but Alexis had gotten around people like Iris Darcy before. She had ingratiated herself with the other members and Iris had been outvoted.

A smug smile curved Alexis's hot-pink lips. In whatever realm of the afterlife Iris now resided, Alexis fervently hoped she was aware that little old Alice Mae Murphy from Wichita, Kansas, had beat out Iris's handpicked successor to The Club's presidency.

Struck by an even more delicious thought, Alexis giggled and hugged herself. Iris Darcy had more than one reason to be spinning in her grave. It was a sure bet it had never entered that old spinster's mind, while she was among the living, that the niece to whom she'd willed the Darcy family home would have the poor taste to turn it into a tourist trap.

God, how the old bat used to go on about the Darcy family and its grand traditions, as though they were royalty. Which, Alexis supposed, they were, in the view of most of Victoria Springs's few thousand permanent residents. The Darcys were the town's first family. Big fish in a very small pond. Iris and Dahlia's grandfather had been among the town's original settlers. In fact, he'd named the settlement for his mother, been elected the first mayor, and built this big, Victorian-style house, one of the first residences in what, in the early days, had passed for Victoria Springs's Nob Hill.

Now, Tess Darcy was renting out the upstairs bedrooms. Grandpa Darcy had lived and died before the era of fashionable bed-and-breakfast establishments. Fancy as it was, he would consider this a common boardinghouse.

Doubtless, so would Iris. What a comedown! Or comeuppance, depending on your point of view.

"Iris, old gal," Alexis said aloud, "the times they are a-changin'."

Laughter bubbled up in her throat. She smothered it in a lace-edged throw pillow. Lordy, Lordy, when you thought about the situation from what would surely have been Iris Darcy's viewpoint, it was hysterically funny.

Chapter 3

Reva Isley awoke to the sound of the shower going full blast. A deep bass voice issued from the bathroom, bellowing—one couldn't by any stretch of generosity call it singing—a country western ballad, off-key:

> "Those barroom beauties,
> those wild, painted women.
> They'll make you crazy,
> they'll drive you insane . . ."

Reva groaned and pulled a pillow over her head, succeeding only fractionally in muffling the caterwauling. She muttered an oath and threw the pillow on the floor. Swinging her legs over the side of the bed, she sat up. Didn't Randall know she was asleep? Stupid question. Of course he knew, if he'd bothered to think of her at all. Which he hadn't done in twenty years, so why should he start now? Other people's comfort, least of all his wife's, did not figure largely in her husband's universe.

> "They'll tease and they'll taunt you,
> And act like they want you . . ."

Reva peered at the pristine white ceiling, replete with carving and crown moldings. *God in heaven, strike him dumb.* The braying continued.

9

Either God had a tin ear, or He was busy elsewhere.

A shaft of bright sunlight from the window next to the bed struck her face, making her suddenly aware of the faint ache behind her eyes. She got up and adjusted the blind. She *wouldn't* have a headache on the first day of the conference. Damned if she would let Randall spoil it for her.

She padded across the room to the white wicker dresser and rummaged in her purse for the aspirin tin. Then she stepped into the steam-filled bathroom for a glass of water and swallowed three tablets.

> *"So kiss 'em and squeeze 'em
> and take 'em to dine,
> But don't expect nothin'
> but a roarin' good time."*

Hastily, Reva closed the bathroom door and pulled on her robe. With a resigned sigh, she stretched out on the wicker chaise and waited for Randall to finish in the bathroom.

Leaning against a lacy white pillow, she surveyed the Annabel Jane Room, their accommodations for the next five days at Iris House Bed and Breakfast. A framed watercolor of the ruffled lavender iris, for which the room was named, hung over the delicately scrolled white-and-brass iron bed, setting the tone for the room's color scheme.

The chaise was upholstered in lavender and spring-green floral chintz, the same fabric used in the puffy quilted coverlet. The wallpaper was striped in lavender and white, and the carpet was a soothing gray with the barest hint of a lavender undertone. Antique lace adorned the bed's dust ruffle, the shade of the porcelain lamp on the bedside table, and numerous throw pillows. Wicker baskets overflowing with greenery filled two corners, another hung suspended on a brass hook over the lace-curtained window.

It was a graceful, lighthearted room and Reva had anticipated a relaxing few days there—alone—when she wasn't attending sessions of the Four-State Iris Growers Conference at the Hilltop Hotel a block away. She'd looked forward to it for months. Until Randall had announced, out of the blue, that he believed he'd join her at Iris House.

She had tried to talk him out of it, the dutiful wife concerned for her husband's well-being, the only sort of appeal Randall understood. She would welcome his company, of course, but he'd be utterly bored with the talk of irises and mulching and watering and the mundane business of the Victoria Springs Garden Club, of which Reva was the program chairperson. Her subtly worded arguments had fallen on deaf ears.

She bitterly resented Randall's imposing his loud, uncouth presence into the one area that had always been hers alone, her Garden Club activities. With his usual obliviousness to her feelings, he hadn't noticed.

It wasn't as if she had wanted to loll away five days in some posh out-of-town resort. The Isley house, with its well-stocked larder and freezer, was only six blocks from the bed and breakfast.

Amazingly, Randall, who wouldn't notice a whole houseful of new furniture unless he fell over it and broke both legs, had professed an unquenchable curiosity over what Tess Darcy had done with old Iris Darcy's house. He didn't want to be a bother, naturally, so Reva was not to worry her fussy little head about him. He'd spend the days from ten until five, as usual, at the Isley Previously Driven Automobile Emporium. After hours, when Reva was busy with conference activities, he'd occupy himself somehow. Reva must go on to her meetings and not spare a thought for him. (This had been delivered with a brave smile.)

Then he'd rubbed his big hands together with an air of making the best of an inconvenient situation. Come to think of it, he'd said, he couldn't wait to tuck into

Gertie Bogart's breakfasts. Gertie had cooked for Miss
Iris and had returned to take charge of the remodeled
kitchen for Tess Darcy when the old Darcy family
home had been converted to a bed and breakfast.

Randall's expressed desire to sample Gertie's breakfasts was another spur-of-the moment lie. Reva was
no slouch in the kitchen herself, and Randall was no
gourmet, usually bolting his food, giving himself hardly
enough time to notice the taste. It was true, however,
that Gertie Bogart was generally conceded to be the
best cook in Victoria Springs, Missouri. Obtaining her
services had been something of a coup for Tess Darcy
who was, in spite of her family connections, a stranger
in town.

"Reva, sugar," Randall had drawled, tweaking her
cheek, "it'll be like a second honeymoon." At which
point Reva had cringed, remembering their first—three
days and nights in a frigid cabin with a frozen water
pump and an outhouse two hundred yards straight up
the side of a mountain. Three eternal days and nights
during which she had, at last, come to realize that her
father had been right all along. She had married far beneath herself. But that was water under the bridge.

It was Randall's current behavior that infuriated her.
All in all, Reva had never seen such a performance in
her life as Randall's. But dammit, she could act, too. In
response to his mention of a second honeymoon, she'd
said, "Why, Randall, darling, how sweet of you," while
she had boiled inside.

Reva Isley had been born forty-three years ago come
June—not yesterday. She knew full well that Randall's
presence at Iris House had nothing at all to do with the
house, or Gertie Bogart's cooking, or his wife's company. What it had to do with was that bleached-blonde
slut, Lana Morrison.

Chapter 4

Chester Leeds, The Club's vice president, had been up for hours. By seven A.M., he'd already showered, shaved, and dressed in a gray three-piece suit, one of four identical suits, the other three of which were perfectly aligned in his large closet back home in another Victorian-style house three doors south of the bed and breakfast. His closet at home also contained three identical black suits—the fourth he'd brought with him to Iris House—and four identical brown ones. All of Chester's suits were specially made for him by a Kansas City tailor in the conservative style and colors that befitted a bank president.

At seven-thirty, he'd walked to his own house to retrieve the *Wall Street Journal* from his front walk. He'd stepped inside only long enough to say hello to his mother, who was being served breakfast in bed by their maid. As expected, Mother had gone on eating her oatmeal and pretended not to hear him. Damn fool woman. Undaunted, he'd returned to the Black Swan Room in Iris House, detouring past the kitchen for a cup of coffee.

Having finished his coffee and read the *Journal* from front to back, he folded the newspaper neatly and laid it on the cane side table. He much preferred being in his own house, with his greenhouse and his books and other familiar comforts, even though it meant subjecting himself to his mother's childish piques.

13

After the conference, however, he could look forward
to a short period of peace and quiet, as Mother would
sulk for a week over his "desertion." She'd spent the
past two days trying to shame him out of "moving out,"
as she insisted upon calling it. What if she became ill
in the night? What if she had a heart attack and died?
"I'll stink," she had whined, "by the time you come
home and find my corpse."

I should be so lucky, Chester had thought as he
pointed out that she wasn't alone. The maid was there,
and he'd only be gone five days. Besides, he was convinced his mother would outlive him. Furthermore,
he'd had no choice but to move into Iris House for the
conference. Otherwise, people would think he was sulk-
ing over losing The Club's presidency to Alexis
Dinwitty. The back-stabbing floozy. To think he'd actually recommended her for membership. Not that he'd
had much choice in the matter. Harley Dinwitty was, by
far, the bank's biggest depositor.

Chester looked around and told himself that, if he
had to leave home, his present accommodations could
hardly be improved upon. Like all the rooms in Iris
House, the Black Swan Room's decor began with a
well-known iris. The Black Swan—the flower, not the
room—depicted in a miniature framed print on the wall
above the cane side table, was a tall-bearded variety,
reddish-black with a brown beard. A self, in the language of iris breeders, meaning it was a single color.

The massively scaled bed was lacquered in the same
reddish-black color as were the huge bureau and
marble-topped washstand. Attached to the wall above
the bed's headboard were two gooseneck reading lamps
with white fluted shades. The ruffled side draperies on
the windows and the paneling above the wainscotting
were white, too. Below the wainscotting the walls had
been papered with a bold black-and-white print.

An intricately patterned rug covered most of the pol-
ished oak floor, its black and gray tones relieved by

bright splashes of lemon-yellow. The room had been
rescued from dullness by other touches of yellow, in
throw pillows, bed linens, and the comfortable wing-
backed chair which swaddled Chester at the moment.

On the whole, the Black Swan Room had a fine,
manly look which, doubtless, was why Tess Darcy had
put Chester there. Unfortunately, he had arrived at the bed
and breakfast simultaneously with Lana Morrison, who
had glanced into his room on the way to her own.

"Isn't this nice, Chester?" she'd chirped with a snide
sideways glance at him. "So masculine." He'd wanted
to murder her.

In spite of a brief, youthful marriage, rumors circu-
lated periodically that he was gay. In less provincial
places such gossip would be met with bored yawns, but
among the social elite of Victoria Springs, any sexual
diversity was treated as scandalous, at least outside of
their bedrooms.

Chester had briefly suspected that the latest round of
rumors had been started by Alexis Dinwitty during her
campaign for The Club's presidency, a position that was
rightfully his. But once he'd calmed down, he'd realized that whispering sordid gossip wasn't Alexis's style.
She was the head-on type. It was more like that bloody
Lana Morrison. Lately Lana and Alexis had become
bosom pals. Lana had campaigned tirelessly for Alexis
prior to the Garden Club's recent election of officers.

Like Alexis, Lana had married money. Her third husband, a physician, had been worth several million and,
rumor had it, she'd left the marriage with a nice, fat settlement. With prudent investment guidance, the settlement would have provided comfortably for Lana the
rest of her days. But no one would ever call Lana prudent. She had no money sense, so the settlement
wouldn't last long. In fact, he'd heard talk recently that
Lana was already well-nigh penniless. Since Lana was
The Club's treasurer, he was keeping an eagle eye on
their checking account, which was deposited in his

bank. Lana wouldn't be above "borrowing" a few dollars in a pinch. Oh, God, he'd love to catch her at it.

Imagining Lana reduced to penny-pinching and embezzlement caused Chester's thin lips to quirk in a smug smile. As much as he despised Alexis, Chester could tolerate the woman's lack of class and nauseatingly conspicuous consumption of her husband's wealth. But he could hardly stand to be in the same room with Lana. He was convinced Lana Morrison had single-handedly cost him The Club presidency. In the process she had gained a lifelong enemy.

Lana Morrison was destined to learn that he was a force to reckon with. Sooner or later, he would have his revenge. Lana would rue the day she had spread her nasty lies about Chester Leeds.

In actual fact, Chester had no sexual interest in men, and not much in women. His sexual appetite was satisfied during the two or three "business" trips he took each year to Kansas City where he paid handsomely for services rendered. These encounters were silent and brief, furtive somehow, and he barely looked at the women. They meant nothing to him. His mother and the girl he'd married and divorced twenty-five years ago had scotched any interest he might have had in female companionship. Most women were parasites.

Now, pride was forcing him to spend five days in a house otherwise occupied by numerous females. Except for Randall Isley, with whom he had no intention of passing the time of day if he could avoid it.

Reva Simpson's long-ago marriage to Isley had shaken Victoria Springs to its foundations, for Isley would have been a disgrace to any respectable family. Reva's poor mother had gone into seclusion for two years after the elopement. Eventually, The Club's membership had gotten over their shock at Reva's unsuitable marriage and had taken her in, like her mother and grandmother before her. After a time, the Simpsons had resumed their relationship with their daughter, though it was still tense, and had learned to love Reva's two sons, who were now off at college. But Randall had never really been treated like a member of their family.

Chester suspected that Reva had long regretted the adolescent streak of rebellion that had caused her to marry Randall in the first place. She was simply too proud to admit it. Ah, well, Chester understood pride. But a used-car salesman. Really! Chester certainly could not envision engaging in friendly chats with Randall Isley during their sojourn at Iris House. Good God, what would they talk about? Not alternators and transmissions, for a start. Anything mechanical was Greek to Chester.

On the whole, Chester preferred his own company to that of most of the human race. Spending five days in close proximity to the other occupants of Iris House would be a severe trial.

Might as well make the best of it, though. Living with his mother had certainly taught him how to do that. He would occupy himself in studying Lana Morrison for chinks in her glossy armor. With a purposeful squaring of his narrow shoulders, he stood and prepared to go down to breakfast.

Chapter 5

Tess hurried down the bottle-green–carpeted hall to her office. Where *had* she put the day's schedule? She had been certain she'd left it on the kitchen table, but it wasn't there or in her bedroom. She would be lost without it. She chewed her bottom lip anxiously as she turned the corner into the office.

She noticed that she had failed to close the roll top on the oak desk. Primrose, the gray Persian she had inherited along with the house, was napping on it in a puddle of sunlight from the tall bay window. Spying a sheaf of papers beneath the cat, Tess picked her up. "Sorry, sweetie, but I think you're lying on my schedule."

Primrose blinked her yellow eyes and growled crossly as Tess deposited her on the padded window seat beneath the bay window. To further manifest her displeasure at having her nap interrupted, the cat twitched her fluffy tail, leaped down, and stalked out of the room.

Primrose had still not fully accepted the young upstart who had supplanted Aunt Iris in the house. During the renovation, she had spent the days hiding in closets, coming out at night, when the workmen were gone, to eat and demand with loud yowls to be let outside.

But Tess and the haughty Persian were making progress. In the past few weeks Primrose had finally deigned to acknowledge Tess's existence. She allowed Tess to brush her coat now. And last

18

evening, when a harried Tess had collapsed in a chair long enough for a cup of chamomile tea, Primrose had actually jumped into her lap. Still, she wasn't about to let Tess forget which of them was the interloper here.

Tess shuffled through the papers, which were still warm with Primrose's body heat, and found the elusive schedule. She must have carried it back from the kitchen last night, where she'd worked on it over dinner. After a long day of checking last-minute details for the opening, she'd been so exhausted she couldn't remember what she'd done before staggering off to bed. Then she'd been awakened in the middle of the night by Lana Morrison, who had looked Tess in the eye and lied through her teeth. Why? And where had Lana been going when Tess saw her in the backyard?

She shook the questions aside. She couldn't worry about Lana right now. She scanned the schedule, mentally checking off the important highlights. Gertie had begun serving breakfast at 8 A.M., ten minutes ago. The premiere breakfast in what Tess hoped would be the long and prosperous history of Iris House Bed and Breakfast.

At ten, or as soon as the last guest left the table, Tess and Gertie would begin arranging food on large silver trays in preparation for the first of three Victorian teas to be served that afternoon.

Tess glanced at the bed of irises beyond the bay window, hoping she could find time in her busy day for a walk through the garden to enjoy the glorious riot of color surrounding her. Beyond the window, the giant rust-wine blooms of tall bearded Infernos filled the center of an oval bed. They were surrounded by clumps of shorter Dreaming Yellow Siberian irises the color of rich cream. Tess congratulated herself on recalling the two varieties. She was still working on learning all the names of the dozens of different varieties her aunt had cultivated.

The lacy white wrought-iron settee beside the iris

bed looked so inviting that she longed to toss the schedule aside, go out, and spend ten minutes in the settee, admiring her house and garden and watching the red birds cavort in the nearby birdbath. But alas, she wouldn't be able to relax.

Reluctantly, she stopped woolgathering and returned her attention to her schedule. At one P.M., the first group would arrive to tour the garden, ending with tea served in the gazebo. The second tour group was due at 2:30, the third at 4:00.

Tess would be running all afternoon, helping Gertie replenish trays and carrying food from the kitchen to the gazebo and leftovers from the gazebo to the kitchen between tour groups. All on her opening day.

Oh, dear. She must have been mad to let The Club talk her into putting the iris garden on their annual garden tour. Fortunately, Aunt Dahlia was coming to act as tour guide, but it was the least she could do. It had been Dahlia who'd insisted that Tess must continue with Iris's teas in the gazebo during the garden tour. Traditions were *so* important, didn't Tess agree? The tea was always the highlight of the tour, Dahlia had stressed, and as a nice bonus for Tess, a great number of tourists would be introduced to Victoria Springs's exquisite new bed and breakfast. Why, by the time they left, they'd be planning another trip, dying to stay at Iris House.

That conversation had taken place three months ago, when a Victorian tea had sounded quite wonderful. At that point, Tess had been so pleased with the renovations being made to the house that she'd felt capable of anything. Three months later, she was still wildly in love with the house, but after the last two weeks spent dealing with a million glitches in her well-thought-out plans, Tess barely felt capable of sleepwalking through her opening day.

The telephone on the desk jangled as she tucked the schedule into the pocket of her navy cotton skirt. She jumped and glared at the old-fashioned ivory phone as though it had suddenly sprouted legs and was hunkering down into attack position. She took a deep breath. She'd better get a handle on her jitters, or she'd never make it through the day.

The phone pealed again as she reached for the receiver. "Iris House Bed and Breakfast."

A deep male voice greeted her cheerily, "Good morning, Tess. I see you survived to enjoy your opening."

"Oh, Luke." She hadn't meant to sound so desperate, but he had caught her in a weak moment. "Barely, and I wouldn't say 'enjoy' is precisely the right word."

She and Luke Fredrik had seen quite a lot of each other the past two months. When she moved to Victoria Springs from Atlanta, she had been determined to wait at least a year before even thinking about men; she would have more than enough on her plate, renovating the house and getting the bed and breakfast off the ground, without that distraction. An eminently sensible plan, the only problem being that she had never expected to meet anyone like Luke in Victoria Springs. Merely hearing his voice caused a little flutter in the pit of her stomach.

They had met under less than ideal circumstances. As chairman of the board of the Chamber of Commerce, he'd dropped by to welcome her to town and offer the chamber's services if she should need them in her new business venture. Her auburn curls a tangle, she'd been grimy and bedraggled from stripping layers of varnish from the golden-oak rolltop desk that had come with the house. She'd tripped over a roll of old carpet as she ran to answer the doorbell and was barely able to keep from sprawling. Blowing a copper curl out of her eyes, she'd thrown open the door to find a dashingly handsome blond man lounging against the door frame. He looked like a young Viking explorer in a business suit, or what she imagined those romantic adventurers must have looked like.

Mortified, she had stammered thanks for his thought-fulness and watched him stroll off down the street, whistling. He should have phoned first, she'd told her-self; it was just as well that she wasn't looking for a man at the moment. Luke Fredrik would certainly not have the slightest interest in a drudge smelling of var-nish remover with streaks of brown wood stain on her face. To her amazement, she had been wrong. Luke's attentions had sent her sensible vow to remain unat-tached flying out the window. When Luke was around she had to work at concentrating on anything else.

But this was no time to take that mental byroad. "Thanks for calling to wish me well, Luke, but I don't have time to talk now."

"You sound as though you've already had a catastro-phe."

"Bite your tongue. Fortunately, things are going smoothly so far, but I don't know how I'll get every-thing done today. Why did I let Aunt Dahlia bulldoze me into serving tea?"

"You're panicking, Tess," he drawled in that deep, lazy tone that sent a shiver up her spine. "Take a few deep breaths and calm down."

Had Luke ever been uptight over anything in his life? How could he always be so sensible? Well, for one thing, he'd never had to worry about money. A few months after graduating from Columbia, where he'd studied finance, his father had died and left him a large portfolio of stocks and bonds. Under Luke's superin-tendence, the portfolio's value had multiplied several times over. He had an instinct for when to be in a par-ticular market and when to get out with his profits in-tact. He managed his investments, as well as those of a few, carefully selected clients, from an office in his home where he was linked by computer, modem, and fax machine to Wall Street.

"Some of my guests are already at breakfast," Tess said, "and I haven't even left my quarters. I should have been in the dining room to greet them when they came down. Now I have to go and make like a hostess. I'll talk to you when I have more time."

"Rather what I had in mind. I'll pick you up for dinner at seven."

"Tonight?"

"Of course. We'll celebrate the successful opening of Iris House. It'll be behind you then and you can relax."

Tess couldn't think beyond the next five minutes, much less to the end of the day. Would she ever relax again? "Don't you mean expire? Luke—"

But she was talking to the dial tone.

Frowning, Tess replaced the receiver. Apparently Luke didn't comprehend how much pressure she was under today. Of course, he would say it was self-imposed. In her place, Luke would probably be strolling through the garden right now with a big mug of Gertie's coffee in his hand. She allowed herself another brief, longing glance out the bay window at the settee before pulling her mind back to business.

Luke always expected things to work out well. After all, they always did for him. No wonder his inclination was to relax and go with the flow. If only she could! But she couldn't forget that she had spent her cash inheritance from Aunt Iris as well as her own savings to renovate the house. She had to succeed in this venture or she'd be bankrupt, and they would sell her beautiful house to the highest bidder. Who wouldn't be worried?

Besides, she couldn't change her approach to life in the next two minutes. As for Luke, she would deal with him tonight. If she fell asleep over dinner, well, he could just deal with *that*.

Tess's living quarters, which occupied half of the first floor of Iris House, had two entrances—a private one through a side yard into a small entryway off the sitting room, the other through the oversized front door of the house, with its stained-glass panes, and the main foyer. Having left her quarters by the second route, she walked across an expanse of mahogany-colored glazed tile and entered the parlor.

A wide archway led from the parlor to the dining room, one of Tess's two favorite rooms in the house. Her other favorite was the library in the circular tower room on the third floor.

As for the dining room, with its latticework ceiling, heavy, dark, carved fireplace mantel, sideboard, and buffet, colorful sea-green-and-raspberry needlepoint rug, twenty-lamp brass chandelier, massive oval table, and Windsor chairs, it was the essence of the elaborate Mid-Victorian Age.

Four people were seated at the table. In the six months since she'd moved to Victoria Springs, she'd come to know these people and her other guests pretty well. Even though her father had not returned to the home of his youth, except for short visits after his college graduation, Tess was still a Darcy and, as such, was considered "one of us."

After her mother's death when Tess was twelve, her father had married a woman only ten years older than Tess and proceeded to have another family. He was with the State Department, currently stationed in France with Zelda and their two children. Tess didn't see them often, which she suspected suited Zelda just fine. But she and her father corresponded regularly and talked by phone when they could, and she would always be grateful to him for refusing to follow the Darcy family tradition—which started with Aunt Iris's mother, Rose—of naming female offspring, even pets, for flowers. Iris's sister, Dahlia, had named her daughter Hyacinth. Tess's cousin was a pretty blonde who didn't seem to mind her flowery name. Tess would have hated it.

Lana Morrison, Alexis Dinwitty, and Randall Isley sat at one end of the long dining table, Chester Leeds at the other. Tess had the feeling that if Chester could have removed himself even farther from his table mates, he would have.

The new guest china was in use for the first time. Specially made for Iris House, it was decorated with hand-painted irises the color of ripe raspberries.

Breakfast this morning was cheesecake crepes garnished with pineapple-strawberry sauce and served with Canadian bacon. As Tess walked in, Gertie ladled a second helping onto Randall Isley's plate and, with a reassuring smile for Tess, returned to the kitchen.

"Good morning," Tess greeted the four cheerfully. "Isn't it a lovely day?"

"Absolutely gorgeous!" caroled Alexis. She turned to beam at Tess, her large dangling earrings reflecting sparks of light. Good heavens, those were real diamonds, and a third, even larger, sparkled at her throat! "One can never be sure about April," Alexis was saying, "but we couldn't have had better weather for the conference."

"Your irises are at the height of their beauty, too, Tess," Lana Morrison said. When Lana had arrived last night, her platinum hair had been arranged in a chignon. This morning she wore it in loose waves about her shoulders, as it had been last night when she'd gone for that mysterious nocturnal stroll. It made her look younger than her true age, which was in the late forties. Her ice-blue dress with a single strand of pearls and small pearl ear studs added to the look of youthful innocence. The effect was obviously false, and deliberate. In her own way, though, Lana was as striking as Alexis.

Randall Isley certainly thought so. He'd had his gray-green eyes glued to Lana since Tess came in. The only way he could have sat any closer to her would have been by sharing her chair.

Chester Leeds, on the other hand, was looking at his plate, pale brows drawn down in an irritable frown. For all the attention he was paying the others, he might as well have been breakfasting alone. He couldn't possibly be disappointed in the food, Tess thought anxiously.

She reached for the silver pot from the sideboard and replenished his coffee. "Is breakfast to your liking, Chester?"

"Oh, yes," he said curtly. "Satisfactory indeed."

"Good. When I came in, I thought you looked unhappy about something."

"Chester seems to have gotten up on the wrong side of the bed," Lana purred.

Alexis exchanged a sly look with Lana. "Perhaps he didn't sleep well. Are you upset, Chester?"

Chester glared at the two women. Tess was shocked by the smoldering hatred in his hazel eyes. "What is there to be upset about?" he spat. "And I slept like a baby, thank you very much." A muscle twitched once in his jaw. He lifted his cup and took a sip of coffee, his grip so tight Tess feared he would break the china cup's handle.

Chester Leeds was slight of build, his light-brown hair thinning. Sparse as it was, every hair was combed away from his face with no effort to camouflage the receding hairline. In a dark suit, pristine white shirt, and striped tie, he looked as though he were about to leave for an important business meeting, though Tess had understood he was taking a few days' vacation from the bank. He didn't look like a man who would ever be a threat to anybody, but the glitter in his eyes troubled Tess.

"What you got stuck in your craw, then, old buddy?" Randall asked jovially. He wore a blue-plaid Western shirt and string tie with a silver medallion. Though his feet were out of Tess's sight, she knew they were encased in hand-tooled Western boots. She'd never seen him wear any other footwear.

Chester shuddered. His haughty sneer would either have shriveled or enraged a more sensitive man. "I am not your buddy, as you so quaintly put it."

Randall laughed good-naturedly. "Didn't mean to insult you, Chet my man."

Chester clenched his teeth. "And don't call me Chet."

Tess frowned and tried to catch Randall's eye. He ignored her, scowling and drawing back like a rowdy puppy who'd been whacked across the nose with a rolled newspaper for piddling on the carpet. "What's wrong with Chet?"

"I don't like it," Chester snapped. "Furthermore, you don't know me well enough to use a nickname in addressing me."

Randall's eyebrows rose comically. "Well, who died and made you king? Excuse me all to hell, Mr. Leeds."

"Gentlemen, please," Tess pleaded.

Lana grinned and tilted her head coyly. "You're a case, Randall."

Chester shot her a withering glare.

"Chester, how can you be so prickly on such a gorgeous day?" Alexis put in.

Chester's head whipped around as his snapping hazel eyes bored into Alexis. "You expect me to sit here and let this ridiculous drugstore cowboy make fun of me?"

"I don't think Randall meant—" Tess began.

Randall overrode her. "Now, just a cotton-pickin' minute. Who're you calling a drugstore cowboy?"

Chester's look was venomous. "Would you prefer used-car salesman? Or how about con man?"

Randall flushed. *"Con man!"*

"Exactly. I don't think you ever set foot on a Texas ranch, much less grew up on one as you claim."

Randall's face had gone rigid. "Why, you prissy little queer—"

"Randall!" Lana shrieked as she struggled to keep from laughing.

Alexis's face had turned rosy and she covered her fuchsia lips with her fuchsia-nailed hand to hide their twitching.

Tess felt like crying. These two idiots were ruining the very first guest breakfast served in Iris House. Alexis and Lana weren't helping the situation one bit, either.

His face ashen, Chester threw down his linen napkin, pushed back his chair, and stood. He was shaking and his hands were clenched at his sides as he stared at Randall. "You—you pathetic buffoon!" With that, he stalked out of the room. After a moment, they heard his steps on the stairs.

Randall half-rose threateningly from his chair and was pulled back down by Lana. Tess longed to strangle the two middle-aged men for being so childish. She had so wanted everything to go smoothly on her opening day. Breakfast wasn't even over yet, and already two of her guests were squabbling.

"Randall," she said, "I don't know what's going on between you and Chester, but I'd appreciate it if you'd wait until you've left Iris House to settle it. I'm very disappointed in your behavior."

"Me?" Randall squawked, outraged. "I was only trying to be friendly to the little pervert."

"Now, that's what I mean," Tess retorted sharply. "Please refrain from childish name-calling in this house. If you can't keep from insulting Chester, I suggest you avoid talking to him altogether."

"And *I* suggest you tell Chester to stay out of my way."

"I intend to."

Randall continued to bluster. "I'll hurt that whining pansy if he even looks at me crossways again. Who in tarnation does he think—"

Lana laid a crimson-nailed hand on his arm. "Ignore him, Randall. Actually, I feel sorry for poor Chester, having to live with that mother of his."

"Mama's boy," muttered Randall.

Lana dimpled and tapped a playful finger against Randall's lips. "Now, you stop that, Randall. You're upsetting Tess. You hear?"

Randall's outrage melted and was replaced by a wolfish grin. "For you, Lana, honey, I'll do just about anything."

"If I were you, Randall, I wouldn't let Reva hear you say that," Alexis advised.

"Reva knows we're not serious," Lana said, picking up her coffee cup and winking at him over the rim.

He winked back.

Alexis shrugged her shoulders, as though to say, *Let it be on your heads.* Then she excused herself to go upstairs.

Lana and Randall put their heads together as Randall whispered something and Lana laughed. Tess hesitated, wondering if she should add a warning to Alexis's advice. But why should they listen to her?

Tess retreated to the kitchen, where Gertie was taking down trays and the silver tea service from a tall pickled-pine breakfront topped with crown molding. Tess began setting the trays out on the large center island, her thoughts still in the dining room with Randall and Lana. Lana might not be serious, but Tess wasn't so sure about Randall. She hoped there wouldn't be another unpleasant scene when Reva came down and found her husband fawning over another woman. She wished Randall had stayed at home. Or Chester. Come to think of it, she wished they both had.

Chapter 6

The next five days could well be the most important in Marisa Stackpole's young life. What if it didn't turn out as she hoped? Could she face an existence without joy or purpose again, after she'd had a glimpse of how different life could be?

No. Oh, no. She wouldn't even entertain the thought of failure.

For at least the tenth time, she consulted the gold wristwatch Johnny had given her last month for her twenty-fourth birthday.

She had felt terribly let down that it wasn't an engagement ring, but it had been easy to mask her disappointment. She had known, from childhood, how to hide her feelings. And it *was* a beautiful watch, with ruby chips beneath each of the twelve numerals. At the moment, it read eight-twenty, a minute later than the last time she'd checked.

Nervously, she paced the width of her room—the Carnaby Room—and back again, her heels sinking into the carpet's rose-red plush, the same color as the iris for which the room was named. If the painting on the wall was an accurate representation of the Carnaby iris, its rose-red petals—or falls as Fern insisted she must call them—were edged with pink.

She flopped down on her back on the four-poster bed and stared up at the white canopy. The room's wallpaper and matching ruffled draperies were splashed with rose, pink, and blue tulips. The overall effect was unabashedly romantic. She only wished Johnny were sharing the canopied bed with her. It seemed a shame to waste all this atmosphere.

She sighed disconsolately and looked at her watch again. Eight twenty-three. Fern had asked her to knock on the door of the Arctic Fancy Room at eight-thirty so that they could go down to breakfast together. Marisa didn't want to be late, but if she was early, Fern might be alerted to how eager Marisa was to please her. Marisa's future happiness depended on Fern's liking her.

In fact, her main reason for joining The Club was that Fern was a member. Secretly, Marisa thought it was downright silly how people in Victoria Springs considered membership such a big status symbol. She wasn't even very interested in gardening; and, to make matters worse, except for Tess Darcy and two or three others, the members were middle-aged or older. Why, a few of them had to have a cane or a walker to get around. After hearing their conversations, Marisa had concluded they hadn't noticed any changes in the world since the fifties. Lana Morrison was the only one of the bunch who wasn't an old fuddy-duddy.

It was hard to believe Lana was as old as Fern. Lana was one of those rare individuals who never seemed to age at all. It had something to do with their attitude toward life, Marisa thought. People like Lana seemed to possess a boundless energy that could last into old age.

To Marisa's surprise, Lana had invited Marisa to lunch several times, and the years separating them had melted away as they giggled over some scandalous tidbit like a couple of adolescents. Lana's befriending her had helped Marisa feel more at home in Victoria Springs, which proved Lana wasn't as self-centered as everybody seemed to think.

Lana was easy to talk to, as well as a font of naughty gossip. Great fun to be with, but Marisa couldn't help

wondering if Lana gossiped about *her* when she was
with somebody else. Not that the possibility concerned
her greatly. Marisa's life since coming to Victoria
Springs had been circumspect. Quite ordinary, really.
There was nothing even remotely scandalous for Lana
to gossip about. Marisa liked Lana, but, all the same,
Lana wasn't a person she'd confide in, had she anything to confide.

In spite of Lana's presence, the monthly meetings of
The Club bored her to death, but she had perfected the
technique of looking raptly attentive while her mind
traveled far afield. Usually to the last time she and
Johnny had been together.

Naturally, it had been a foregone conclusion that William Stackpole's granddaughter would be thrilled to become a member, and, as Lana had pointed out, she
didn't want to get off on the wrong foot. It was important to fit in.

Marisa felt compelled to look at her watch again.
Eight twenty-five. She took a deep breath, got off the
bed, and resumed pacing. Occasionally she wondered if
her decision to settle in Victoria Springs after William
Stackpole's death had been wise. At the time, she
hadn't doubted. It was the sort of friendly, close-knit
community she'd always dreamed of being a part of.

The phone call from William Stackpole's nurse
couldn't have come at a better time. The old man
wanted to see his only grandchild before he died.

When she had recovered her voice, she had told the
nurse she would come right away. Her job was nothing
special; she could find another one as good or better
whenever she wanted. More to the point, she was happy
to leave the silent apartment where she was surrounded
by reminders of her late roommate.

She still got teary when she remembered the good
times they used to have before her friend's unexpected
death following emergency surgery for a ruptured ap-

pendix. She had felt as though a piece of her heart had been torn away.

She had left Chicago with vast relief. She arrived in Victoria Springs two days before William Stackpole's death. There had been nothing left of the arrogant, stubborn man she'd heard about.

She had spent the next forty-eight hours sitting beside his bed, holding his hand and talking to him during his periods of lucidity. The last thing he said to her was, "I've left it all to you, Marisa."

That, of course, was what she'd hoped for, though she hadn't dared count on it. She'd told herself that, even if he'd left all he had to charity, she would at least have had an expense-free vacation.

As it turned out, the estate wasn't a fortune, but it was enough to provide the security she'd never known, if she was careful with her money.

Because she had always been frugal out of necessity, she managed very well on the income from the trust William Stackpole had set up. Equally important, it had seemed at the time, she had also inherited his house and the standing of a Stackpole in the community.

It had all seemed like a dream come true then, before she realized that her standing in the community would compel her to spend a great deal of time with people who, on the whole, she found tedious and stultifying. People like Fern Willis. But if she hadn't stayed in Victoria Springs, she wouldn't have met Johnny. It was unfortunate that he happened to be Fern's only son. Even more unfortunate that, for a twenty-five-year-old man, he seemed to be inordinately concerned with his parents' approval. He even lived with them, though he claimed that was only to save money.

The Willis family continued to be held in high regard in Victoria Springs, even though their fortune had been lost when the family business went under years ago. Johnny and his father, the minister at Hope Community Church, worked for a living, like ordinary people. At least no one could say she wanted Johnny for his money. She was madly in love with him and, once they were married, his salary combined with her trust income would provide a very comfortable living.

There remained one large fly in the ointment. Marisa feared there would be no marriage without the approval of Johnny's parents. Reverend Willis, a sweet, gentle man, was no problem. But it was Fern who ruled in that house, so it was Fern she had to win over. Which was why she subjected herself to those dreary Garden Club meetings, why she had agreed to be the Club secretary and keep their deadly boring minutes. It was why she was determined, in the next five days, to convince Fern she would be an ideal daughter-in-law. Pleasant, proper, and, most of all, malleable. No doubt she would spend much of that time biting her tongue but, considering what she had to gain, she could surely play the role for five days.

Once she and Johnny were man and wife, she would relish telling Fern to take a flying leap. If Fern wanted to see her future grandchildren, she'd learn to keep her long nose out of her son's marriage.

Standing before the mirror in the Arctic Fancy Room, Fern Willis gave herself a critical inspection. Sighing, she plucked at the waistline of her navy linen dress. The dress, with its white-piped collar, had looked so crisp and springlike in the shop. The salesgirl had raved about how slimming it was, but now, suddenly, it looked like a potato sack bunched up with a belt at the waist. It made her look dumpy, and the color was too dull. She looked as though she were dressed to attend a funeral. Undoubtedly, Lana and Alexis would be decked out in bright hues or feminine pastels. Why hadn't she worn one of her simple shirtwaists and saved her money?

The mirror reflected her unhappy face with crows' feet at the corners of her eyes and a straying wisp of graying brown hair dangling across one cheek. With fingers that trembled slightly, she tucked the strand into the fat coil at the back of her head, wishing she'd followed her impulse to have her hair cut and permed before the conference. She might start coloring it, too. The gray made her look older than forty-eight.

Her heart thudded. It was disheartening to see what a sharp contrast there was between her drab image and the deep violets, blues, and whites of the Arctic Fancy Room behind her.

Until now, Fern had taken a certain pride in never trying to be anything but what she was, a proper, middle-aged matron whose life revolved around her family, her church, and The Club, for which she served as newsletter editor and publicity chairperson.

The same certainly could not be said for her cousin, Lana Morrison, who was neither proper nor looked her age, which was the same as Fern's. Remembering that she was going to spend the next five days in the same house with Lana made her stomach churn. Oddly, she didn't feel safe here, as she did in her own home.

Turning away from her reflection, Fern closed her eyes and took several deep breaths. *Good Lord, Fern,* she lectured herself, *you and Lana haven't been teenagers for more years than either of you cares to recall. Why were the memories still so vivid after all this time?*

Lana had made her high-school career miserable, but, as painful as it still was to remember, that was long in the past. And it really wasn't Lana's fault that she'd been pretty and popular, while Fern had been plain and bookish. It was their mothers who had insisted that Lana must include Fern in outings with her friends. Lana, never known for her compassion, had blamed Fern, of course, and made fun of her with her crowd, sometimes in Fern's presence.

To be fair, on the one occasion when Fern had desperately needed Lana's help, Lana had come through for her. Which was certainly fortuitous since, at the time, there had been nowhere else to turn. Of course, Fern had spent the last thirty-one years regretting that, in the process, she'd given Lana a powerful weapon to be used against her. To Fern's knowledge, Lana had never breathed a word about it to anyone else, nor had she mentioned it to Fern since they were seventeen. But that didn't keep Fern from worrying that she might someday blurt out the whole sordid story. Lana had the power to blow Fern's safe little world apart.

But she wouldn't. Of course she wouldn't, not after all this time.

Fern took another bracing breath and smoothed her dress down while sucking in her stomach. She turned her thoughts to the young woman her Johnny seemed seriously interested in, Marisa Stackpole—an interest that made Fern uneasy. They knew so little about the girl. What Fern had managed to learn had come from people who'd grown up with Marisa's father in Victoria Springs. He had been estranged from his parents before Marisa was born. Nobody seemed to know the reason, but William Stackpole declared that he had no son. One of Fern's informants had told her the old man hadn't even sent word to his son when his mother died.

Then Marisa's parents had died in a car wreck when she was eight. Thereafter, Marisa had told Fern, she'd lived in foster homes until she was eighteen. According to the girl herself, the closest thing to a family Marisa had known since early childhood was Janet Forsythe, the young woman with whom she'd shared an apartment in Chicago. Both of them orphans without brothers or sisters, it seemed they had recognized in each other a kindred spirit from their first meeting.

Fern had often wondered if William Stackpole had known about the foster homes. She suspected that he had. Even though the prideful old man had never laid eyes on his only grandchild, he must have kept track of her from afar, for he'd sent for her when he was dying.

All those years, he'd let them go on shifting her from
one foster family to another when he could have
brought her to live with him. Perhaps, as he was dying,
he regretted disowning his only child and repented
leaving his granddaughter to strangers. But in Marisa's
place, Fern would have been extremely bitter.

At exactly 8:30, there was a hesitant knock at Fern's
door. Marisa was prompt, as usual. The girl thought she
was clever, but Fern knew exactly what she was up to.
She'd known almost as soon as Marisa had that she had
set her cap for Johnny. Fern was far more intelligent
than most people gave her credit for; she was also re-
alistic. To imagine that her darling boy would never
marry and leave her was delusion. And, as sad as it
made her to contemplate his going, she didn't want him
to turn out like Chester Leeds. Therefore, it behooved
her to choose her daughter-in-law herself, while allow-
ing Johnny to think it was solely his own decision.

She knew exactly how to manipulate events in her
family to her liking, while Richard and Johnny remained oblivious to the fact that she was in control. In
her more reflective moments, Fern was aware that she
had to be in control of her little world. Losing control
was like falling into a black abyss. It had happened
once; if it happened again there would be no sound
footing anywhere.

So, she would choose Johnny's wife just as she had
made the other important decisions in his life. Perhaps
it would be Marisa, but she wasn't yet sure. Who knew
how seriously Marisa's psyche had been damaged by
her unsettled, unhappy childhood? Also, Fern had to
admit it rankled that Marisa's father had been a member
of Lana's popular clique when they were teenagers, but
that was hardly Marisa's fault. The girl barely remembered her father.

Fern admitted grudgingly that she had found no ir-
reparable flaws in Marisa so far, but the next few days

would be the acid test. Arranging her face in a pleasant expression, Fern opened the door.

Marisa forced a smile as Fern's door opened. "Am I too early?"

"No, dear. Right on time," Fern assured her as she gave Marisa's demure cotton dress, with its Peter Pan collar, an approving once-over. "Why don't you run ahead and tell them they can serve our breakfast now. I'll be along in a minute. Insist on real cream for the coffee, although I can't imagine Tess Darcy serving anything less. Oh, and don't let them pour my coffee until I'm seated. I must have it piping hot."

Marisa swallowed hard. It appeared she was to be Fern's errand girl, not an auspicious beginning for the day. "All right," she said, smiling amiably before she turned away, lest Fern see the flash of anger in her eyes. "I'll see you downstairs."

"Oh, and Marisa," Fern called after her. "I can't eat pork, can't even stand the smell of it. So if they're serving bacon, tell them to leave it off my plate."

"Of course," Marisa mumbled without turning around. She knew she would not be able to force another smile. The amount of simpering she could manage at one time was limited and, at the moment, she'd run out of simper.

Chapter 7

Tess slid the last foil-covered tray of finger sandwiches—watercress and cucumber with mint butter—into the giant-sized refrigerator. Also on the tea menu were salmon mousse, lemon bread and ginger-flavored honey, madeleines, and thin slices of blackberry jam cake made from an old family recipe that Iris and Dahlia had always refused to share with outsiders—except Gertie and Dahlia's housekeeper, of course. Tess had inherited the recipe with the rest of Aunt Iris's estate. When Dahlia's daughter, Hyacinth—Cinny for short—married, she would be presented with her own copy, along with other recipes handed down in the family. Probably in a locked box. Though Tess found it difficult to imagine her often frivolous cousin in an apron with flour on her nose.

"Now, where's the cake knife?" Tess inquired, turning from the refrigerator.

Gertie, who'd been arranging the last of the breakfast dishes in the dishwasher, punched the button that started the machine. She wore a bright flowered tent dress with a white bibbed apron tied around her ample waist. Like many good cooks, Gertie enjoyed her own creations a little too much. "In that drawer right beside you. And be careful. I just sharpened it."

Tess laid the gleaming knife on the counter. "All that's missing now are the napkins."

"I saw them on the top cabinet shelf, in the corner there." As Tess stood on tiptoe to reach the

39

shelf, she was aware of Gertie studying her with sturdy, capable hands planted on wide hips. "Stop fussing, Tess. I helped Miss Iris serve these teas for year. Be thankful it's not raining. A couple of years ago it poured all afternoon. The garden tour was canceled, leaving us with enough food for a battalion. Watercress sandwiches don't keep worth a hoot, either."

Tess smiled. "I only wish I could go to sleep and wake up when the afternoon is over."

"I'd tell you to go take a nap, but you wouldn't hear of it."

"Gracious, no. There's too much to do." Tess still had not even found time for a garden break.

"It'll all come out in the wash."

Gertie's placid confidence reminded Tess of Luke's advice. *Take a few deep breaths and calm down.* "Oh, you're right, Gertie. But I could never manage this without you, not even with Aunt Dahlia's help." She glanced at the clock on the wall. "Speaking of Aunt Dahlia, it's twelve-twenty. She should be here. The first tour's at one."

"She'll show up before then," Gertie said calmly.

Tess actually felt herself relax a little. Gertie's attitude was catching. She found the napkins and set a stack on the center island, then resettled the ribbing of her yellow cotton sweater at her waist. Tea would be served in the gazebo. The garden-tour guests would then take their china plates to the small metal tables that were scattered around the backyard for the occasion. Each table was spread with a white, lace-trimmed cloth, there being plenty of extras to replace soiled ones between tour groups. Aunt Iris's linen closet had been very well supplied.

The tablecloths, of course, meant more laundry for Nedra to do. Tess had given in to Aunt Dahlia on the cloths, but had stood firm on her decision to use paper napkins. When Dahlia realized Tess had dug in her heels on the subject, she'd ordered the napkins herself.

They must have cost a pretty penny, too. The paper was so fine it looked like linen, and there was a lengthy inscription engraved in gold.

Idly, Tess picked up one and read the words Dahlia had chosen, a quotation from a Victorian-era minister: *What would the world do without tea?—how did it exist? I am glad I was not born before tea.—Reverend Sydney Smith*. Tea *was* a most civilized convention, Tess admitted to herself, replacing the napkin. In fact, she was thinking of starting a new tradition: as soon as she had the library ready for guests, she would serve tea in the tower on Sunday afternoons.

Tess's housekeeper, Nedra Yates, marched into the kitchen, carrying a plastic bucket containing her cleaning supplies. She set the bucket on the floor and plunked into a chair at the sturdy oak table. Wisps of straw-colored hair stood out around her angular face. It made her look like Medusa in a cotton shirt and jeans. "If they keep out from underfoot," she announced, "I can do the first floor right after lunch."

Which Tess interpreted to mean Nedra was finished on the second floor. The housekeeper's brain sometimes ran ahead of her mouth, causing her to start talking in the middle of a thought. It had frustrated Tess in the beginning, but, after getting used to Nedra, she could usually fill in what the housekeeper left unsaid. And she wouldn't trade Nedra now for three other housekeepers, although Nedra's gauntness had worried her at first. She looked so frail, which only proved once more how deceiving looks could be. The woman was a workhorse.

"I don't expect any of the guests back until later this afternoon," Tess said. "What are you having to drink, Nedra?"

"None of that minty stuff you're giving the tourists. The regular kind."

Iced tea, Tess translated. Glad to have something productive to do, she poured three glasses and set them on the table with a bowl of fruit while Gertie made tuna-salad sandwiches. No time for a hot lunch today.

Tess stirred sugar into her tea. To divert her mind from worrying about all she had to do that afternoon, she admired the kitchen. It was a wonderful room. In fact, she had a smaller version of it in her apartment. Glass-fronted white cabinets, airy lace curtains, and a pressed tin ceiling softened the effect of contemporary recessed lighting, modern appliances, and brick-colored ceramic tile floor.

Gertie brought the plate of sandwiches to the table and sat down. Nedra immediately ate a whole sandwich, hardly pausing to draw breath, and reached for another. It was amazing, Tess mused, how the woman could eat like that and stay so thin.

"By the way," Gertie said, as though the thought had just popped into her head, "what's wrong between Randall Isley and Chester Leeds?"

Tess suspected that Gertie had been waiting for her to mention the altercation that had occurred at breakfast. Since Tess had not cooperated, Gertie was taking the direct approach. "Oh, I don't know what got into those two this morning," Tess replied. "Randall was apparently trying to be friendly." Her brow puckered. "At least, I don't think he was deliberately goading Chester. But you can never be sure, and you know Chester. He decided to take exception."

Gertie nodded. "I heard that part. Called Mr. Isley a drugstore cowboy, didn't he?"

Nedra snorted and her green eyes swung to Tess questioningly.

"That and more," Tess said. "He said Randall was a con man and a buffoon. Randall, of course, responded in kind."

"Mad as hops when he came upstairs. Almost ran over me," Nedra commented, swiping a wisp of hair out of her eyes.

"Mr. Leeds, you mean?" Gertie asked.

Nedra wrinkled her freckled nose. "That's what I said, didn't I?"

"Well, Randall Isley better watch his step, is what I say." Gertie spoke authoritatively. "Carrying on with Lana Morrison in front of everybody. If that's not asking for trouble, I don't know what is."

"He really did that?" Nedra asked eagerly.

"It was disgusting," Gertie told her. "What if his wife had come down in the middle of it?"

"Luckily," Tess said, "Lana went up as Reva was coming down."

Gertie hurrumphed. "That close, huh?"

Tess's head bobbed in agreement. "I was ready to strangle Randall. Honestly, I don't know what he's doing here, anyway. He's not even a member of the Garden Club."

"Obvious," Nedra chortled.

Tess looked glum. "You mean he's here because Lana is."

"Yep."

After what Tess had observed at breakfast, she suspected Nedra was right. "If he must make a spectacle of himself, I wish he wouldn't do it under Reva's nose. It's so—well, insulting and— Oh, my—" Tess paused to ponder a new thought. "I just remembered something ... Oh, no, you don't suppose ... ?"

Gertie and Nedra watched her with avid curiosity. "We don't suppose what?" Gertie prompted.

Tess looked from one raptly inquisitive face to the other. She thought she could trust these two to keep a confidence. "Something very strange happened last night. A little after one A.M., a noise awakened me. Eventually, I realized it was the back door closing. I looked out my bedroom window, and what do you think I saw?"

Nedra scowled intently, so absorbed in what Tess was saying she had forgotten the half-eaten sandwich on her plate. Gertie's round face flushed with impatience and she fidgeted in her chair. "Don't play twenty questions, Tess," she wailed. "Tell us what you saw."

"Lana Morrison, in her negligee, tripping across the backyard and disappearing through the hedge."

Nedra gave her disheveled head a quick shake. "I'll be switched." Her eyes narrowed speculatively. "Maybe she and Randall Isley had a—what do you call it?"

"Assignation," Tess supplied. "That's exactly what I was thinking, Nedra."

Gertie's face creased in thought. "Did you see Mr. Isley out there, too?"

"No, only Lana," Tess mused. "But what other explanation is there for Lana to be wandering around outside in her nightgown at one A.M.? I started to go after her last night—once I'd thought about it, I wondered if she was sleepwalking. But by the time I reached the parlor, she was back inside, and she definitely was not asleep."

Gertie leaned forward to ask earnestly, "How long was that after you saw her in the yard?"

Tess tried to recall. She'd gone back to bed and had lain there, awake, for some time. She'd started to get sleepy when she'd finally decided to check on Lana. "I don't know. Maybe half an hour. It could have been even longer. Anyway, when I found her in the parlor and suggested that somebody had been in the backyard, she batted those big blue eyes and said she'd only been in the kitchen looking for something to eat, and that must have been what I heard."

"Lying like a dog," muttered Nedra.

"Yes," Tess agreed. "Now, why would she have lied if she hadn't been sneaking out to meet somebody else's husband?"

"Oh, I expect it was somebody else's husband, all right," Gertie said. "I'm not convinced it was Mr. Isley she was meeting, though. Or calling on, I should say."

Tess and Nedra stared at Gertie blankly. Gertie's gray

eyes had taken on a shrewd look and Tess could almost see her mind working out its own scenario.

"But you saw them acting like two teenagers at breakfast," Tess said.

"Think about it, Tess," Gertie suggested. "You've known Lana Morrison long enough to realize she has a champagne appetite. Almost spent her first husband into the poorhouse, they say."

"Aunt Dahlia said Lana got a big settlement from her third husband," Tess put in.

"It won't last. Lana Morrison can go through money faster than water through a sieve." Gertie's eyes puckered in a thoughtful squint. "I'd say she's about had enough time to go through what she got out of the doctor. Which means she's in the market for husband number four." She paused dramatically, looking from Tess to Nedra to make sure they were with her.

"Hasn't got a pot to pee in," Nedra snorted.

Gertie could fill in the blanks in Nedra's conversation as well as Tess. "Randall Isley? No, he doesn't," she agreed.

"I heard tell," Nedra said, "her daddy fixed hers and the grandkids' money so Randall will never get his hands on it."

"Reva's father, you mean," Tess mused.

"That's common knowledge," Gertie said dismissively. "What it means is, Lana's not looking to break up the Isley marriage. She's only having a little fun with Randall."

"Always stirring things up," was Nedra's observation.

Tess pondered Gertie's words. They made a lot of sense. Still . . . "But the only other man here is Chester Leeds, and he's made no secret of his dislike for Lana," Tess reasoned. "Besides, I can't see Lana being attracted to Chester, even if he does have the first dollar he ever made. At least, that's what Aunt Dahlia says. So it *has* to be Randall Lana was meeting."

"Couldn't have been anyone else," Nedra agreed. "Must be true love."

Gertie waved the suggestion aside. "Oh, please. Use your noggins, you two. Whose house is on the other side of the hedge?"

Nedra looked puzzled, and then her mouth dropped open.

Tess shook her head impatiently. *Now* who was playing twenty questions? Whose house . . . ? Tess's hand flew to her cheek as the answer came to her. "Oh, dear heaven. The Dinwitty house. But Alexis is here."

"And Harley Dinwitty is there," Gertie finished for her, with the air of a magician turning a hat upside down to reveal that the rabbit has disappeared.

"Tess?" At the sound of the voice from the kitchen doorway, all three women jumped, like children caught in some forbidden mischief. It was Chester Leeds.

Flustered, Tess rose and walked to the door. "May I help you, Chester?" He was supposed to be lunching at the conference, after which sessions were scheduled for the early afternoon. What was he doing back at this hour?

"I wanted to ask if I can have another kind of soap. I'm allergic to anything with perfume in it."

She had the distinct feeling he'd fabricated the allergy on the spur of the moment. "Of course, Chester. I'm sorry. I wish you'd mentioned it earlier. How is the conference going?"

"Smoothly, on the whole. But lunch disagreed with me. I think it was the chicken Kiev. I'm going to lie down for a bit."

"Can I get you something to settle your stomach? I have an over-the-counter remedy."

"No, I'm sure I'll be fine in a little while."

"I'll put a different soap in your room later this afternoon, then, after you've rested."

Tess hesitated in the doorway as he walked away from her. He did look a little green around the gills. She still hadn't spoken to Chester about Randall, but now wasn't the time.

Tess couldn't shake an uneasy feeling of foreboding. She hadn't heard Chester come in, and he hadn't made a sound walking through the house to the kitchen, as if he hadn't wanted them to know he was there. What an odd, sneaky little man.

How long had he been standing there before he spoke?

Dahlia breezed in at ten minutes before one, lavender silk swishing about shapely nyloned legs, every curled and frosted hair in place. "Yoo hoo, Tess!"

Dahlia was three years older than Tess's father, but she took very good care of herself. She was still the family beauty; it was easy to understand why so many young men had swarmed around the Darcy house before Dahlia's marriage. Tess could remember, as a young child, hearing her father lament, "It doesn't seem fair that Iris didn't get a fraction of Dahlia's looks. She was obstinate besides. She refused to cultivate a pleasing personality to make up for her plainness. Dahlia used to try to pass off some of her boyfriends to Iris, but it just made Iris more strident than ever." According to her father, Iris, who had been the eldest of the three Darcy children, had been born an old maid.

"Thank goodness!" Tess greeted Dahlia. "I've been calling your house for the past fifteen minutes." She had also aged ten years in that time, imagining the worst. Dahlia had been in an auto accident. Dahlia had had a sudden onset of amnesia and had no memory of promising to act as tour guide. Dahlia had left town.

Tess was not familiar enough with all the names of the irises to narrate a tour through the garden. Besides, she had to help Gertie transfer the food to the gazebo and serve tea. She couldn't be in two places at once.

The scent of Chanel No. 5 wafted to Tess as Dahlia patted her shoulder with a slim, freshly manicured

hand. "Luella must have gone grocery shopping."
Luella was the Forrests' cook-housekeeper. "Or she
would have told you I was at the beauty parlor, dear. I
did mention to you that I was going there before I came
here."

"No, you didn't," Tess said in exasperation.

Dahlia smiled fondly at her niece. "Of course I did.
You've simply forgotten in the excitement of your
opening day." When Tess had announced that she intended to turn Dahlia's childhood home into a bed and
breakfast, Dahlia had been aghast at the very idea. But
she'd come around when she saw the finished product,
pronouncing Tess's taste exquisite.

Tess shrugged helplessly. "Well, you're here now.
That's what counts."

Deep-set dark eyes peered at Tess. Reproachful
eyes. "Did you ever doubt, Tess?"

Tess chose diplomacy over truth. "Not really, Aunt
Dahlia."

The clouds cleared and Dahlia smiled. "My hair-
dresser was running a bit behind because the woman
before me was nearly twenty minutes late. Can you
imagine?" She clicked her tongue. "No concern for
other people's time. But I was prepared to leave with
my hair half-combed if it became necessary." She patted her coifed and sprayed locks.

Tess didn't believe a word of it. No one was more
meticulous about her appearance than Dahlia.

"Don't dawdle, Tess," Dahlia said briskly, taking
charge. "I want to see what Gertie has prepared for tea."

Tess couldn't decide whether to laugh or be angry. But
as she followed Dahlia to the kitchen, she decided that,
late or not, her aunt would be a far more charming and
knowledgeable guide than Tess could have hoped to be.

"Hello, Gertie," Dahlia said as she inspected the arrangement of food on the silver trays, which Gertie had
just set out of the refrigerator.

"Afternoon, Mrs. Forrest."

"Very nice, Tess," Dahlia pronounced, even though she couldn't resist rearranging the sandwiches on the nearest tray. "Remember, now, you are to be in the gazebo, ready to serve, at one-thirty."

"I'm not likely to forget."

The doorbell chimed melodically. "That must be the first tour group," Tess said.

Dahlia looked displeased. "They're six minutes early." She hurried from the kitchen, muttering, "People have no respect for schedules nowadays." She threw open the front door, her tone changing to that of a Southern belle greeting a contingent of beaux. "Good afternoon, all you lovely people! Welcome to Iris House." She went out, closing the door behind her. Tess could hear her sketching the house's history as she led the group toward the garden.

Tess sank into a chair. "Whew! That was close."

Gertie chuckled. "I told you she'd be here."

Tess grinned. "You did. I admit it."

"Now, if it had been her daughter Hyacinth you were expecting, you'd have had reason to get in a dither. That girl will be late for her own funeral. Miss Iris always said it took Cinny an hour just to put on her makeup."

"I know better than to depend on Cinny." Tess's cousin lived as if clocks had never been invented. Tess had wondered for weeks how Cinny managed to keep her part-time job in a local bookshop. The mystery had been solved when she'd learned that the Forrests owned fifty-one percent of the business.

Tess rose from her chair reluctantly. "We'd better start carrying the food out."

"Yep," Gertie agreed, lifting a tray. "Now that Mrs. Forrest is here, things will go like clockwork."

"Uh huh," Tess murmured. "I'm actually beginning to believe we're going to sail through this afternoon without a crisis."

Those words would come back to mock her.

Chapter 8

By three o'clock, all seven of Tess's guests had returned to Iris House, the conference having adjourned until evening. But it was too beautiful an afternoon to stay indoors. As Tess carried trays, served tea, changed tablecloths, and chatted with people who had toured the gardens, she caught sight of most of her guests at one time or another.

Fern and Marisa strolled among the irises, taking their own private tour while the second tour group enjoyed tea. Tess envied them; she couldn't even find a few minutes to sit or walk in the garden, much less an hour to attend one of the conference sessions. Perhaps tomorrow. For now, she had to content herself with waving at Fern and Marisa, but they were engrossed in their conversation and didn't see her.

Fern, looking frumpy in a navy dress that had been designed for a taller, thinner woman, seemed to be doing the talking, while Marisa nodded and smiled valiantly. In spite of fine, flyaway brown hair, Marisa was a pretty young woman in an undramatic sort of way, but her smile definitely looked forced, as her hands, linked behind her, clenched and unclenched nervously. She seemed distracted, as though she wanted to get away from Fern and was looking for a convenient break in the conversation. Too much gardening talk, Tess supposed. In the few Garden Club meetings she had attended, Marisa hadn't seemed very interested. Tess wondered why she bothered with the meetings at all.

After a while, Marisa and Fern turned back toward the house, Marisa looking less tense now that they were leaving the garden. A few minutes later, Reva and Alexis appeared beside a bed of clear yellow standards with violet-blue falls, their blue beards tipped with orange. Now, what was the name of the irises in that bed? Tess pondered. A woman's name, probably the one who'd bred that particular variety. Edith something, wasn't it? Yes, she had it now. Edith Wolford.

Reva, in a red shirtwaist dress, seemed to be explaining something to Alexis as she stooped to part the yellow standards of a large bloom for Alexis's inspection. Alexis nodded and bent to peer into the iris. Where were Randall and Lana? Tess wondered uneasily. Not together, she hoped. Randall had gone to work earlier, but he'd come back a short while ago, saying that business was slack today.

Privately, Tess thought she knew the real reason for his reluctance to stay away, as Reva must also, and it had nothing to do with the used-car business. Randall didn't seem particularly concerned with keeping secret his interest in Lana. The foreboding that had attacked Tess in the kitchen earlier came back. Could they possibly get through the next few days without an unpleasant scene between Reva and Lana, or Reva and Randall, or Chester and Randall?

As though thinking of Chester had conjured him up, Tess, watching from the gazebo, saw him stride purposefully through the garden, ignoring the riotous blooms all around him. He seemed recovered from his stomach complaint, however. He went straight to Alexis and Reva and spoke to Alexis, who frowned a little and walked away with him. They disappeared from Tess's sight as they rounded a front corner of the house. Reva straightened, but remained beside the iris bed, looking after them quizzically. Then she, too, moved slowly back toward the house.

Apprehensive, Tess stared at the place where Alexis and Reva had been standing when Chester joined them. What had Chester said to Alexis to make her go off with him? Everybody knew there had been bad blood between the two of them since The Club's last election of officers. At Club meetings, Alexis often treated him with disdain, as though his opinions were of little value.

As for Chester, who probably knew more about flower gardening than Alexis, he thoroughly disliked her and made little effort to hide it. But then, Chester didn't seem particularly fond of anybody. One assumed he loved his mother, although Tess rarely saw them together. What could Chester and Alexis have to discuss? Club business, Tess told herself, but at the back of her mind another question nagged: How much *had* Chester heard of her conversation with Gertie and Nedra in the kitchen?

Tess pulled her mind back to more immediate concerns, chatting with the lingerers in the second tour group and refilling teacups. Several of them asked about her bed-and-breakfast rates and on which weekends she had openings in the next few months. She handed them all business cards, which she'd had the forethought to put in her skirt pocket, and suggested they phone later when she could check the reservation book.

By three-thirty, the last of the second tour group had gone. Except for the used plates and silverware on a few remaining tables, the backyard looked as color-photograph–perfect as it had that morning. Lavish with bright-colored irises. Charming. Edenic.

The gazebo, with its cupola and white latticework, sat invitingly in a back corner of the yard. Cobblestone paths meandered through stretches of brilliant green grass, iris beds, and more beds where petunias, geraniums, impatiens, and other summer annuals were beginning to bloom. Two wrought-iron lampposts were placed on either side of the backyard. At night, they emitted dim golden light, leaving the interior of the yard mysterious with shadows.

The back and side yards were surrounded by a white wrought-iron fence in an elaborate pattern of vines and grapes. Sugar maple and oak trees shaded several wrought-iron settees and benches which were scattered about the yard. Tess still had trouble sometimes believing all this was hers.

Gertie had gone inside with the empty serving trays from the gazebo. Dahlia came to help Tess finish clearing tables, still looking as if she'd stepped out of the beauty parlor only minutes earlier. Tess wondered how she did it. She herself felt too warm and sticky, and she had chewed her lipstick off hours ago.

Dahlia stacked three plates and handed them to Tess, then whipped a stained cloth from a table, rolling it into a ball. "Tess, I'm concerned about Alexis. I don't think she's feeling well."

Tess added three forks to the stack on the metal tray she was using to transport dishes to and from the kitchen. "She seemed in great spirits at breakfast."

"She was fine this morning at the opening session of the conference, too. In her element. I had to leave the hotel soon after that to keep my appointment at the beauty parlor. But just now, as I was seeing the tour stragglers off, I noticed her sitting in one of the wrought-iron chairs on the front lawn. She looked— well, miserable."

"Was she alone?"

"Quite alone. She didn't even see me until I spoke to her. She had her head bent, looking down at the ground. She just seemed to be staring. I asked if she was all right, and she looked up at me and—" Dahlia batted her thick lashes in bewilderment. "Her eyes were all glittery—the way they can be when you've got a fever."

"Or when you're very upset or angry," Tess said half to herself.

Dahlia looked at her sharply. "Why, yes, I suppose so. Now that I think about it, she went all stiff and rigid, as if I'd intruded where I shouldn't have." Dahlia's lips pursed in a rueful pout. "For an instant, I had the feeling she wanted to yell at me to leave her alone."

How baffling, Tess thought. "Merely for asking if she was all right?"

Dahlia cocked her head, bemused. "I was only being solicitous, not nosy. She *did* look unwell, Tess. Strange, isn't it?"

"Mmmm," Tess murmured. "What did she say?"

"That she was fine—very curtly, I might add—and then she got up and practically ran into the house."

"You probably startled her," Tess said, moving to another table. Oh, dear, what had Chester said to Alexis?

Dahlia followed Tess, inspected the cloth on the table from which Tess was removing dishes, and evidently decided it would do. "You're probably right. I mean, why would she be angry with *me?*" Dahlia said it as though she could hardly imagine such a turn of events. "But she definitely wasn't herself. Tess—"

Dahlia broke off and watched as Marisa hurried across the backyard, her face pale. "Uh oh. Do you suppose she's losing patience with Fern already?" Dahlia inquired dryly, gazing after Marisa. "Not that one can blame her."

"I saw them in the garden together earlier," Tess said. "Fern did seem to be lecturing Marisa—on the subject of gardening, I suspect. But if Marisa doesn't like it, why doesn't she avoid Fern?"

Dahlia laughed. "Innocent Tess."

"What?" Tess asked blankly.

"Surely you've noticed that Marisa and Johnny Willis have gotten awfully thick the past few months."

"I've been preoccupied with the house."

"My dear, those two young people are in love. But

Fern Willis has that boy—and his father the reverend, too—under her capable thumb."

Tess had difficulty seeing Fern Willis in such a domineering role. But then, Reverend Willis did seem the sort of man who would want peace at any cost. She didn't know Johnny Willis well enough to form an opinion about him.

"Little Marisa," Dahlia continued, "is beside herself, trying to please Fern. If Fern takes a notion that Marisa isn't right for Johnny, I don't hold out much hope for the relationship."

"Are you saying," Tess asked, "that Fern would actually interfere in her grown son's personal life?"

Dahlia looked at her pityingly. "My naive niece—"

At that moment, Randall Isley trotted across the backyard, taking the same route Marisa had taken before him. "Marisa! Wait a minute!"

"Oh, my," Dahlia observed, "the plot does thicken, doesn't it?"

Great heavens, what tempest was Randall stirring up now? "Randall!" Tess called. "What's wrong with Marisa?"

Randall stopped long enough to wail, "I don't know. What's wrong with everybody today? I didn't do anything except try to be friendly." He trotted on around the house.

"That's what he said this morning when he made Chester so mad," Tess murmured. "I wish Randall would go to work and forget being friendly with my guests."

Dahlia's plucked brows rose. "Randall appears to have found a new object for his attentions. Lana must have gotten bored with him since breakfast. With Randall, that would be easy to do." She flicked a crumb off the nearest table.

"You heard about that?" Tess asked, surprised.

"Gertie did mention it," Dahlia said, brushing at another crumb.

Tess looked skeptical. "I'll bet you pried it out of her."

Dahlia straightened and met Tess's gaze directly. "Don't fret, dear." She looked the soul of demure innocence. "Gertie dropped a passing remark, nothing more."

"What else did Gertie mention in passing?" Tess inquired sharply.

"Why, nothing else, Tess. Are you suggesting I didn't get the whole story?"

"No," Tess assured her.

Dahlia peered at her for a long moment. "Any woman with sense would tire of Randall quickly." She paused, then added with a small shake of her head, "That doesn't say much for Reva, does it? I mean, they've been married for more than twenty years."

"People stay married for all sorts of reasons," Tess pointed out.

"True. Anyway, it looks like Marisa wants nothing to do with Randall. She's probably terrified of Fern seeing them together and drawing the wrong conclusions. Or pretending to, and running to Johnny with it."

Was it possible that Randall had made a pass at Marisa? With Randall, it wasn't something you could rule out completely. Faithfulness didn't seem to be one of his virtues, and it would explain Marisa's obvious distress. Really, Reva Isley ought to keep her husband on a leash.

"Where is Lana, by the way?" Dahlia asked.

"I haven't seen her since she came back to the house about two-thirty. She must be in her room. Let's take these things inside and have a cup of tea before we prepare for the arrival of the last tour group." After that, Tess could relax in her apartment for a short time. In spite of the evidence of trouble brewing among her guests, there had been no major crisis.

Now, if Randall would pay some attention to his wife and leave the other female guests alone—and if Chester would stop sneaking up on people and eavesdropping on private conversations—Tess could look forward to an enjoyable dinner with Luke.

A few minutes later, as they sat at the kitchen table, Dahlia said, "You know, Tess, I'm beginning to understand why you wanted to open a bed and breakfast. So many interesting people coming and going. All the little intrigues."

Tess looked at her reprovingly. "I'd rather not know about their intrigues."

"That's what makes life exciting, Tess. Relationships."

"I'll stick to my own, thank you."

Dahlia studied her across the circular expanse of the oak table. "You refer to that darling Luke Fredrik," she cooed. "How *are* things progressing with your young man?"

"I don't know what you mean by progressing, Aunt Dahlia," Tess said primly. "Luke and I like each other's company on occasion. We've become—friends."

"Tess, Tess, Tess," Dahlia remonstrated, wagging her head. "You can't fool me. Romance is my middle name. I've certainly had enough in my time to recognize it when I see it."

"I've no doubt," Tess muttered, and drank the last of her tea. Dahlia looked ready to pursue the topic when the doorbell chimed. "Your last tour group, Aunt Dahlia," Tess said, relieved.

Dahlia patted her hair. "The tea was lovely, dear. I'm off now."

Watching her go, Tess decided there was time to check on Alexis. What Dahlia had reported of Alexis's behavior in the front yard earlier worried her. She ran upstairs, her destination the Darcy Flame Suite at the far end of the wide hall.

The scent of Nedra's lemony furniture polish hung in the air. Tess stopped midway down the hall to straighten a mauve-matted print that hung on the wall—it was of two Victorian ladies ice-skating in bonnets and fur-trimmed capes. The picture was one of several flea-market finds that Tess was proud of. She stepped back, checking to see if the picture hung level now. Satisfied, she went on.

As she neared the Arctic Fancy Room, she heard Fern Willis's voice. Hearing no response to what Fern was saying, Tess deduced that she was on the telephone. Tess was already past the door when Fern's voice rose shrilly.

"How can you do this to me?"

Tess hesitated. Never before had she heard Fern raise her voice. She was always so controlled. But at the moment she sounded almost unhinged, certainly frantic. Should she knock at Fern's door on some pretext, Tess wondered, to see if Fern was all right? That would mean admitting she'd heard Fern. But if she passed on, as though she hadn't heard, and Fern needed help, that would be worse. Tess raised her hand to knock.

"You know I can't do that!" Fern cried. "No. It's out of the question."

She was still extremely upset, but she seemed to be getting control of herself. She would be mortified if she knew Tess had overheard her end of the conversation. Tess decided to wait and perhaps speak to Fern later if she still seemed troubled. She lowered her hand.

"What do you imagine that will gain you?" Fern demanded. She had dropped her voice and she spoke slowly, as if making a conscious effort to at least sound calm. But there was something almost too calm about her tone when she spoke again. "I'm listening." There was a pause, and then Fern said, "Now, you listen to me. I'll kill you before I let you do that." The threat was issued in the same deadly quiet voice, which somehow made it more frightening than if she'd shouted it.

The slam of the receiver in the cradle made Tess jump. She backed away, lest Fern open the door and find her eavesdropping.

* * *

Fern Willis's hands were shaking so badly she barely managed to hit the phone's cradle with the receiver. She clutched her head with both hands to keep from ripping the telephone from the wall and throwing it across the room.

Then, dropping her hands, she sagged onto the bed and tried to hold back the tide that threatened to engulf her in a flood of panic. That loathsome, evil woman! Thirty-one years hadn't changed her. Selfish. Vain. Manipulative. How could she. How *dare* she! Fern clenched her hands into fists to stop the shaking.

Unclenching one hand, she rubbed two fingers over the lines between her brows. She had to think. What if she went to Richard herself and told him everything? He would have to forgive her—Richard always did his Christian duty—but it would be just like him to insist on a public confession, total humiliation in front of the whole congregation. Richard was so naive that he really believed other people were as understanding and compassionate as he. Fern, on the other hand, knew people for what, with few exceptions, they were. Cruel and self-righteous. Delighting in other people's misfortunes. No. Going to Richard was not an option.

Her mind skittered desperately for another solution. How could she get her hands on the money? She could sell her car, tell Richard she needed to walk more, and she could always use his when she needed to go out of town. How much was her old Ford worth? Two thousand, maybe three. She covered her face with her hands. Dear God, this wasn't clear thinking. It was delusion. If she sold the car and everything else she owned, she couldn't come up with enough cash. And the only money they'd saved was in Richard's IRA. Even if she could get to it, she would have to explain what she had done with it. Besides all that, meeting a blackmailer's demand was futile. There would be another . . . and another.

If only she hadn't gone to that party so long ago. She groaned aloud, remembering that horrible day almost two months later when she finally accepted the truth. She couldn't remember how it had happened, but it had happened and she had done the only thing that had seemed possible at the time. Now everyone would know. Shame rose like hot bile in her throat. Oh, God, the shame. She felt it as intensely as she had at seventeen. Richard had once told her, in his own kind way, of course, that pride would be her downfall. Richard was right, as usual.

She lifted her head and stared at the lush green branches of the oak tree outside her window. But what she saw was the truth that she had kept buried for years. She had committed a grievous sin, and all her charitable acts, even the public demonstrations that had been so difficult for a private person like Fern to take part in, could not erase that sin. Now the whole town would know. And through no fault of her own, except that of being too trusting.

It was *her* fault. She and her friends had fed Fern punch laced with vodka until Fern was so drunk she didn't know what she was doing. She didn't even know who had committed that final outrage; she had never wanted to know. He probably hadn't known what he was doing, either. In the most secret part of her mind, she had sometimes wondered if there had been more than one. She shuddered and pushed the thought back in the black corner where it belonged. She didn't really want to know.

Besides, if *she* hadn't been the instigator, none of it would have happened.

Then, to compound her crime, *she* had pretended to be Fern's friend. She must have been feeling so superior all the time. The embraces, the sympathetic words. Lies. While she'd held the secret close, all these years, until the time finally came when she needed to make use of it.

That brought Fern to the last option. The black-mailing whore had to be stopped. Fern could not live with any other outcome. That's what it came down to. The bottom line.

Her hands were still now and she felt calmer. The decision had been made. All that was left was to work out how to implement it.

When Tess reached the Darcy Flame Suite, she paused a moment to collect herself. Who had Fern been talking to? And what terrible thing had the caller said to make Fern threaten him or her with death? Of course, Tess didn't believe Fern had been speaking literally. People made such exaggerated threats all the time without meaning them. Earlier in the afternoon, she herself had said she'd like to strangle Randall Isley. But it was unsettling to hear it from Fern Willis, the minister's wife, who was usually so reserved and soft-spoken.

Tess had found it difficult to accept Dahlia's assertion that Fern was an interfering mother and a domineering wife. But after hearing Fern on the telephone, Tess realized there was another side to the minister's wife that she usually kept well-concealed.

She knocked on Alexis's door, waited a few moments, and tapped again. It seemed Alexis wasn't there, or she was napping. Tess hesitated and was about to retrace her steps when the door finally opened.

"Yes?"

Tess tried to hide her shock at Alexis's appearance. The always-perfectly-groomed hair had come loose, and black strands straggled down her neck. Her face beneath the blush and powder was unnaturally pale, her lipstick gone. Her eyes were swollen, as though she'd been sleeping. No, crying, Tess thought, seeing a streak of mascara on one cheek. Tess was embarrassed to have caught Alexis in such an un-Alexis-like state.

"I woke you. I'm so sorry," she apologized.

"No, I wasn't sleeping." Alexis composed herself

with a clear effort and began smoothing her hair off her neck and repinning the French knot. "I was on the phone." She didn't invite Tess in but Tess felt like an intruder anyway.

"I wanted to check on you. Aunt Dahlia said you weren't feeling well earlier."

"Oh . . . it's nothing, really. A little nausea, but I'm better now."

"Chester had an upset stomach, too. It must have been something you both ate at lunch."

She gave Tess an odd look. "That's probably it." She closed the door except for a narrow crack.

"I won't keep you. Do let me know if there's anything you need, anything I can do for you."

"Thank you." The door closed. The lock clicked.

Tess turned around, glancing longingly at the spiral staircase that led to the library in the tower. How she would love to slip away, curl up on the library sofa, and lose herself in a good book. But it was impossible today.

Thinking about Alexis, she walked along the hall and down the stairs. Alexis had been on the telephone. With Fern? Oh, it couldn't be. Ordinarily, Alexis and Fern didn't even move in the same circles. Alexis involved herself in various society functions. Except for The Club, Fern's activities were all church-related, like the Mission Society and the shelter for the homeless. The usually retiring Fern preferred working behind the scenes, except for the few times she'd taken part in a demonstration at an abortion clinic. Alexis had nothing to do with Fern's favorite charities. When she was involved in a project, she always had a visible role. If there was any glory to be garnered, Alexis was there to get her share.

The women did occasionally work on Garden Club projects together. As far as Tess knew, they got on well enough at those times.

Then why was Alexis so obviously distraught? It

must have to do with her conversation with Chester in the garden.

Who had Fern been talking to, if not Alexis? Marisa? Could Fern have heard about Randall's attempts to "befriend" Marisa? If Dahlia was right, Fern might be looking for an excuse to separate Marisa and Johnny, and the little contretemps in the garden could provide it. But what could Marisa possibly have said to make Fern so furious?

Well, it wasn't her business, Tess decided. She had meant it when she'd told Dahlia that she preferred to remain ignorant of her guests' intrigues.

Now it was time to prepare the gazebo for the last tea of the afternoon.

Alexis Dinwitty lay on the bed in the Darcy Flame Suite, aswim in the cold, hard anger that had overwhelmed her when Chester had dropped his bomb, his thin lips pursed disapprovingly, his face long with false concern for her. The conniving snake had enjoyed telling her. She had wanted to attack him, but the feeling had lasted only a moment before the focus of her anger had settled on the appropriate target.

It all made sense now. Lana's sudden friendship, her tireless efforts to get Alexis elected president of The Club, the clever way she'd maneuvered Alexis into suggesting the officers stay at Iris House during the conference. It was all a carefully-thought-out campaign to gain Alexis's trust and get her out of the house for several days so that Lana could make her move.

And she'd played right into Lana's hands, lowered herself to Lana's cheap, conniving level. Her face heated as she remembered how proud she'd been that morning, how sure of herself. How she'd preened before the iris growers, welcoming them to Victoria Springs as if she owned the town, turning this way and that to show off her diamonds. While Lana sat in the audience with that knowing smile on her face, looking as if butter wouldn't melt in her mouth.

The woman was totally without principle or conscience. *That* was what Alexis couldn't stand. To be taken in by a stupid, good-for-nothing tramp.

But her eyes were open now.

She was glad she had stopped herself from confronting Harley in the heat of anger. Harley was a wizard at business, but when it came to women he was a babe. It was Lana she had to deal with. Fortunately, Alexis had learned all the ways to fight for what was hers in that trailer park back in Wichita. Forget rules and giving people the benefit of the doubt and fair play. This called for back-alley tactics. Lana Morrison would think she'd tangled with a buzz saw before Alexis was finished with her.

Chapter 9

By four P.M., when Dahlia stepped out the front door to meet the last tour group, the final tea of the afternoon was spread in the gazebo. Tess and Gertie, weary with the not-unpleasant tiredness that comes from a job well done, admired the laden table.

"One more time, Gertie," Tess said, "and then you can go home. I'll clean up."

Gertie scanned the table. "Where's the cake knife?"

"It's here somewhere." Tess lifted several trays to look beneath them. "That's funny. I took it inside to wash it, but I was sure I brought it back out with the cake tray."

"Maybe it fell off." Gertie stepped back and bent over to look beneath the table. She straightened up again with a puzzled frown. "Not there. We must have left it inside."

"I'll go," Tess said, and ran down the gazebo steps and across the yard.

Nedra was finishing off a piece of blackberry jam cake and iced tea at the kitchen table before leaving for the day. Tess's gaze swept the countertops. "Have you seen the cake knife, Nedra?"

"Nope," mumbled Nedra around a bite of cake. "Dishwasher?"

"Good idea," Tess said, but the knife wasn't among the silverware in the dishwasher's webbed plastic basket. She looked in all the kitchen drawers, too, but didn't find the cake knife.

65

Nedra finished her tea and pushed back her chair. She went to the sink and stuck her hand down through the opening for the garbage disposal. Her hand came up empty. "Thought it might've fallen down there, but nope."

Tess looked around helplessly. "Where could it be?"

"Out in the yard, maybe," Nedra suggested. "In the grass."

Tess thought she would have noticed if she'd dropped the knife in the yard. There wasn't time to look for it now, anyway. She got another knife from a drawer. "This will do, if Gertie still hasn't found it in the gazebo. I hope it turns up. It was one of my grandparents' wedding gifts."

"Didn't evaporate," Nedra said. "It's around here somewhere." She followed Tess out the door. "I'll look in the yard before I go home."

"Thank you, Nedra."

Tess left Nedra walking in circles, scanning the grass, and returned to the gazebo. "I couldn't find the knife," she reported to Gertie. "We'll have to use this one."

"It's not in this gazebo," Gertie said. "I've looked everywhere." She craned her neck around the gazebo's latticework. "Why's Nedra going around in circles? Makes me dizzy, just looking at her."

Tess watched Nedra complete another circle and start slowly along the side of the house. "She's searching for the knife."

"She won't find it over there," Gertie observed. "Neither one of us has gone into the side yard with food or dishes. If we dropped it, it'll be in a direct line between here and the back door."

"Maybe she's given up and decided to go home," Tess sighed. She was too tired to go and see. Nedra knew what she was doing. From the north side of the house, Tess could hear Dahlia, reeling off the names of several varieties of iris as easily as she could have recited the alphabet. The four o'clock tour should be nearly finished. Within the next few minutes, the tour group would descend on the gazebo.

"I think they're headed this way," Gertie announced.

Tess nodded and took up her position behind the buffet table next to the teapot.

A woman screamed.

People with the garden tour started surging around the corner of the house to see what was happening.

Tess and Gertie exchanged a look of incomprehension and left the gazebo. The scream had come from the south side of the house, where Nedra had disappeared a few minutes earlier, the opposite side from where the garden tour had ended. Tess began to run toward the south side yard. She could hear Gertie behind her, grunting as she struggled to keep up. It must have been Nedra who screamed. Tess hadn't seen anyone else go around to that side of the house in nearly half an hour.

It's nothing serious, Tess told herself. Nedra hadn't been watching where she was going; she had probably run into something. Maybe twisted an ankle. That could keep Nedra off her feet for days. Tess groaned. How would she manage with a house full of guests and no cleaning woman?

Now, that was a selfish thought. Poor Nedra might have a broken limb and here Tess was, worrying about who would change the bed linens. She would do it herself. It wasn't as if she hadn't changed her share of sheets in her time.

She had a full view of the side yard now, and there was Nedra, standing beside a bed of Darcy Flame irises, blocking Tess's view of what Nedra was staring at. At least Nedra was on her feet, so she couldn't be seriously hurt, thank God.

Nedra staggered back a few steps, exposing a slender leg to Tess's view. Someone screamed again, but this time the scream came from Gertie, who was still behind Tess.

Tess circled around Nedra, then stopped short and clutched Nedra's thin arm.

Other voices reached Tess as some of those with the garden tour arrived at the back corner of the house and ventured a few steps into the south side yard. Gertie crept up to stand on the other side of Tess beside the iris bed, panting, her face flushed with exertion and shock.

Tess would always remember that moment. The scent of the lilac bush beside the house. The warmth of the afternoon sun on her arms. The way Lana Morrison looked as she lay lifeless on her back, her platinum hair spread out, as if it had been arranged for a photograph, over crushed coral petals of the irises she had knocked to the ground as she fell. The blade of Grandmother Darcy's cake knife was buried in her chest, and gushing blood had created a dark stain on the bodice of her pale-blue dress.

Tess started to tremble. She had never liked Lana much. Lana was the sort of woman other women didn't fully trust. But that didn't make it any easier to see Lana like this.

An elderly man came up behind Tess and peered over her shoulder. "Oh, my word!"

Tess tore her gaze from the body in the Darcy Flame bed and turned around. The man's bald head glistened in the sunlight, his blue eyes bulged. Dahlia was but a few steps behind the man, her lovely face pale. "Get back," Tess said, taking the man's arm and urging him toward the backyard. "Aunt Dahlia, help me keep everybody away from here."

Dahlia pulled herself together and brusquely took charge, issuing directions to the tourists in a voice that no one thought to disobey. She shooed them out of the side yard and planted herself at the corner of the house to keep them out.

Gertie and Nedra, mute in the face of the horrible scene, turned away from the corpse. Gertie's face was

ashen with red splotches high on her cheeks. Nedra's
tall, thin body seemed somehow to have shrunk.

Tess was suddenly concerned for both of them.
"Gertie, would you call nine-one-one, please?" she
asked. "And Nedra, you'd better go with her. You look
as if you need to sit down." They left without argument, and Tess went to stand beside Dahlia at the corner of the house.

Dahlia shot a grim glance in Tess's direction before
turning back to stare at the crowd in the backyard. She
twisted a lace-edged handkerchief in her hands and
cleared her throat. "You don't go around setting fires,
Tess, without eventually getting burned," she said, as if
pronouncing the world's doom.

Tess studied Dahlia's patrician profile. "What are
you talking about, Aunt Dahlia?"

"Lana Morrison and the way she toyed with people's
lives."

Tess looked down at her low-heeled navy shoes in
the thick green grass, feeling uncomfortable about
speaking ill of the dead. "I don't really think she meant
to cause trouble."

Dahlia sniffed. "People don't become saints just because they're dead."

Tess couldn't argue with that.

How many people had Lana angered with her flirtations and her barbed taunts? Reva Isley and Chester
Leeds. Alexis Dinwitty, who by this time had surely
heard of Lana's excursion through the hedge last night.
There was no other explanation for the change in
Alexis described by Dahlia and which Tess had seen
with her own eyes when she knocked on Alexis's door.

Several of The Club's officers had reason to dislike
and distrust Lana, but enough to push them to the act
of murder? Surely none of them could have done this.
It was madness.

"Regardless," Dahlia went on, "it appears Lana
picked the wrong person to toy with this time, wouldn't

you say?" There was an adamant edge to Dahlia's words, as though Lana Morrison's violent death had been inevitable, as if Dahlia had expected it, sooner or later.

"Do you know something I don't know?"

"Any number of things," Dahlia replied with a glimmer of irony. "I've lived much longer. I would have to be pretty dense not to have learned more."

"You know what I mean, Aunt Dahlia." Tess glanced briefly at the body in the iris bed, catching a flash of colors from the corner of her eye. The blazing coral of the Darcy Flames. The soft blue of Lana's dress. Dark-red blood. "Who do you think could have done this?"

Dahlia's intelligent dark eyes moved over Tess's face, as if to discover if Tess were being deliberately obtuse. Dahlia looked shrewd and unwaveringly sure of herself. "Why, one of your guests, of course. You don't think a tourist did it, do you? Or one of your employees?"

"Gertie or Nedra? Don't be ridiculous!" Tess chewed her lip before admitting, "I don't think it was a stranger, either." The knife buried in Lana's chest spoke of unbridled passion. Hatred. Rage. People didn't harbor such strong feelings for strangers—unless they were certifiably insane. Nor could Tess picture a mere casual acquaintance getting worked up enough to commit murder. It was somebody Lana knew well, somebody who shared a long history with her.

"Then?" Dahlia queried.

Still, Tess didn't want to accept Dahlia's conclusion. "That doesn't mean it was one of the guests," she protested.

"It's a simple process of elimination," Dahlia said firmly. "The police will discover they all have motives. Mark my words."

"What motives?"

"I don't know yet. But anybody who was close to Lana could have reason to wish her out of the way.

Trust me, Tess. I've had dealings of my own with Lana Morrison. She was a truly loathsome person." Spots of high color burned in Dahlia's pale cheeks now.

Tess wondered if Dahlia realized that her words could be taken as self-incriminating. "What kind of dealings?"

Dahlia shrugged. "The details aren't important. It was a while ago."

Tess stared at her. "You can't mean Lana and Uncle Maurice—?"

Dahlia's dark eyes locked with Tess's reprovingly. "I shall pretend I didn't hear that, Tess."

Tess felt herself flushing. "I'm sorry if I misunderstood."

Dahlia looked away, dismissing the subject.

But Tess could not dismiss it so easily. What had Dahlia meant? Had Dahlia's husband had a fling with Lana sometime in the past? But Maurice seemed devoted to Dahlia. Tess simply could not believe he'd ever strayed.

Well, it didn't really matter now. Whatever it was, it had happened a long time ago, so it could have nothing to do with Lana's murder.

The tour group milled aimlessly around the backyard, unwilling to leave before they knew more about what had happened, but not knowing what to do with themselves in the meantime. The sudden silence between Tess and Dahlia was tense. Tess spoke merely to break it. "I can't bring myself to go to the gazebo and serve tea as if nothing had happened."

"If they're barbaric enough to eat at a time like this, let them serve themselves," Dahlia said, her voice cracking a little around the edges. She still twisted the handkerchief in her small, manicured hands. "Look at them—gawking, trying to get a look at Lana. They're like hungry wolves with the smell of blood in their nostrils. We should send them away now."

Tess put an arm around her aunt's narrow waist and

felt a tremor run through Dahlia. "The police may want to question them."

Dahlia seemed to relax as she looked at Tess, her forehead puckered. "Oh, you're right. I wasn't thinking."

"Are you sure you don't want to go in the house and wait?"

"What? Leave you here to deal with this rabble alone?" Dahlia snapped.

Tess understood what she was doing. Dahlia needed a target for her anger at the murderer, and the tourists were there. They were wandering around, murmuring quietly to one another, behaving themselves very well, all things considered. If they wished to help themselves to the food in the gazebo, Tess thought, then more power to them. As for herself, she didn't think she would want to eat again for days.

A siren sounded in the distance.

Chapter 10

Victoria Springs's chief of police, Desmond Butts, stepped into the room, his piercing gaze sweeping the apprehensive assemblage. He had ordered them into the parlor as soon as he arrived, and they had been waiting for him for half an hour.

As they waited, they had talked in hushed tones while, outside the house, the medical examiner arrived and made the official pronouncement of death, then the chief and two of his officers had secured the scene of the crime and, after the body had been removed, questioned the people in the four o'clock garden tour.

The questioning of the tourists had been brief which, Tess guessed, meant nothing very helpful had come of it.

The talk in the parlor, as Tess, Dahlia, Gertie, Nedra, and those currently in residence in Iris House waited for the chief, had been mostly in the "I can't believe Lana was murdered" vein. Blame-placing, even blame-hinting, was studiously avoided. Nobody admitted to having seen or heard anything even remotely related to Lana's murder.

As for Tess, she mainly watched and listened to the others, unable to believe that one of them was a murderer. She knew these people. Wouldn't she have noticed *something* if one of them harbored such a violent streak in his character?

Butts, bushy-headed and spectacled with a ruddy, blunt-featured face, folded his arms across his broad chest and cleared his throat portentously. Plainly, he was in a bad temper, as though he'd been called away from something more important. Tess wondered what could be more important than murder.

"Now then—" Butts's wide nostrils flared and his eyes traveled slowly around the circle of faces, stopping for a moment to squint at each one.

Gertie, seated in a sculptured cane chair, looked back at him expectantly, as though she believed he was about to solve the case and make an arrest on the spot. She had not completely recovered her color, and her fingers rolled and unrolled the hem of her apron nervously.

Nedra, perched on the edge of a skirted chintz chair, stared at the bony hands clasped tightly in her lap. When Butts's eyes lit on her, she muttered darkly to herself.

"What's that, Miz Yates?" Butts demanded.

"Not talking to you," Nedra said.

A muscle in Butts's jaw twitched as he shifted his gaze to Reva and Randall Isley, who shared the moss-green velvet settee. Randall, uncharacteristically subdued, seemed belatedly to have remembered that he was married and had thrown himself into the role of the attentive husband, his arm wrapped protectively around his wife's shoulders.

Tess only wished it hadn't taken the shock of Lana's death to remind Randall where his duty lay. Every once in a while he glanced concernedly down at Reva, who pointedly ignored him and gave her attention to the toe of her shiny red patent leather shoe as it traced and re-traced the gold diamond design in the hunter-green carpet.

Fern leaned forward as Butts's gaze reached the sofa, where she sat beside Tess. Her face looked washed out in contrast to the cheerful rose-and-green chintz of the sofa behind her. She was clutching a gold fringed cushion to her breast, as if for solace.

When Butts got to Tess, she held his eyes without blinking, and he sniffed and moved on.

Marisa, huddled on the low ottoman near the sofa, ignored Butts's perusal, staring fixedly at the cherry grandfather's clock in one corner and gnawing unhappily on a thumbnail.

Butts's eyes lifted to take in Chester, who stood with his back to a lace-curtained front window, his shoulders back, his hands clasped behind him, as rigidly straight as a military guard on duty. Tess couldn't see Chester's eyes—they were lowered in what might have been solemn contemplation of the tragedy of Lana's murder—but his mouth had a satisfied set to it. Tess gave a tiny shake of her head, thinking she must be misinterpreting Chester's attitude.

The chief's glance slid to Alexis, whose makeup and hair had been restored to a semblance of their customary perfection. She seemed to have aged ten years since morning. Deeply grooved lines—Tess wondered how she could have overlooked them before—led from her nose to the downturned corners of her mouth, and her eyes were lusterless.

Dahlia, as meticulously turned out as when she'd arrived at Iris House, tilted her chin and smiled sadly at the chief as his gaze snagged hers.

Butts flushed. "Let's get on with it, people. If one of you wants to confess now, it'll save us all a lot of time and grief."

The parlor went absolutely still for a moment. Then Randall boomed, "Are you suggesting one of *us* killed Lana?"

More than suggesting, Tess thought glumly as Dahlia caught her eye and nodded. Hadn't she already told Tess it had to be one of them?

Butts shot a hostile glance at Randall. "You gonna tell me who did, Isley, if not one of you?"

Chester took a step away from the window. "Now, see here!"

"Haven't even read us our rights," huffed Gertie, who was a great fan of TV cop shows.

"I wish I'd never heard of the Garden Club," Marisa murmured, and a little sob escaped her.

Alexis hugged herself and made a strange moaning sound in her throat.

"Quiet!" Butts yelled.

Startled silence followed the chief's outburst, then Fern spoke hesitantly. "There was a garden tour here. Dozens of people, any one of whom—"

"Get real, Miz Willis!" Butts barked so loudly that Fern jumped. "I talked to those people. They were rank strangers, for God's sake. None of them even knew Lana Morrison's name. Half of them didn't even know we had a corpse on our hands until the ambulance attendants carried her off in a body bag."

Tess winced at the image his words evoked. Lana the flirt. Lana the gossip. Lana and her schemes within schemes, zipped into a plastic shroud and hauled off like so much unsightly litter.

"Of course, the murderer wouldn't admit to knowing Lana," Fern Willis said.

Butts waved this away as if it were unworthy of any response.

Chester shifted restlessly, running one hand down the back of his head over the already smooth sparse strands of his hair. "Fern has a point. If a tourist murdered Lana—somebody from her past, perhaps—naturally they'd say they didn't know her," he muttered irritably.

Butts looked him up and down, then turned away as if Chester's observation were the babbling of a two-year-old. He scanned the room again. "Oh, you'd all like nothing better than for me to run around chasing wild geese. But we all know the killer's in this room."

"You can't accuse *me* without evidence," Randall sputtered. "I won't stand for it. I barely knew Lana Morrison. I demand—"

"Shut up, Randall!" Reva snarled. "Nobody's fooled

by your stupid lies." She jerked away from him. "And get your sweaty arm off me."

Every eye in the room had focused on the Isleys. Randall slumped back in the settee as though he were trying to disappear into the velvet upholstery.

"Care to explain what lies you're talking about, Miz Isley?" Butts inquired with mock friendliness.

"No!" Reva responded, and covered her face with her hands.

Butts rolled his eyes toward the ceiling. "If you ya-hoos had to murder one of your own, I wish you hadn't picked the first week of tourist season."

Tess bridled. One of their *own?* What did he mean by that? Butts made it sound as if they were all involved in some sort of conspiracy to get rid of Lana. To him, the murder was apparently just another inconvenience. Tess had to clamp her lips together to keep from telling him what she thought of his unprofessional attitude.

Butts whipped out a small spiral notebook from his shirt pocket and flipped back the cover. "Okay, let's get down to business, and remember, withholding evidence is a serious offense." He looked around the room and let his words sink in. "Now, Miz Yates, you found the body—is that right?" Nedra nodded apprehensively, and Butts went on, "What time was that?"

"Well, uh—" Nedra gulped and looked at Tess for help.

"It was about four-thirty," Tess supplied. "The garden tours took half an hour. The last tour group arrived at four and they were heading toward the gazebo, where Gertie and I were waiting to serve tea, when we heard Nedra scream."

Butts scribbled in his notebook. "Why were you out in the yard anyway, Miz Yates? Don't you work in the house?"

Nedra shifted uncomfortably. "Looking for Tess's knife."

Butts gave her a narrow-eyed perusal. "The one used to stab Lana Morrison?"

Nedra cast a sorrowful glance at Tess and nodded. "Didn't know it'd been used for that then."

Butts ignored her and wheeled around to jab a blunt finger in Tess's direction. "So the murder weapon belongs to you, Miss Darcy?"

Tess drew herself up. "Of course it does. This house and its contents were left to me in my Aunt Iris's will. The cake knife originally belonged to my grandparents, and then it came to Aunt Iris. Gertie and I had been using it in the gazebo all afternoon. During the third garden tour, we noticed it was missing."

"Check Iris Darcy's will," Butts muttered, and wrote in his notebook while Tess fumed. Did he think she was lying about the inheritance?

"So when did the murder weapon disappear?" Butts asked, emphasizing the last word as though he were placing it in quotation marks.

"I've already told you. Gertie and I noticed it was missing when we were getting ready to serve the four-thirty tea," Tess said through clenched teeth.

"The last time I remember seeing it in the gazebo was after the second tour group left," Gertie added. "That was about three-thirty."

Butts's brow furrowed. "You people in the habit of leaving dangerous weapons laying around like that?"

"A cake knife?" Tess flared. "And how were we to know there was a murderer on the loose?"

Butts studied her with lowered brows for an instant. "So sometime between three-thirty and four-thirty, the murderer snatched the knife from the gazebo. Who was in the gazebo during that time?"

"Gertie and I were in and out," Tess said.

Nobody else uttered a word. "Did either of you see anyone else in there during that hour?" Butts asked.

Tess and Gertie looked at each other in dismay and shook their heads.

Butts sent a surly glance around the room. "Did *anybody* see someone else in the gazebo between three-thirty and four-thirty?"

Still nobody spoke.

Butts turned to Nedra and pounced. "Then how did you know the knife was missing, Miz Yates?"

"I told her," Tess interjected impatiently, "when I went into the kitchen looking for the knife."

Butts scribbled some more. "Okay, did any of you see Miz Morrison over there in the side yard before Miz Yates found her body?"

A ring of blank faces met the chief's narrowed eyes; nobody admitted to seeing Lana in the side yard. "Innocent as newborn babes, the whole bunch of you," Butts said sarcastically.

"You can't see very much of the south side yard from either the front or the back of the house," Tess pointed out. "You have to go over there to get a full view."

Butts grumbled crankily and wrote in his notebook.

"Perhaps I can be of some help, Chief Butts," Dahlia said sweetly.

Butts wet the lead of his pencil with the tip of his tongue and all but smacked his lips. "Maybe we'll get someplace now. Tell me exactly what you saw, Miz Forrest."

"Nothing," Dahlia said with the lift of an elegant brow.

"Pardon?" Butts said blankly.

"It's what I didn't see. I conducted the garden tours, and I started with the south side of the house. There's a huge bed of Darcy Flames over there, you see."

"Flames!" Butts bleated. "Don't try to tell me there was a fire, too, because—"

"No, no, Chief Butts," Dahlia interposed reasonably. "Darcy Flame is the name of an iris which was bred by my late dear sister, Iris."

"Those orange-looking flowers where the body was found?"

"Coral," Dahlia corrected.

Butts waved the hand clutching the notebook. "Whatever. Are those the flowers you're talking about?"

"Yes, those are Darcy Flames. As I was saying, I started each tour with the Darcy Flames. Their beauty is quite overwhelming to people when they first see them. You should have heard the ooh's and ah's. It got the tour off with a bang, so to speak. Ooh," Dahlia sighed, pressing fingertips to her temples. "I'll never forget the sight of Lana lying there among those gorgeous irises. Everybody said they were the best part of the tour."

"I don't gave a tinker's damn about the confounded garden tour!" Butts bellowed. "I thought you said you could help with the murder investigation."

Dahlia dropped her hands to her lap. "I'm getting to that," she said with the patient tone of one dealing with a stubborn child. "I began the four o'clock tour as I had the previous ones, with the Darcy Flames."

Butts heaved a put-upon sigh. "Get on with it, please, Miz Forrest. I don't have all day."

"I'm trying to. You keep interrupting me." Butts looked furious but kept quiet. "We left that side yard perhaps five minutes after four," Dahlia went on. "Lana wasn't there then."

Butts hastily began to scrawl in his notebook. "I want to know where you all were between four and four-thirty. I also want to know when and where you last saw Lana Morrison." He swung his big head toward Tess. "We'll start with you, Miss Darcy, since you and Miz Bogart seem to be the only ones who had access to the knife."

Tess tensed. *"Anybody* could have taken it from the gazebo during one of our trips to the house."

Butts nodded sagely. "So you say. Now, will you answer the question?"

"Between four and four-thirty I was running back and forth between the house and the gazebo. As for the last time I saw Lana—" She closed her eyes to shut out Butts's meaty face and thought back over the day. Lana flirting outrageously with Randall at breakfast, later leaving with Alexis for the conference at the Hilltop Hotel, returning alone in the afternoon and going straight upstairs.

"She came back from the Iris Growers Conference at the hotel about two-thirty and went up to her room. That's the last time I saw her—" Tess swallowed hard. "—alive."

Chapter 11

When Chief Butts finished grilling those assembled in the parlor as to when and where they had last seen Lana Morrison alive, he cautioned them—actually, it was more like a command—not to spread "loose talk" around town about the murder. Then he dismissed them curtly with a look that said: *You people are trying to pull the wool over my eyes, but you won't get away with it.* Finally, he ordered Tess to show him the room assigned to Lana in Iris House.

Tess left him in the Cliffs of Dover Room, sent Gertie, Nedra, and Dahlia home, and hurriedly cleared the gazebo, put the food away, and cleaned up the kitchen.

While she worked, her thoughts kept going back over the exchange between Butts and her guests in the parlor. Was there a clue to the identity of Lana's murderer in what they had told the chief?

If so, it escaped her.

Of course, their collective attitude did leave something to be desired. When Butts released them, Tess's guests had retired to their rooms to get ready for the evening session of the Iris Growers Conference. This business-as-usual attitude had struck Tess as shockingly unfeeling but, as Dahlia had pointed out, The Club was hosting several hundred out-of-town iris growers, few of whom knew Lana. Canceling the evening session at the last minute would serve no purpose. The conference must go on as scheduled.

What Dahlia left unsaid was that none of Tess's guests, all of whom knew Lana well, appeared to be deeply cut up over her death. They all said it was a terrible thing, naturally, and Lana would be sorely missed, both as friend and fellow Club member. But Tess wondered how many of them really considered Lana a friend. Before today, she would have said Alexis and Fern certainly. Now, even that was questionable.

According to what her guests had told the chief, none of them had seen Lana after she returned to Iris House at 2:30 that afternoon. If one of them was lying, he or she was very good at it.

Twenty minutes after Butts went into the Cliffs of Dover Room, Tess heard his heavy steps descending the stairs. She gave the range top a final swipe, tossed the damp cloth in the sink, and met Butts in the foyer.

"Did you find anything helpful, Chief?" Tess inquired.

Butts drew himself up importantly and looked down his nose at Tess. "You should know better than to ask a question like that, Miss Darcy," he clucked. "All information relating to a police investigation is confidential." Tess would not have been surprised had Butts patted her on the head and told her to run along.

"Can we clean Lana's room now?"

"Why?" he asked suspiciously.

Tess sighed. Did the man think she wanted to get rid of evidence he might have missed? "To make it ready for another guest—if you're finished in there, that is."

"Oh." He opened the door. "You go ahead. I gave that room a good once-over." A quick one, too, Tess thought critically. He turned back and pointed a finger to emphasize his next words. "But I don't want anybody in that side yard until we're finished with it. Inform the others and leave our tapes up until I say you can take them down." Evidently the word "please" was not in the man's vocabulary.

"Of course," Tess agreed, irritated at the way he kept barking orders, as though she were one of his officers.

"Oh, and by the way, Miss Darcy," Butts added as he went out the door, "if the lab gets any clear prints off the murder weapon, I'll be back to fingerprint everybody."

Tess found herself staring at the red and yellow irises in the stained-glass panes of the closed door. Furious, she paced across the foyer, Chief Butts's parting words ringing in her ears.

She raked a hand carelessly through her thick auburn hair. He'd be back, all right. For some reason, Butts seemed to dislike everyone in Iris House, including her, and she'd never even met him before today. "He's dying to fingerprint us like common criminals!" she fumed aloud.

Tess's heart skipped a beat. Her fingerprints, as well as Gertie's, would be on the knife handle; they'd been using it all afternoon. Surely Butts couldn't turn that into evidence against them. Could he?

Tess feared he might try to do just that. She'd gotten the distinct impression that she and Gertie were Chief Butts's prime suspects. She stopped pacing. Butts couldn't arrest them based on finding their fingerprints on the knife, she told herself. He first had to prove motive and opportunity. Neither she nor Gertie had a motive to murder Lana. Tess supposed, from Butts's viewpoint, they'd had opportunity, but so had everybody else in the house.

Shaking off these worrisome thoughts, she ran upstairs to see what condition Butts had left Lana's room in.

Walls, carpeting, love seat, gauzy lace side curtains, and quilted and lace-trimmed bed coverings in the Cliffs of Dover Room were all creamy white, like the tall, bearded iris of the same name. In dramatic con-

trast, the bed and bedside lamp were of sculptured
brass, and the skirted armchair and several throw pillows were covered with crisp red-and-white-patterned
glazed chintz. A white ironstone pitcher on the intricately carved white dresser overflowed with red silk
carnations.

Tess had thought the cheerful elegance of the sur-
roundings suited Lana, who had been delighted with the
room assignment.

Had it really been only twenty-four hours ago when
Lana had arrived at Iris House so pretty and full of life?

And now ...

Tess shuddered and tried not to imagine the inelegant
environment of the county morgue where Lana's body
must be at that very moment.

The condition of the Cliffs of Dover Room was not
as bad as Tess had feared, given Butts's surly attitude.
The contents of the bathroom wastebasket—a few wadded and lipstick-smudged tissues—had been dumped on
the bathroom floor. Evidently Butts felt it was beneath
his dignity to clean up after himself. Tess picked up the
tissues and dropped them in the basket. The closet
doors stood open. The chief must have gone through all
Lana's pockets.

Lana's handbag lay on the bed. Butts had pawed
through its contents and left them strewn across the
puffy white comforter. It would have taken less than a
minute to put everything back where he'd found it, Tess
thought crossly as she returned the items, one by one,
to the handbag. A blue leather billfold containing
seventy-six dollars in cash and three major credit cards;
a checkbook; a packet of tissues; a zippered clear-
plastic case containing mascara, eyebrow pencil, several
shades of lip liner and lipstick, a small bottle of co-
logne and another of moisturizing lotion; a credit-card
receipt; three ballpoint pens; a ring of keys; and three
four-by-six-inch lined index cards covered with notes in
what Tess recognized as Lana's cramped handwriting.

Frowning in puzzlement, Tess read what was written on the cards which, at first glance, might as well have been a foreign language.

Bacterial soft rot
    Symptoms: yel. leaf tips; squishy, foul-smelling rhizomes
    Treatment: cut back rhi. to clean white tissue, remove tainted soil, ster. knife
Leaf spot
    Symptoms: sm. black spts. on lvs.
    Treatment: spray with cop. fung.
Gray mold
    Symptoms: yel./br. leaf tips, gr. mold at fan base
    Treatment: spray benomyl, carbendazim or thiophanatelmethyl
Ink disease
    Symptoms: premature yellowing of bulbous irises, blk. strks. on bulb
    Treatment: no cure—dig up & burn plants, sterilize soil
Mosaic virus
    Symptoms: deformed, striped, mottled blooms
    Treatment: same as ink dis.

The third card contained only two words: *Malignant hyperthermia.*

The writing made little sense to Tess, but these were apparently the notes Lana had used for the session she had conducted that morning at the Iris Growers Conference. Tess wondered if the handbag had contained anything Butts considered relevant to his investigation. If so, he had taken it with him.

She dropped Lana's note cards in the handbag, then hesitated, retrieved the cards, and stuck them in the pocket of her skirt. As an afterthought, she took out the checkbook and looked at the balance. Three hundred and four dollars and ten cents. If this was all the money Lana had in the bank, Gertie was right—Lana had been running desperately low on funds. But she could have had other accounts.

Tess returned the checkbook to the handbag and snapped the clasp shut. She packed the bag, with the rest of Lana's belongings, in the suitcase Lana had brought with her.

Tomorrow, she would find out where she should send the suitcase. As far as Tess knew, Fern Willis was the only relative Lana had in town. Would Fern be in charge of the burial? At any rate, Fern would know what should be done with the suitcase and Lana's car, which was parked at the curb in front of Iris House.

Tess looked around the room one last time, making sure she hadn't missed anything of Lana's, and a wave of sadness engulfed her. Lana might have been a gossip and a troublemaker, but she hadn't deserved such an untimely and bloody death. Blinking to keep back tears, Tess left the room.

In the hallway, she hesitated for a moment, wondering if she should speak to Fern about Lana's belongings right away. No sound came from any of the rooms around her. To Tess the silence was almost sepulchral. But that was only because she'd been thinking of Lana, she told herself.

The silence could probably be explained by the fact that all the guests were trying to rest before getting ready for the evening session of the conference. However, Tess doubted if they were any more successful at turning off thoughts of the murder than she was. In spite of their attitude toward Lana, surely they were still dealing with the shock of the murder and trying to accept what had happened.

All but one—the murderer—if Chief Butts and Dahlia were right. He or she was probably feeling pretty smug, pleased with having gotten through the police interrogation without calling special attention to himself.

Remembering Fern's tense, drawn face in the parlor, Tess decided not to bother her now. Tomorrow would be soon enough.

As she hurried toward the stairs, she glanced at her wristwatch. The time had gotten away from her. She could barely manage a quick shower and change of clothes before Luke came to take her to dinner. Dear Luke. How glad she was now that he'd insisted they go out for dinner.

She didn't want to spend the evening in this big house alone.

Chapter 12

Wearing a lime-green dress piped in white and fresh makeup, her auburn curls temporarily tamed by a brush and hairspray and arranged in a smooth, turned-under style, Tess felt sure she looked like a carefree young woman enjoying an evening out with nothing on her mind but the blond man in the navy suit who sat across the small table from her. That is, unless one looked closely enough to see the haunted look in her brown eyes, which she knew was there, from a glance in the mirror before leaving Iris House. Since the intimate little restaurant, one of Victoria Springs's finest, was dimly lit, it was unlikely that anyone but Luke had noticed.

But like most small towns, Victoria Springs fed on gossip. News of the murder had already spread, and several diners who were known to Tess had stopped her on the way to the table, wanting to hear the gory details. Tess had declined to satisfy their curiosity.

Now, she poked unhappily at her smoked salmon. "Chief Butts's attitude really ticked me off," she said. Since word of the murder had made the rounds, Tess saw no reason to heed Butts's caution to keep mum with Luke. She had spent the past ten minutes telling him about the session in the parlor with Chief Butts and what he'd said to her as he left Iris House. She spoke in hushed tones, aware that several ears were cocked in their direction.

She put down her fork and looked at Luke disconsolately. "He doesn't even know me, Luke, so how can he dislike me?"

Luke laid his fork aside and reached out to cover Tess's hand with his own. "It's not you, Tess." Following her lead, he also kept his voice low. "It's what you stand for. You're a Darcy. Old family, social connections, money."

"Money, hah!" Tess muttered. "All I have to my name is in Iris House."

"That looks like a lot to Butts," Luke said. "He grew up in poverty. A sick mother and a father who drank too much and wouldn't work." Retrieving his fork and knife, he cut a bite of rare steak and chewed it thoughtfully before he went on. "Butts went to school with an older cousin of mine who told me he never saw Des Butts wear a pair of shoes without holes in them. Or any coat at all. When it was cold, Butts came to school wearing three or four layers of clothes."

"That's terrible," Tess said, sympathy for the young Desmond Butts momentarily overcoming anger at the officious man she'd met that day. "It must have taken a lot of courage to keep going to school under those conditions. I'll bet the other kids made fun of him, too."

Luke buttered a fat whole-wheat roll. "Probably. You know how kids are. Anyway, the result is that Butts resents people who are socially or financially better off than he is."

"I guess I can understand that," Tess admitted grudgingly, "but it doesn't give him the right to—" She looked around and leaned closer to Luke. "—to practically accuse me and Gertie of murder."

"It's probably some kind of police routine."

"Like good cop–bad cop—except without the good cop?"

"Yeah. Butts was in a room full of some of Victoria

Springs's civic and social leaders, one of whom he thinks is a murderer."

Tess reached for her fork and stabbed a piece of potato. "He made *that* perfectly clear."

"You think he's wrong?"

Tess hesitated and finally shook her head. "I don't know. It's hard to imagine any of those people as a killer. They're all responsible, upstanding citizens, and murder—especially *this* murder—is so ugly."

Luke ate another bite of steak and washed it down with water. His warm blue eyes held hers. "Butts probably started out on the offensive to make sure you all understand he's in charge and doesn't intend to make any concessions simply because he's dealing with influential people."

Bless him. He was doing his best to soothe her worry, but it wasn't working.

"That's ridiculous," Tess protested. "I have about as much influence as—as Primrose." Remembering that the uppity Persian usually managed to have things to her liking around Iris House, Tess amended, "Less, even."

Luke grinned at the reference to the cat, who had yet to let him get close enough to pet her. Leaning forward, he reached for Tess's hand, enclosing it in both of his. For one moment, Tess wished that she could fit all of herself into that strong, capable shelter. "Don't fret, honey," he murmured. "Your fingerprints on the cake knife don't mean a thing. Butts can't build a case against you or Gertie since you're innocent."

"Innocent people have been arrested before."

"You won't be arrested." He gave her hand a final squeeze before releasing it. "There's no real evidence against you."

Tess wished she was as sure of that as Luke seemed to be.

They finished eating and lingered over cappuccinos. Finally, Tess said, "I've been over and over everything that happened today, looking for a clue to Lana's murderer. It's all so baffling."

A small frown marred Luke's handsome face. "Forget it, Tess. It's not up to you to figure it out."

Ignoring this sensible bit of advice, she took a pen and notepad from her purse. "Aunt Dahlia agrees with Butts that one of my guests killed Lana. But each one of them told the chief they didn't see Lana after two-thirty when she returned from the conference and went up to her room. If Dahlia and Butts are right, one of them is lying."

Luke was being drawn in, clearly against his better judgment. "It *must* be one of them. I find it hard to believe, too, but who else could it be?" He watched her write something on the pad. "What are you doing?"

"I saw most of my guests during the afternoon. Maybe if I make a list of what I saw in chronological order, we can figure out who's lying."

Luke lifted a blond brow. He seemed to be thinking that talk was one thing, but putting it in writing quite another. "I don't like the idea of your playing detective, Tess. Isn't that Butts's job?"

"I don't trust Butts to be impartial. He's already zeroed in on me and Gertie. It can't hurt to get down what I remember while it's fresh in my mind." She wrote *Where guests were from 2:30 P.M. to after 6 P.M. All times approximate.*

Tess had the bit in her teeth and was going to run with it. Regardless of his obvious doubts, Luke's look was endearing.

Tess scribbled hurriedly for several minutes.

> 2:30 P.M.—*Lana returned alone from conference and went to her room.*
> 3:00 P.M.—*By this time all other guests back at Iris House.*
> 3:15 P.M.—*Marisa & Fern seen in garden. Fern not seen after approx. 3:20.*

She was aware that Luke watched her with indulgent affection. He must know it was useless trying to talk Tess out of something when she was this determined.

Tess stopped writing and chewed reflectively on her bottom lip. What was Lana doing between 2:30 and the time she was killed? Did she talk to any of the other guests? Who? When did she leave her room and why was she in the side yard? Had the murderer arranged to meet her there?

For the moment oblivious to Luke's appreciative gaze, she bent her head over her notepad again.

> 3:20 P.M.—*Chester seen in garden speaking to Alexis and Reva. Alexis and Chester left garden together (probably talked in front yard—Dahlia saw Alexis there a short time later. Alexis upset).*

Tess lifted her head. "I forgot to tell you that I saw Lana in the backyard last night about one A.M. She went through the hedge into the Dinwitty yard. When I went to check on her a while later, she was back in the house, and she said she'd never left, that she'd been in the kitchen the whole time."

Luke's fond look became intrigued. "Did you tell her you saw her?"

Tess shook her head. "No, I didn't think it was any of my business."

He glanced aside as a new couple, strangers, were seated at the next table, then asked quietly, "What was she doing?"

"Gertie thinks she went to the Dinwitty house to see Harley."

"What?" Luke's whisper was incredulous.

"Yes. Chester heard Gertie, Nedra, and me talking about it and I think that's what he told Alexis. It would explain why she was so upset."

"Good God! That sure gives Alexis a motive for murder. Did you mention any of this to the police?"

"I might have if Butts hadn't made me so mad," Tess said defensively.

"Is that a no?"

Reluctantly, Tess nodded.

Luke looked at her dubiously, less indulgent now. "That's called withholding evidence, Tess."

Tess shivered, remembering Butts's warning that withholding evidence was a serious crime. "I'll tell him later if it seems relevant."

"Relevant? To whom? You?"

"Well—"

"Hell's bells, Tess. This could get you and Gertie off the hook."

"But at Alexis's expense," Tess said unhappily. She looked down at her notepad. "Let me finish this and I'll show it to you."

Reva left garden shortly after Alexis & Chester (claims she went straight to her room).

3:30 P.M.—Second tour group left. Dahlia and Tess began clearing tables in yard. By this time, Alexis in her room, upset (over what Chester told her?).

3:40 P.M.—Marisa & Randall crossed backyard. Marisa seemed agitated by something Randall had said or done—did Randall make a pass?

3:55–4:05 P.M.—Tess went upstairs to check on Alexis. Heard Fern on phone in her room. (Fern sounded angry. Talking to whom?) Alexis came to door of her room disheveled. (Said she had been on phone. With Fern?) She'd been crying.

4:05 P.M.—Dahlia & last tour group left side yard where body later found. All guests claim to have been in their rooms by 4 P.M., resting, getting ready for evening session of conference

at 7 P.M. *Claim they didn't leave rooms until they heard ambulance siren about 4:40 P.M.*
4:30 P.M.—*Lana's body found by Nedra.*
4:40 P.M.—*Ambulance arrived.*
4:42 P.M.—*Chief Butts & medical examiner arrived.*
4:50 P.M.—*Body removed. Butts ordered all occupants of Iris House to meet him in parlor for questioning.*
Everybody in parlor by 5:05 P.M. Chief arrived there about 5:30 P.M.
5:55 P.M.—*Butts finished questioning guests and they retired to rooms. Butts searched Lana's room.*
6:15 P.M.—*Butts left Iris House.*

Tess stopped writing and handed the pad to Luke. While he read her notes, she finished her cappuccino, still mulling over the afternoon's sequence of events. Somehow, Lana's murderer had slipped out of Iris House. He or she had taken the cake knife from the gazebo, met Lana, killed her, and returned to Iris House, all without being seen.

The killer could have exited by the foyer door when there was no one else in the front yard. Then he would have lurked in the south side yard while the last tour group continued on the final tour of the afternoon. When the killer was sure Tess and Gertie were both in the house, he'd run to the gazebo, grabbed the knife, and dashed back to the side yard where he met Lana. So he must have known Lana was coming; the meeting had been prearranged.

But if he'd arranged the meeting in order to murder Lana, why hadn't he brought a weapon with him? Maybe the murder had been a decision made on the spur of the moment, while the killer waited for Lana to arrive.

Whose idea had it been to meet in the side yard,

Lana's or the murderer's? Why not in one of their rooms? Obviously, the murderer hadn't wanted to run the risk of being seen entering or leaving Lana's room. And neither of them had wanted to be overheard.

Tess had the feeling that if she knew the purpose of the meeting she would know the identity of the killer.

Luke finished reading and handed Tess's notepad back to her. "All I can deduce from your notes is that three of your guests were agitated at some point during the afternoon, for reasons we don't know."

Tess smiled at the "we." Luke was fascinated by the puzzle, in spite of being worried that she was getting in too deep. "I'm pretty sure Alexis was devastated over whatever it was Chester told her. That could only be what he overheard Gertie, Nedra, and me talking about in the kitchen earlier."

Luke scratched his chin contemplatively. "You mean Lana's supposed secret night meeting with Alexis's husband." He chuckled. "I have to tell you, I don't think Harley Dinwitty's the kind of man who has lovers' trysts with his wife's friends. Or anyone else, for that matter. I've never heard a suggestion that Harley was ever unfaithful to Alexis. He's too busy wheeling and dealing."

Tess gnawed the plastic tip of her pen for a moment. "It could have been Lana who was the aggressor. Gertie says she'd probably spent the settlement from her last divorce and was looking for another rich husband."

Luke cocked his head. "Seems to me you and Gertie have engaged in a lot of speculation without much evidence."

"We were having a *private* conversation," Tess said, nettled by the implied criticism in Luke's words. "Chester had no right to repeat it."

Luke backpedaled. Plainly, he knew when to drop a subject. "Let's get back to why your other guests were upset."

Tess nodded, glad that he had finally given up telling

her to mind her own business. "As for Marisa, I strongly suspect Randall made a pass at her and she's afraid Fern will find out about it and tell Johnny, who might think she'd encouraged Randall."

Luke shook his head doubtfully. "That's all pretty iffy, Tess. And it doesn't give Marisa a motive to murder Lana. From what you've said, if she murdered anyone, it would be Fern. But why was Fern Willis so agitated? Who was on the other end of that telephone conversation?"

"I have no idea," Tess admitted, "but I intend to find out."

"How?"

"If I have to, I'll ask Fern point-blank," she said firmly. "I heard her threaten to kill whoever she was talking to. It could have been Lana."

Luke grinned. "Can you really picture Reverend Willis's wife stabbing somebody?"

Tess sighed. "It does boggle the mind, doesn't it? But Luke, I wouldn't have believed Fern could go into a rage and say the things I heard her say, either."

Luke contemplated her words. "If she threatened Lana and then killed her, she's not going to admit a thing."

Tess was still thinking about what she'd overheard Fern say in the telephone conversation. "If Lana was desperately in need of money, I wouldn't put it past her to have been blackmailing Fern."

Luke covered another laugh with a cough. "That's really off the wall, Tess. In order to be a victim of blackmail, Fern Willis would have to be harboring some terrible secret." He shook his head in disbelief. "It's impossible, my sweet Tess. Fern Willis has never done anything scandalous in her life. Why, she doesn't even say 'darn.' "

"She hasn't always been a minister's wife," Tess argued a bit feebly. "Lana was her cousin. They grew up together right here in Victoria Springs. Maybe it was something that happened a long time ago, something only the two of them knew about."

"And they managed to keep it hidden all these years? In this hotbed of gossip and innuendo? No way, Tess."

Tess's shoulders sagged. "Maybe you're right." She looked down at the notepad which she still held in her hand and sighed. Picking up her pen, she turned to a new page and wrote:

SUSPECTS & POSSIBLE MOTIVES
Alexis Dinwitty—Lana having an affair with Harley Dinwitty.
Fern Willis—Lana blackmailing her. (Why?)
Chester Leeds—Lana responsible for his losing The Club's presidency to Alexis.

Tess stopped writing and said dolefully, "Every one of these motives is a pure guess."

Luke, who had been leaning over the table, reading as she wrote, agreed. "The one you've assigned to Chester isn't strong enough to be a motive for murder, either."

"Not for most people, Luke, but being president of The Club is very important to Chester, almost an obsession. Lana campaigned tirelessly for Alexis. I doubt that Alexis would have won otherwise. Chester has been in a dreadful funk ever since."

Luke waved this away. "No sane person would commit murder for such a reason. Chester may be a little eccentric, but he's not nuts."

Tess studied her notes again, but left Chester's motive as she had written it. "I can't even make a guess about the other suspects," she said as she stuffed pen and notepad back in her purse. "I'll have to find out more before I can complete the list."

He eyed her gravely. "Would it do any good if I suggested again that you leave the investigation to Chief Butts?" But it was a halfhearted plea.

Tess waved an impatient hand. "This *is* my business, Luke. First of all, I'm a suspect. Secondly, a murder in Iris House on opening day isn't exactly good for business. The sooner the case is solved, the sooner people will forget."

As they left the restaurant, new questions swirled in Tess's mind. Why had the murder been committed at Iris House? Was it simply because that's where the opportunity presented itself? Or was it a calculated choice?

Luke slipped an arm around her shoulders. "Tess?"

His voice scattered her troubled thoughts. She looked up at him. Light from the street lamp had turned his handsome face into an arresting landscape of shadows and angles.

"I'd better take you straight home, sweetheart. You need a good night's rest."

"I have a better idea," Tess said huskily. "Let's go to your place first."

Chapter 13

The next morning, when Tess left her quarters, instead of the early-morning noises Gertie usually made—water running, pots banging, dishes clinking, drawers opening and closing—dead silence reigned on the ground floor.

On most mornings, when Tess crossed the foyer she could hear Gertie humming contentedly to herself as she worked. But there was no humming this morning. For a moment, Tess feared that Gertie had been so undone by Lana Morrison's murder that she'd decided to avoid the scene of the crime today. Not that Tess would blame her much, but it wasn't like Gertie to miss work without letting Tess know. In fact, there had been times that Gertie came to work when she should have stayed home in bed.

Anxiously, Tess tried to think of a quick and easy dish she could fix for breakfast. Surely, her guests would expect to be fed, regardless of yesterday's events. As she reached the dining room, Tess caught the scent of fresh-brewed coffee and heaved a sigh of relief. Arriving at the kitchen doorway, she found Gertie, in another of her bright tent dresses, gazing disconsolately out a window at the backyard.

Whatever was baking in the oven smelled scrumptuous.

"Morning," Tess said.

Gertie started nervously and jerked around, her characteristic calm having deserted her.

"Mercy! You scared me, Tess. Don't sneak up on me like that."

"Sorry."

Gertie's round face was drawn with fatigue. "You're up and about early."

"I couldn't sleep," Tess admitted. She took down a cup and helped herself to coffee.

"You, too?" Gertie asked. "I don't think I closed my eyes until after midnight. Woke up again about four and couldn't get back to sleep. Couldn't stop my mind from going over and over what happened and trying to make some sense out of it."

Tess sat down at the oak table. "Did you have any luck?"

Gertie puffed out her cheeks and expelled a long breath. "After all that thinking, the conclusion I reached was that only one person had a strong motive to do away with Lana Morrison, and it's not you or me. I don't care what Desmond Butts thinks."

"You believe Alexis Dinwitty did it," Tess murmured.

Gertie picked up a pot holder and opened the oven door. "Don't you?"

"If I thought so, I'd have told Chief Butts about seeing Lana in her nightgown heading for the Dinwitty house. *If* that's where she was headed, which we don't know for sure."

"Your loyalty to Alexis is commendable," Gertie responded, "but it may be misplaced."

Was she merely denying the evidence because she liked Alexis? Tess wondered. She didn't know.

She sipped her coffee and watched Gertie take several baking pans from the oven and set them on top of the range. "That smells wonderful," she said as Gertie straightened up. "What is it?"

"Carrot and bacon quiche," Gertie told her. "I'm serving it with fresh fruit cups." She came over to the table, sat down, and looked at Tess.

Seeing the question in Gertie's eyes, Tess squirmed in her chair. "Okay," she said unhappily. "Sooner or later, I'll have to tell the police about seeing Lana going toward the Dinwitty house night before last. It just makes me feel like a traitor."

"Well, don't get in a tizzy about it. You might not have to make that decision. Chester Leeds could decide to tell them, if he hasn't already."

Tess frowned and set her cup down. "I hadn't thought of that, but I'll bet you're right. Oh, Gertie, I should never have told you and Nedra about seeing Lana in the backyard that night. If I'd kept my mouth shut, Chester wouldn't have overheard and run to Alexis with it. Lana might still be alive."

Gertie eyed her solemnly. "You *do* think Alexis did it."

Did she really? Tess wondered. To give herself time to frame a reply, she went to the refrigerator and got one of the individual crystal fruit bowls lined up on the top shelf. Plump strawberries, glistening blueberries, and chunks of melon, peach, and pineapple filled the fluted bowl.

Taking the fruit and a spoon back to the table, Tess said, "Luke says Harley Dinwitty isn't the type of man to be messing around with another woman, especially someone like Lana."

"The most rational men have been known to make fools of themselves over a woman."

"But Harley?"

"If he wasn't carrying on with Lana, why was she going over there in the middle of the night? And don't tell me she might have been going somewhere else."

"I didn't actually *see* her go in the Dinwitty house."

At Gertie's exasperated sigh, Tess went on, "Oh, I'll admit, from what we know Alexis seems to have the best motive. But what do we *not* know, Gertie? That's the question."

Before Gertie could respond, they heard steps de-

scending the stairs and shortly Reva and Randall Isley
came into the dining room together. Tess made a valiant
effort to chat cheerily with them while Gertie served
breakfast. It was tough going. Nobody mentioned what
was foremost on everyone's mind, the murder investigation.

Randall was uncharacteristically subdued, though he
made a few feeble attempts at solicitous conversation
with Reva, which were met with tense monosyllables.
Once he even jumped up to fetch the coffeepot and re-
fill Reva's cup before Gertie could get to it.

Tess couldn't help thinking the one good thing result-
ing from Lana's murder was that it appeared to have
shaken some sense into Randall. Belatedly, it seemed to
have dawned on him that Reva could actually reach the
end of her patience with his flirtations. He was worried.

Watching him, Tess asked herself if he could be the
murderer. But what reason could he have had for killing
Lana? Had she suddenly turned on him with contempt,
scorned his advances? Laughed at him? At breakfast
the previous morning, Tess had seen how quickly Randall could be angered when Chester insulted him. If
Lana hadn't stopped him, he might well have attacked
Chester.

Suppose Lana had led Randall to believe she was interested in him, then ridiculed him for believing it. He might
have grabbed a knife and stabbed her in a burst of rage.
Picturing such a turn of events was not impossible for
Tess. What she couldn't imagine was Lana waiting pa-
tiently in the side yard while an enraged Randall went after the knife. Either he got it before she met him in the
yard—which made the murder premeditated—or she'd
believed he was going to the gazebo for another reason. Perhaps . . .

Someone came up behind Tess and cleared his throat.
She turned to find Chester hovering in the doorway.
The man could enter a room more quietly than anyone

she knew. This morning he looked like an undertaker in his black suit.

"Come in, Chester," Tess said, moving aside.

"Only coffee this morning, Gertie," he said briskly, sitting down. "I don't have time for breakfast."

While Gertie poured Chester's coffee, Randall eyed him with smoldering hatred. Chester gave the Isleys a frigid glance and reached for his cup.

"I trust you had a restful night, Chester," Tess said.

Chester ran a hand down his somber black-and-gray tie to make sure it was in place. "Eventually. I had a decision to make, but once I'd made it, I dropped right off." He threw a smug glance in the Isleys' direction.

Tess did not like the sound of this.

Chester took a swallow of coffee and again looked at Randall as he said, "I have to conduct a morning session at the conference, but before that I have an appointment downtown with Chief Butts."

Randall snorted. "Going to confess, Chet?" he snarled.

"Hardly," Chester said with a smirk. "But since the rest of you don't seem inclined to cooperate with the police, it's my civic duty to report what I know."

"Are you saying you know who the killer is?" Tess asked.

"He knows diddly squat," Randall muttered.

Chester set his cup down and stood. "I was not an eyewitness to the murder, if that's what you mean, but I do possess certain relevant information."

Randall suddenly straightened up and planted his hands on the table, as though to push himself to his feet. "What information, you little wimp?"

Here we go again, Tess thought, and shook her head at Randall.

Chester flashed him an evil smile. "Wouldn't you like to know, Isley?" He hurried from the room before Randall could get up.

Tess watched him leave, thinking, *Poor Alexis.* She

knew Chester wouldn't listen if she tried to stop him. Should she warn Alexis?

Before she could decide, Marisa Stackpole walked slowly into the dining room.

"Good morning, Marisa," Tess said distractedly, her greeting echoed disconsolately by Reva. Randall had slumped back into his chair, but was still staring in the direction Chester had gone. They heard the front door open and close.

"Hi," Marisa replied dully, taking a chair across the table from the Isleys. There were dark smudges beneath her eyes. Clearly, Marisa, too, had had a restless night.

As Gertie set Marisa's breakfast in front of her, Marisa said, "Fern doesn't feel up to coming down for breakfast. She wants me to bring her tea and toast when I go back upstairs."

"You take your time with breakfast," Tess said, seizing on the opportunity to talk to Fern alone. "I'll take a tray up to Fern."

Marisa brightened. "Oh, would you? Thank you so much," she said, her gratitude out of all proportion to Tess's simple offer.

Reva, whose conversation had been confined to one- or two-syllable words until now, spoke up suddenly. "Fern will run you ragged if you allow it, Marisa. You should start as you mean to go on."

Marisa stared at Reva as color crept up her neck. The look she gave the Isleys was fraught with embarrassment, but all she said was, "Oh, I don't mind, really." Marisa, Tess decided, was humiliated to learn that her reasons for kowtowing to Fern were obvious to others.

Reva shrugged. "She might have more respect for you if you'd stand up to her."

Marisa didn't reply. She lowered her eyes to her plate, her expression unreadable, and picked up her fork.

Aunt Dahlia's right, Tess thought. *The girl is terrified*

*that Fern will turn against her and destroy her chances
of marrying Johnny Willis.*

Was it possible that Lana had threatened to tell Fern
something damning about Marisa? That she was carrying on with Randall, perhaps?

Oh, now you're really reaching, Tess told herself.
Besides, she couldn't imagine this pale, anxious girl
stabbing anybody.

"If you'll all excuse me," Tess said, "I'll go and prepare Fern's tray."

Minutes later, Tess was knocking on the door of the
Arctic Fancy Room.

Fern called languidly, "Come in, Marisa."

"It's me," Tess said, entering. "I talked Marisa into
letting me bring up your tray. I wanted to see how
you're feeling."

Fern shrugged as if it made no difference. In a gray-
and-white-striped shirtwaist dress, her hair pinned up in
a neat bun, Fern sat at the small chintz-draped table
near the window. She watched Tess place the tray on
the table without comment.

"I'm sorry you're under the weather," Tess said.

"I'm not sick, only tired," Fern replied with an edge
of distraction. She spooned sugar into her teacup. "Not
up to making conversation with the others at breakfast.
I didn't get much sleep."

"I don't think any of us did," Tess said sympatheti-
cally, sitting down with Fern and resting her elbows on
the table. "Little wonder."

"Mmmm." Fern tasted the tea and added more sugar.

"I wanted to talk to you about something else, too,"
Tess said, fingering the delicate gold chain in the vee of
her royal-blue cotton dress. "After Chief Butts searched
Lana's room, I packed her belongings and—"

Fern laid her spoon down and stared at Tess. "Butts
searched Lana's room?"

"Yes—naturally. I mean, that's the logical place to look for clues."

"What clues?"

What was going on here? Was Fern afraid Butts might have found something in Lana's room that implicated her? "Well—I don't know. I suppose anything that might point to somebody Lana was at odds with."

"An enemy," Fern mused. "Did Butts find what he was looking for?"

"If he did, I'd be the last person he'd tell."

Fern held Tess's eyes for another instant, then dropped her gaze. She picked up a triangle of toast and bit off a corner, which she chewed meditatively. After a moment, she said, "The police won't have any trouble finding people who despised Lana."

"So I've gathered," prompted Tess, hoping to encourage Fern to be more explicit.

"They can start with her ex-husbands."

Except that none of Lana's ex-husbands had been anywhere near Iris House yesterday.

Tess waited for more, but Fern didn't name any other enemies of Lana. Tess decided to be more direct. "Fern, was Lana having an affair?"

Fern's expression was cynical. "Probably. Reva thought she was, anyway."

"With Randall?"

Fern nodded. "I heard them arguing in their room. Randall denied it, and Reva called him a liar and said she wasn't going to put up with it."

Did she, indeed? "When was this?"

"Yesterday afternoon. It must have been a little before four o'clock because I'd come in from the garden. My bathroom is next to their room. I'd just stepped out of the shower when I heard them." She broke another corner off the toast triangle. "Frankly, I was surprised at Reva. Randall has always had a wandering eye, and she's tolerated it for years." She frowned thoughtfully.

"Maybe she was waiting until her boys were out of the house to confront him."

Was Fern exaggerating what she heard to divert suspicion away from herself? Tess wondered. If Fern had finished showering shortly before four o'clock, would she have had time to get dressed and meet Lana outside? It was possible.

"What do you think?" Tess asked. "Was Lana having an affair with Randall?"

"It wouldn't surprise me." She ate the broken-off bit of toast and dabbed at her mouth with her napkin. "If not Randall, there was likely somebody else. Lana usually had a man on the string. She never had a problem attracting men." She gave Tess a look of prim satisfaction. "Her problem was she couldn't keep one."

"Do you have any idea who else she might have been seeing?"

Fern gazed at her for a long moment. "No," she said finally. "I wasn't particularly interested in Lana's pathetic back-street liaisons. We were cousins, but we never saw eye-to-eye on much of anything."

"That's too bad. Relatives ought to get along."

Fern smiled with her lips only. "You're very young, Tess. Relatives can be the bane of one's existence. As for Lana, I kept my nose out of her business. The less I knew about it, the better I liked it."

She'd been very well occupied elsewhere, according to Dahlia—orchestrating the lives of her husband and son. Tess's instincts told her that Lana had not reciprocated by staying out of Fern's business, though. Fern's reaction to hearing that Butts had searched Lana's room gave credence to Tess's suspicion that it was Lana whom Fern had raged at on the telephone. It had sounded like a response to a threat. *Could* it have been attempted blackmail?

As Fern spread blackberry jam on a piece of toast, Tess silently concocted a possible scenario. Suppose Lana *had* tried to blackmail Fern. When Fern threatened to kill her, it made sense that Lana would have written something implicating Fern and left it in her room, just in case. The possibility must have occurred to Fern, too—if she was the murderer. Or even if she wasn't. Unfortunately, Chief Butts had not left Tess with the impression that he had found anything like that.

Tess gazed out the window at a bed of white bearded irises in one corner of the front yard, while she pursued the notion that Lana had been blackmailing Fern. She kept going back to the fact that the two had grown up together in Victoria Springs. If there were any skeletons in Fern's past, Lana would have known about them.

An idea flickered at the back of Tess's mind, but she couldn't quite get hold of it.

"You're awfully quiet all of a sudden," Fern remarked.

Tess turned away from the window. "I was thinking how bizarre it seems that there was a murder in my yard yesterday."

"Well, I've been thinking about what you said—that Lana was having an affair that went wrong. Do you know something I don't?"

It was a moment before Tess understood what she meant. Fern was asking if Tess knew for certain of Lana's involvement with Randall Isley or some other man.

"No," Tess said quickly. Fern obviously had no inkling of Lana's interest in Harley Dinwitty, if it existed.

So Chester had not mentioned Lana's trip through the back hedge to anyone but Alexis. Until now. At the moment, Tess suspected he was spilling his guts, trying to implicate a woman whom he had known and worked with in the Garden Club for years. Tess didn't think Chester had any real loyalties to anyone. Maybe he wanted to throw suspicion on Alexis to turn it away from himself. Tess would have to think about that later.

"I was wondering," she went on, "if you will be in charge of winding up Lana's affairs."

Fern looked startled and set her cup down abruptly. It clattered against the saucer. "I hadn't even thought about it." She chewed the inside of her cheek for a moment. "Well, I am as close a relative as Lana had, and the only one in Victoria Springs." She looked pained as she added grudgingly, "I suppose I'll have to check with her attorney and see what's being done about funeral arrangements. I only hope there's enough money left to bury her."

"Her suitcase is upstairs and her car's out front. Her house and car keys were in her purse. Lana's belongings should be returned to her house. I'd be glad to take care of that for you. One less thing you'd have to worry about."

Something shifted in Fern's eyes. "I'll do it. After all," she added with an air of martyrdom, "it's my Christian duty. Marisa can follow in my car and bring me back."

"I'll follow you," Tess said hastily. "Marisa can stay here and rest." She had every intention of taking a look around Lana's house. Since it appeared she would have to hand over the keys, accompanying Fern was the only way to get in without breaking the law.

"Marisa won't mind."

"I'm sure she wouldn't, but Marisa looks beat this morning. She should go back to bed. Frankly, she's seemed stressed ever since she arrived here. Do you know what's bothering her?"

"I've no idea," Fern said crossly.

She's lying, Tess thought. *She knows perfectly well that she has Marisa scared half to death.* It would serve Fern right if Marisa and Johnny presented her with a fait accompli by eloping.

"I'll get the suitcase and meet you in the foyer," Tess said.

Chapter 14

Tess pulled into the driveway behind Fern, who was driving Lana's car. Fern got out quickly, carrying Lana's suitcase. "Don't bother coming in," she called from the end of the front walk. "I won't be long."

Tess nodded and counted to fifty, her fingers drumming on the steering wheel impatiently. Then she got out of her car.

Finding the front door unlatched, Tess eased it open noiselessly and stepped into a small entryway. Fern wasn't in the living room, which opened off the left of the entry, or the kitchen, which opened off the right. Muffled sounds came from somewhere beyond the kitchen.

Determined to make the best use of the brief time she had, Tess looked quickly around the living room. The walls and carpeting were champagne-colored. In contrast, the chairs and sofa were upholstered in bright hues—jade, rose, and blue. Tess gazed across the trackless carpet; the room didn't appear to have been inhabited since it was last vacuumed. She took a step, leaving the faint impression of her shoe behind.

Well, there was no help for it. She hurried across the room and shuffled through the items on the coffee table which, it turned out, consisted of nothing but a silver candy dish filled with Hershey's Kisses and a half dozen fashion magazines.

Discarding *Glamour* and *Vogue*, Tess moved to

a lamp table and pulled open its drawer. Inside were several ballpoint pens and a small blank notepad. Tess held the pad up to the light from the window and peered at it closely, hoping to find impressions of the last message which had been written on a sheet that was torn off. As often happened in detective novels. But Lana's was no fictional murder, and Tess could detect no impressions on the notepad. She replaced the pad and looked through the only other drawer in the room—it was in a second lamp table—with no fruitful results.

There being no other obvious place in the living room where a clue might be concealed, Tess moved on to the kitchen, tiptoeing when she stepped off the carpet to cross the flagstone floor of the entryway.

The muffled sounds from the back of the house were louder in the kitchen. Fern muttered something that Tess couldn't decipher, and then there was the sound of a drawer being slammed shut and another jerked open.

Keeping an ear cocked, Tess rifled gingerly through the kitchen drawers, taking care not to make enough noise for Fern to hear, but she found nothing useful to the murder investigation. As she closed the last drawer, it occurred to her that if Lana had left anything incriminating in writing, it would probably be in a desk, or perhaps in her bedroom.

Since she couldn't tell which of the rooms opening off the hallway Fern was in, Tess hesitated at the door leading to the hall. On the wall near her were a telephone and a small corkboard. A pencil dangled on a string beside the phone. She scanned the items thumbtacked to the board—a grocery list, a past-due notice from a local dress shop for a hundred and sixty-two dollars, and a reminder of a dental appointment for Tuesday of the coming week. An appointment that Lana would never keep, Tess thought sadly.

Her gaze slid to the white telephone which hung beside the corkboard and snagged on the redial button.

She punched the button and watched ten numerals appear in the plastic-covered panel below the receiver. Quickly, she tore the past-due notice off the board and grabbed the dangling pencil. But she only had time to register that the last number Lana had called from this phone was long distance and scribble the area code before she heard Fern slam another drawer shut and mutter again. She sounded more irritated than before and closer to the kitchen.

Fearing that Fern was about to walk in on her, Tess stuffed the scrap of paper in her pocket, called brightly, "Fern?" and stepped into the hall.

Fern stood in the doorway of a small office, the second room on Tess's right, which was furnished with a large desk, secretary's chair, and a recliner with a pole lamp beside it. Tess was sure that Fern, who stepped back into the office at Tess's approach, had been searching the desk. Wisps of hair had escaped Fern's neat bun and hung down the back of her neck. Beads of perspiration glistened on her upper lip.

From her manner and the fact that her hands were empty, Fern must not have found what she was looking for. Tess glanced at Lana's keys lying on the desk. Fern followed her gaze, snatched up the keys, and dropped them in the pocket of her dress.

Clearly she was not pleased to see Tess, who concluded Fern had been headed for Lana's bedroom next, but didn't want to leave Tess alone now that she knew Tess was in the house.

"I was looking for Lana's will," Fern said combatively, "in case it contained burial instructions."

Tess pretended to believe this patent lie. "Are you sure she had one?"

Fern studied her intently for the space of a heartbeat. "No. At any rate, it's not here." She took a step toward Tess, her chin outthrust. For a second, Tess had the impression Fern wanted to shove her out of the room.

"Didn't you hear me say you should wait in the car for me?" Fern demanded.

Fern was used to being in charge. Being disobeyed upset the status quo, and she resented it. Tess took a step back. "Yes, but I got to thinking that we ought to clean out the refrigerator while we're here. I was afraid you wouldn't think of it, with everything else you have on your mind."

Tess was no slouch at improvising on the spur of the moment herself, and she also took the precaution of positioning herself so that there was nothing between her and the door in case a hasty exit was called for. She was not sure what this unfamiliar Fern Willis would do.

Slowly, Fern's jaw relaxed. "You're right. I wouldn't have thought of it. And we can't leave food to spoil . . ." She made a face, as though she wished Tess hadn't reminded her. "Well, we'd better get to it."

She followed Tess down the hall and into the kitchen, practically stepping on Tess's heels. Her movements jerky with haste, Fern found a large trash bag and they dumped in everything from the refrigerator. Obviously, Fern was eager to leave the house now. Tess suspected she would use the key in her pocket to return alone and continue her search.

She had meant to confront Fern with the overheard telephone conversation, but it didn't seem a good idea to do it while they were in the house. It suddenly occurred to Tess that if Fern was a murderer, confronting her where they could not be seen by anyone else would be reckless.

Having cleaned out the refrigerator, Fern twisted a wire fastener around the open end of the trash bag and set it outside the back door. "If we hurry, I'll be able to get to the eleven o'clock conference session," Fern said, heading for the front door.

Yeah, sure, Tess thought. *You're coming straight back here.* But there was nothing she could do about it. She hit the telephone's redial button again as she passed, her hand dropping away as Fern glanced over her shoulder. Tess could linger no longer without arousing suspicion.

As she left the kitchen, Tess tried to get another look at the number still displayed on the telephone's digital readout panel. But she was no longer close enough to see it clearly. By squinting, she found she could make out most of the numerals: three-one-two-five-five-five-six-seven-four . . .

Fern, having reached the entryway, glanced over her shoulder again. "What *are* you looking at?"

"Nothing," Tess said, and followed Fern from the house.

As she backed her car out of the drive, Tess silently repeated what she had seen of the telephone number, hoping to remember it until she could finish writing it down. If only she had gotten the complete number.

Oh, well. Chances were it had no connection to the murder, anyway.

Next to Tess, Fern sat staring out the car window, engrossed in her own thoughts. *What is going through her mind?* Tess wondered. And what had Fern really been searching for in Lana's desk?

Too bad the phones in Iris House didn't record last number redial information on room-to-room calls. Even if Lana was the person Tess had overheard Fern talking to on the telephone, and neither of them had dialed another number after that, it wouldn't show up on either telephone's readout panel.

Somehow she had to bluff Fern into admitting it was Lana she had talked to.

Tess took a deep breath. "Fern, I know you and Lana had a furious argument the day she died."

Fern's head whipped around. "What?"

"On the telephone."

"I don't know where you got that idea," Fern sputtered, "but Lana and I didn't argue. I told you I had as little contact with her as possible."

Tess could read nothing in Fern's wide-eyed expression. She looked back at the road. She'd gone this far, so she might as well go a little farther. "I overheard you talking to Lana on the telephone. I didn't mean to eavesdrop, Fern. I happened to be going down the second-floor hallway at the time."

Fern gripped her purse to her breast as though it contained the family jewels. "What makes you think it was Lana I was talking to?"

She wasn't as easy to bluff as Tess had hoped. "You said her name," Tess lied, glancing over at the other woman.

Fern was staring at her hard. "You misunderstood."

"No, I didn't," Tess persisted. "You were angry and speaking rather loudly."

Fern released her purse, and it slid to the floor. Her face was pinched. "I couldn't have said Lana's name, since it wasn't Lana I was talking to. It was my husband."

In for a penny, in for a pound, Tess thought. "That's hard to believe since you threatened to kill whoever it was."

Fern shook her head. "Richard did something I disapproved of, and it infuriated me. I'm embarrassed to admit that I have never been able to tame my temper. I overreacted, I'm afraid. I apologized to Richard later."

Alas, Tess thought, bluffing wasn't going to work.

"I hope you haven't gone to the police with your ridiculous suppositions," Fern said.

"I wanted to talk to you first."

"Good. I'm amazed you thought I was arguing with Lana."

"I've heard rumors that Lana was running short of funds."

"You think she was asking me for money? Really! Lana knew I wouldn't give her a dime."

"Unless—" Tess faltered, then pressed on. "Unless she was blackmailing you."

Fern laughed shrilly. "That's preposterous." A vein beat visibly beneath one eye. Tess wondered why she was becoming so agitated if Lana hadn't asked her for money, as she claimed.

Tess was suddenly glad that Iris House was in sight. Fern's legendary composure was a mask hiding a volatile temper and a relentless determination to be in control. Tess turned into the paved parking area which was separated from the north side yard of Iris House by the fence and a waist-high hedge, with a gap where the gate led from the parking lot into the yard. Like most older homes, the original house had had no garage or carport, and Tess hadn't been able to figure out where to put one without spoiling the nineteenth-century effect. So she'd hidden a concrete slab large enough for a half dozen cars behind the hedge.

Fern touched Tess's arm. Her cold fingers made Tess jump. "If you're still thinking of going to the police, don't." The words had the finality of a coffin slamming shut. "You'd look pretty silly when I explained that Richard and I had a marital spat."

Tess shook off Fern's hand. What she had overheard was far more than a spat. They got out of the car and walked toward Iris House. Momentarily, Tess's pleasure at the sight of the Queen Anne–style Victorian supplanted everything else. The house was a soft blue with white shutters and gingerbread, complete with the requisite tower and wraparound veranda. She only wished she had known that Aunt Iris planned to leave it to her so that she could have thanked her.

Before she heard about the terms of the will, Tess had assumed the old family home would go to Dahlia and Tess's father, who would no doubt have sold it. But, according to Iris's will, the estate went to Iris's two nieces. Cinny had inherited Iris's government bonds, while the house and a cash inheritance went to Tess because, the will explained, one Christmas, when Tess was twelve or thirteen, she'd spoken of how much she loved the house and how she looked forward to coming there at Christmas. Tess had forgotten all about that occasion, but would be forever grateful that Iris hadn't.

As they reached the front door, the idea that had eluded Tess in Fern's room earlier floated to the surface of her mind. If something had happened years ago that Lana could have used to blackmail Fern, Tess's father might know what it was. He grew up in Victoria Springs, too, and he was only two or three years older than Lana and Fern.

In the foyer, Tess and Fern ran into Nedra with her cleaning supplies. "Coffee break," she said, evidently to explain why she was downstairs at mid-morning.

Fern hurried up the stairs, taking no notice of the cleaning woman.

Nedra gazed after her, hitching her plastic bucket higher on one bony hip, and muttered, "Out there tromping on all the flowers."

Tess's skill at interpreting Nedra's enigmatic phrases was not up to this one. "Who? Fern?"

"She been tromping the flowers, too?" Nedra inquired as she rearranged the bottles and cans in the bucket.

"No—I thought that's what *you* said."

Nedra looked blank. "Nope."

Tess may have been fully occupied with her own thoughts, but she wasn't hearing things that weren't there yet. "Nedra, you said somebody was tromping all over the flowers."

"Oh. Butts, that's who I said. Plain as day."

Tess didn't want to argue with Nedra right now. "I see. He's out in the side yard then."

"That's what I said."

This conversation was going around in circles. "I'll go out and speak to him," Tess said. As soon as she took care of one small item.

"Don't know why you'd want to do that," Nedra said. "Rude."

"Yes, he is," Tess agreed, "but there's something I want to ask him. Oh, and Nedra, it's okay to clean Lana's room. I got the chief's permission."

Nedra shrugged. "Already did." She turned and went up the stairs.

Before going outside, Tess hurried to her apartment and pulled from her pocket the scrap of paper she'd taken from Lana's house. She stared at the area code she'd scribbled there. Three-one-two. Closing her eyes, she managed to dredge up from memory the other numerals she'd seen on the redial panel on Lana's kitchen telephone.

She grabbed a pen and wrote the next six numerals after the area code. Five-five-five-six-seven-four. Only the last numeral was missing. But did it matter? How could a long-distance phone number have any connection to Lana's murder? She folded the paper, stuck it in one of the secretary's cubbyholes, and left the apartment to confront Chief Butts.

When Tess reached the south side yard, Butts and one of his officers were taking down the yellow scene-of-crime tape.

"Good morning, gentlemen," Tess said, determined to be friendly. The young officer with Butts grinned and dipped his head.

A few brown bloodstains were still visible on the crushed irises in the Darcy Flame bed. Tess averted her eyes.

"You can have your yard back now, Miz Darcy," Butts told her. He wadded up the tape and tossed it on the grass.

Butts could have as easily handed it to her. Tess bent to pick up the balled tape. When she straightened up, Butts was staring at her hard.

"Is something wrong?"

"Hear you've been holding out on me."

Thanks a lot, Chester, Tess fumed. "Whatever do you mean?"

Butts thrust his meaty face forward until it was only inches from Tess's. "I mean that Lana Morrison was playing shaky pudding with Harley Dinwitty and you saw her going over there in the middle of the night. In her nightgown. The night before she was murdered."

Tess pulled her head back. Butts's breath smelled like garlic. "I didn't know hearsay was considered evidence, Chief."

"In court," he amended. "But it can be useful in an investigation." His beetling brows came together over his wide nose. "Besides, what we're talking about here is eyewitness evidence. Did you or did you not see Lana Morrison in her nightgown meeting Harley Dinwitty?"

From the corner of her eye, Tess saw the young officer drifting toward the front yard, as though he feared his boss's anger might spill over on him.

"I did not," Tess replied.

Butts began to bluster. "Now, see here—"

"What I *saw,*" Tess interrupted, "was Lana in the backyard of Iris House. That's it. I didn't see Harley. Nor did I see Lana enter the Dinwitty house."

"And this was the night before she was murdered."

Tess nodded.

"What time was it?"

"A little after one A.M."

"Later, she lied to you about where she'd been. Isn't that right?"

Chester must have repeated her conversation with Gertie and Nedra word for word. "She said she'd been in the kitchen. Which she had. I didn't ask her point-blank if she had been in the yard, too. I certainly didn't ask if she'd gone over to see Harley Dinwitty. It was none of my business."

Butts brushed aside these technicalities. "So, she was secretive about where she'd been and who with."

"I repeat, I did not ask her who she'd been with."

Butts ran a beefy hand through his bushy hair, then poked at her with a thick finger. "Miss Darcy, you are starting to get on my nerves here. I hope I don't have to haul you down to the station to finish this."

His words created an image in Tess's mind of being dragged to a police car and thrown in a cage in the backseat. She strove for calm. "That would accomplish nothing. I've told you all I know."

Butts took out his notepad and pencil. Wetting the pencil lead with the tip of his tongue, he said, "Now, go over it one more time."

Tess did, finishing with, "I want to make myself perfectly clear. I saw Lana go through my back hedge. I got up to check on her. When I stepped into the foyer, I ran into her. That's when she said she'd been hungry and had eaten a cookie in the kitchen."

Butts scribbled for a few moments before looking up. "You're sure there's nothing else you want to add?"

"Absolutely."

He put the pad and pencil back in his shirt pocket. "You may have to sign a statement committing yourself to what you just told me—which you should have told me yesterday."

Tess ignored the criticism. "I'll be glad to sign a statement. When?"

"I'll let you know."

"Okay. What about what you said yesterday? That you wanted to fingerprint everybody."

Butts tilted his head back, sizing her up from beneath eyelids that were at half-mast. "That won't be necessary."

Did that mean they had another suspect, somebody not connected to Iris House? Tess's heart lifted at the thought.

"The murder weapon was wiped clean," Butts said. Tess didn't know whether to be relieved or sorry.

"Somebody's trying to be clever," Butts added, evidently attempting to stare a hole through Tess.

She bridled. "Are you referring to Alexis Dinwitty?"

"Not necessarily." He turned his head to one side and spat on the grass.

Disgusting habit, Tess thought.

"We know for a fact," Butts went on, "that you and your cook had your hands on that knife."

"It would be stupid for us to deny it, since we were using it to cut cake. You can't really believe we had anything to do with Lana's murder."

Butts rocked forward on the balls of his feet. "Why not?"

"Because, if either of us had stabbed Lana, we wouldn't have used a knife we'd been using to cut cake all afternoon!"

"Why not?" Butts asked again in the same maddeningly smug tone as before.

"We're not idiots, Chief Butts! If we wanted to kill somebody, we'd use a weapon that couldn't be traced back to us."

He looked at her in disdain. "Mebbe. Mebbe not. Amateurs don't always think these things through." He spat again. "You didn't like Lana Morrison much, did you, Miss Darcy?"

"I liked her well enough."

"According to my informant—"

"One Chester Leeds," Tess couldn't resist inserting.

Butts ignored her. "—you were outraged over her little trip to the Dinwittys' house. You were still stewing yesterday morning at breakfast."

Thanks again, Chester, Tess thought. "Oh, for heaven's sake!" she exploded. "I was not outraged! Yesterday morning, Randall Isley and Chester Leeds were sniping at each other and Lana was egging them on, while pretending she wasn't. I didn't want my grand opening spoiled by petty squabbling."

"So you were mad at her. Then, when you saw her

yesterday afternoon, you got mad all over again, and attacked her with the knife you happened to have in your hand." His words had gathered volume and speed as he went along.

She glared at him. "Wrong. I didn't see her after she came home from the conference until Nedra found her body in the yard."

Butts gazed at her scornfully, then shrugged as though suddenly bored with the whole thing. "So you say," he muttered, but his mind already seemed to be elsewhere. "Well, if that's your story ..."

Tess threw up her hands. "I give up. I have work to do. If you'll excuse me—"

Butts stepped in her path as Tess noticed Harley Dinwitty getting out of his car in front of Iris House.

"Need to use your parlor for a while," Butts said. "Need to talk to a couple of your guests again."

A couple? Who besides Alexis? "Everybody's probably over at the hotel now," Tess said. "There's a conference going on, in case you didn't know."

"I know all about it, but the people I want to talk to are right here, starting with Miz Dinwitty. I called ahead."

"Should I stay around?"

"I'd rather you didn't," Butts said. "Don't need any nosy females getting in my way."

"I was merely trying to be helpful."

"You should have thought of that yesterday instead of holding out on me."

"Fine." Tess stormed back in the house and threw the ball of tape in the wastebasket beneath the kitchen sink.

Gertie was arranging the last of the breakfast dishes in the dishwasher. "What's got your dander up, Tess?"

Tess folded her arms, fuming. "Desmond Butts."

"He can do it, if anybody can."

Tess repeated what Butts had said about the knife being wiped clean of fingerprints, then added, "He actually accused me of killing Lana."

Gertie's eyes grew wide. "Well, forever more."

"I think he just wanted to see how I'd react," Tess said, reassuring herself as much as Gertie.

"Then I expect I'll be next."

"No, at the moment he's getting ready to question Alexis in the parlor. I guess he called Harley, too—or Alexis did—because I just saw him drive up."

"Chester snitched," Gertie observed.

"As you predicted. Butts invited me to stay out of his way while he questions the Dinwittys in the parlor."

"He didn't say anything to me," Gertie told her, "so I'll keep my ear cocked toward the parlor."

"Don't let Butts see you," Tess advised. "You're not one of his favorite people at the moment."

Gertie sniffed. "Sure breaks my heart."

"I'm going over to my quarters and put in a call to my father. Oh, darn—it's six hours later in Paris. He won't be home yet. I'll have to wait until this afternoon to call Dad."

It might be tomorrow or the next day before she got through to him. Her father was a very busy man. She saw him too seldom since he'd taken the diplomatic post at the U.S. Embassy in Paris three years ago. And given the time difference, it was even difficult for them to connect by phone.

After fixing herself a glass of iced tea, Tess took it outside. She would finally take that walk through the gardens and calm down after her encounter with Butts.

After a stroll along the cobblestone paths crisscrossing the backyard, Tess sat on a wrought-iron bench to finish her tea. The sweet aroma of honeysuckle wafted to her from an overladen vine on the fence. She closed her eyes, inhaled deeply several times, then opened her eyes to concentrate on the scenery.

The bench on which she sat was surrounded by Siberian irises in various shades of lavender and purple. From where she sat, she could read some of the small identifying tags placed in the bed by her late aunt. The pale-lavender irises were called *Pink Haze,* the deep-purple ones with white and gold markings on the falls were tagged *Shirley Pope.* The red-violet irises were *Omar's Cup.*

Tess gazed at the beauty on all sides of her and tried to stop her roiling thoughts, which circled again and again to the murder and its aftermath.

Let Butts handle it.

Good advice, but she was incapable of taking it. She did not believe Butts could be objective.

So, she still intended to phone her father later. She needed to hear his voice, anyway.

In the meantime, it occurred to her, Dahlia had been raised in Victoria Springs, too. She was three years older than Tess's father, which made her five or six years older than Lana and Fern. An eon, when you're young. When Fern and Lana were teenagers, Dahlia was already married, busy with her home and friends. High-school scandals would not have seemed earthshaking to her.

Still, Tess decided to run over to the hotel and see if she could find her aunt. At the moment, she couldn't think of anything else to do. And somebody had to do something before Chief Butts put the wrong person behind bars.

She carried her empty tea glass back to the kitchen, then detoured down the hall to the front of the house. The door to the parlor was closed when she walked across the foyer. Butts was closeted with Alexis and Harley. Tess put her ear to the door and heard Alexis say, "Do you expect me to believe you didn't know she was coming?"

"Yes, I do." That was Harley Dinwitty's voice, calm in contrast with Alexis's angry tone. "I wouldn't lie to you."

"You must have given her some reason to think she'd be welcome," Alexis snapped.

There was a silence, then Butts said, "What do you have to say to that, Mr. Dinwitty?"

"Maybe I did encourage her." Harley's voice was so low that Tess had to strain to hear. "My wife and I were always running into Lana at social gatherings. She flirted with me, and I admit I sort of enjoyed it."

"Male ego!" spat Alexis.

"You're right," Harley said, sounding miserable. "I was flattered. But I never encouraged her to believe I was seriously interested in her as more than a friend. You could have knocked me over with a feather when she showed up on my back step."

"You're asking me and your wife to believe that you didn't invite her in?" Butts inquired.

"I absolutely did not!"

Alexis said something that Tess couldn't understand and then Butts spoke. But he'd lowered his voice, too, and Tess couldn't make out all the words. Something about a woman scorned. Sounded as though Alexis was in deep water.

After that, Tess picked up only an occasional word. She'd better leave before Butts caught her eavesdropping.

Chapter 15

The Hilltop Hotel and the surrounding neighborhood, which included Iris House, sat on the highest point in Victoria Springs. As she walked to the hotel, Tess looked down on winding residential streets and rows of houses which appeared to be caught in the act of spilling down the hillside. Victoria Springs's five-block-square business district lay cupped in a small valley at the bottom of the hill.

The Hilltop Hotel had been built in the late 1800s, when wealthy travelers came to Victoria Springs for the reputed medicinal benefits of the area's artesian waters. At one time there had been half a dozen bathhouses in town; now only one remained, in a rather seedy hotel on the fringe of the town's business district.

These days tourists came to Victoria Springs for the Ozark crafts and the country music shows. The Hilltop had kept up with the times by becoming a regional conference and convention center.

Tess walked around to the wing which housed the meeting rooms. It had been added fifteen years ago, and the architect had done a superb job of making it look as though it had been there as long as the Victorian-era hotel.

Inside, antique Victorian pieces accented the foyer and hallway. Tess consulted the directory to see which rooms were assigned to the Iris Growers Conference. Two sessions were in progress at the moment. Tess scanned both rooms. She didn't

127

see Fern, confirming her suspicion that Fern had returned to Lana's house.

Dahlia, lovely in a pink dress with a pink eyelet
jacket, was seated at the back of the second room Tess
checked.

Tess felt her temper rise upon seeing Chester Leeds
holding forth at the podium. After blithely throwing
Alexis and Tess to the wolves, the traitor. As far as Tess
could tell, he was suffering no qualms whatsoever. He
might at least have given them warning. Had the man
no conscience?

"Of the bulbous varieties," Chester was saying, "the
earliest to bloom are the Reticulata irises."

What a pompous bore!

Tess caught Dahlia's eye and motioned for her to
come out into the hall.

As Dahlia closed the meeting room door behind her,
she whispered anxiously, "What's wrong?"

"Nothing," Tess assured her, taking Dahlia's arm and
leading her farther from the door. "If I'm keeping you
from something you really want to hear, I can wait until
this session is finished."

Dahlia's anxious frown cleared. "Frankly, I'm glad of
the excuse to escape Chester's didacticism. I felt duty-
bound to attend the sessions conducted by our local
people, but good Lord, I've heard it all so many times
before. I was just wondering how I could slip out without Chester seeing me." She studied Tess's solemn face.
"Are you sure there's nothing wrong? Nothing, I mean,
besides the fact that your beautiful Iris House is, even
now, sheltering Lana's murderer."

And I've just been accused of being that murderer,
Tess thought, but there was no point in worrying Dahlia
with it. She wouldn't even mention Chester's meeting
with the chief. Dahlia would hear of it soon enough.

"That's what I wanted to talk to you about," Tess
said. "I'm trying to figure out which of them had motives."

"I'm afraid, if we are to be perfectly candid, Tess, they can all be considered suspects."

Including Dahlia herself? Tess wondered, remembering her aunt's allusion to some trouble with Lana in the past. She shifted to the subject that had brought her there. "Even Fern Willis?"

Dahlia eyed her narrowly, then tapped her chin with a bright-nailed index finger. "Bad blood in the family, cousinly jealousy . . ." she mused. Then she blinked, as though coming out of a trance, and looked at her watch. "I'm meeting Cinny downtown in twenty minutes. Come with me and we'll talk about this over lunch."

Knowing her cousin, Tess expected she and Dahlia would spend a good half hour waiting at the restaurant for Cinny to arrive. Three years younger than Tess, Cinny was twenty-three and had grown up with the people-will-forgive-darling-little-me-anything attitude of many cute, pampered only children.

Yet in spite of Cinny's sometimes self-centered viewpoint, Tess had grown quite fond of her since moving to Victoria Springs. She had even learned to adjust to Cinny's haphazard approach to the keeping of appointments and usually arrived late to such meetings.

Today, however, an uncharacteristically timely arrival at the popular Sampler Tearoom, situated in another of the town's renovated Victorian houses, had caused Cinny to arrive at the meeting place before them. Spotting her cousin holding a table, Tess couldn't suppress her surprise.

"I don't believe it. Cinny's already here."

"Oh, I told her I'd be here thirty minutes ago," Dahlia said, and Tess laughed. Dahlia had discovered the same solution as Tess to the problem of Cinny's penchant for never being on time.

Tess waved at her cousin and glanced around the tearoom. The owners, a couple in their mid-forties, Merv and Marcia Dewhurst, had decorated the restaurant with their enviable collection of hand-stitched antique samplers. Hence the name.

Merv, himself a tall man with chiseled features that reminded Tess a little of Charlton Heston, escorted Dahlia and Tess to their table, placing menus at each place. A reproduction of a child's alphabet sampler decorated the menu covers. Tess remembered that each place setting of the tearoom's china was of a different floral pattern. Part of the tearoom's charm was waiting to see which pattern you'd get.

Cinny jumped up to embrace her cousin. "Tess! What a delightful surprise! I've hardly seen you at all since you got so busy with Iris House." Cinny was exaggerating a bit. Tess had actually seen her several times in the past three months.

When they were seated, Tess apologized anyway. "I know I've been derelict, Cinny. I'll try to do better now that we're open." Not for the first time, Tess regretted that she'd never gotten to know Cinny very well as they were growing up. Her father's job with the State Department had kept the family in Washington during most of Tess's childhood. They'd made it back to Victoria Springs once a year for Christmas. It wasn't until Tess was nineteen that her father received his first foreign posting.

"See that you do," Cinny said with a mischievous grin.

"I've been meaning to come by the shop and pick out some books for the library," Tess said. "Aunt Iris had a lot of nonfiction, but I'd like to add more fiction for my guests."

"People on vacation don't want anything too heavy," Cinny said with a thoughtful tilt of her head. "They want to be entertained. Mystery, romance, science fiction, that's the ticket."

"I'll need some of each."

"I'll make up a list of suggested titles for you," Cinny offered.

"That would be helpful. I'll try to get by the shop in the next few days."

Cinny scooped a handful of long blonde hair away from her pretty face and tucked it behind her small, shell-like ear. With an air of one who had finished with idle chitchat and was getting down to business, she leaned toward Tess and said in a stage whisper, "I know what you've been going through, Tess. Imagine. A murder in Aunt Iris's house." Her bright blue eyes sparkled with avid curiosity. "Do they know who did it yet?"

"No," Tess said, "and the body was found in the yard, not the house."

Cinny cupped her chin in one hand. "Oh, yes, but I don't think that's much better, do you?"

"Well—uh . . ."

"How many cancellations have you had?" Cinny inquired.

"Only one so far, but they said it was because of an illness in the family."

Cinny patted Tess's hand, her look saying plainly, *A likely story, my self-deceived cousin.*

"This," Cinny went on, "is the most interesting thing to happen in Victoria Springs in ages." Her tone seemed to indicate delight in the turn of events.

Could she really be *enjoying* this? Had she not known better, Tess would have thought Cinny was recommending a particularly suspenseful novel, rather than talking about a real murder.

After they had ordered—spinach salads for Cinny and Dahlia, a more substantial chicken-salad croissant sandwich for Tess, and iced tea all around—Dahlia glanced to both sides surreptitiously, then leaned toward the other two and spoke in a confidential tone.

"Now, Tess, you wanted to talk about motives for murder."

Cinny clapped her hands. "Oh, let's."

Cinny was definitely enjoying this. After all, nobody had found a bloody corpse at *her* house.

The sampler on the wall behind Cinny caught Tess's eye. She read the words: *The better part of valour is discretion.*

"I don't want to cast suspicion on anyone," she said, hesitant all at once. Chester was doing enough of that, wasn't he?

Cinny and Dahlia leaned closer. "You can tell us anything, Tess," Cinny whispered. She lifted her hand and pretended to turn a key to lock her mouth.

"Besides, dear," Dahlia said, "you can't leave me dangling after dropping *that* name on me."

She was, of course, referring to Fern Willis.

Cinny pursed her lips, glancing from her mother to Tess quizzically. "What name?"

"Let Tess tell it," Dahlia put in.

Tess still hesitated, and Cinny coaxed, "We're family, Tess. We won't breathe a word of it."

Tess glanced at Dahlia, who assured her serenely, "Of course we won't."

"I'm counting on that," Tess said, glancing at the sampler which urged discretion, then looking severely from Dahlia to Cinny, both of whom smiled and nodded encouragingly.

"First, I have to tell you about a telephone conversation I overheard Fern having yesterday afternoon." Tess repeated what Fern had said, as nearly verbatim as she could remember. "So this morning, I went up to Fern's room to talk to her. Actually, I didn't mention the argument right away. I wanted to ask her what should be done about Lana's clothes and car."

Tess fell silent as the waitress approached with their lunch. While the waitress served them, she could sense Cinny practically jumping out of her skin with the need to talk. Tess ducked her head to hide a smile. Her china pattern, she noticed, was one of delicate pink tea roses.

As soon as the waitress was out of earshot again,

Cinny urged impatiently, "Now, Tess, do get to the part about the argument."

"All in good time," Tess said, and took a bite of her sandwich before continuing. "I offered to go with Fern to return the car and suitcase. She didn't want me to come, said she'd get Marisa to do it, but I insisted."

Cinny sighed impatiently and stabbed a piece of spinach. Dahlia looked at Tess expectantly. Tess described what had happened while she and Fern were in Lana's house.

Dahlia nodded. "You don't believe she was looking for Lana's will, do you?"

"Not for a minute." Tess paused, then plunged ahead. "I think she was looking for written evidence of something that happened in her past that only she and Lana knew about. Something Fern doesn't want anyone else to know."

Dahlia held up a perfectly manicured hand. "I'm confused. You've left something out, Tess. Was it Lana that Fern was arguing with on the telephone?"

"I think so. When I asked her about it, she said it was her husband."

"Oh, pooh," Dahlia clucked. "That's an obvious lie. Reverend Willis is the mildest man you can imagine."

Cinny's head bobbed in agreement. "He's the epitome of the henpecked husband. He would never do anything to make Fern mad enough to threaten violence."

"Exactly," Tess said. "So who else could it have been but Lana?"

"Marisa?" Dahlia suggested, then answered her own question. "No, Marisa is as unlikely to anger Fern as the reverend. Her main goal in life, at the moment, is ingratiating herself with Fern."

"That leaves Lana," Tess said. "I think she'd run through the money from her last divorce settlement and was blackmailing Fern."

Cinny bounced excitedly in her chair. "Oh, this gets juicier and juicier."

"I don't know, Tess," Dahlia said dampingly, "I can't imagine anything Fern Willis could have done that's so terrible she could be blackmailed to keep it quiet." That had been Luke's reaction, too, but Tess wasn't going to abandon the theory yet.

"Oh—" Dahlia's hand flew to her mouth. "You're suggesting Fern *murdered* Lana to keep her quiet." Then she glanced around quickly to see if she'd been overheard. But so many other conversations were going on around them that nobody seemed to be paying any attention to them.

Cinny's blue eyes were as round as her poppy-decorated plate. A small giggle escaped her. "Lana had the goods on Mrs. Goody Two-Shoes Willis. How fascinating!"

"Don't jump to conclusions, Cinny," Tess cautioned. "All I know is that Fern is extremely worried about something and I'd like to know what it is."

"I see what you mean," Dahlia said. "Until we know that, we can't know if Fern had a motive to murder Lana."

"Right. Everybody says Fern is a model of decorum, the perfect minister's wife. If Lana knew something that she could use to blackmail Fern, it must have been something that happened before Fern married Reverend Willis."

Dahlia looked puzzled, then dubious. "As I recall, she married young. I think she'd only finished a year or two of college at the University of Missouri."

"Can you remember hearing rumors that she was— well, wild, or whatever they called it then—in high school or while she was away at college? Maybe she was into drugs and got busted. Or something like that."

Cinny's blue eyes widened again. "She has a rap sheet," she breathed, "and is desperate to keep it from her husband and son."

"Fern?" Dahlia laughed merrily. "Oh, no. No, no, no. Fern was as prim and proper as my dear sister, Iris, even in high school. Of course, she was a bit younger than I, but Victoria Springs was even smaller then than now. I would have known if Fern had gone through a period of rebellion." She lifted her tea glass and ran a slender finger around the rim.

"I thought you would," Tess said.

"Why, Fern didn't even wear makeup until she went to college. Poor thing went around looking like a little mouse." Dahlia took a swallow of tea and set the glass down. "Now, if you wanted to dig up some dirt on Lana . . ."

"I would have guessed Lana was—uh, high-spirited, even as a teenager," Tess said. "There were probably several things in her past she wouldn't have wanted broadcast." Unfortunately, she suspected Lana was the blackmailer, not the other way around.

Dahlia looked sadly thoughtful. "I'm not at all sure Lana would have cared. She did what she wanted and took the consequences. I didn't like the woman, but you had to admire that about her. When she was at Victoria Springs High, she was the most popular girl in school. Had a new boyfriend every week." She pursed her lips. "Pathetic little Fern never had a date, that I know of, during her entire high-school career."

"Really?" Cinny asked, incredulous. As well she might be, Tess thought. From what Tess had heard, Cinny had dated every presentable boy in the junior and senior classes during her last year at Victoria Springs High. During the next four years, she had gone through most of the fraternity men at the University of Missouri. She'd been back for nearly two years now and, even in small Victoria Springs, Cinny had no trouble finding eligible bachelors to date.

It was quite amazing, really. Tess sometimes wondered if Cinny manufactured men in that attractive little house which her father had built for her around the corner from the Forrests' home as an enticement to lure Cinny back to Victoria Springs after her college graduation.

Tess pulled her mind off that particular sidetrack. "Lana and Fern were cousins. Did Fern ever run around with Lana's crowd?"

Dahlia shrugged. "Their mothers tried to throw the girls together, I'm sure. But it didn't work. They were too different. Your father was part of their clique, though a couple of years older than Lana and Fern. He may even have had a date or two with Lana when he was a senior at the high school." She smiled indulgently. "Every other boy in the group did."

"I'm going to call Dad this afternoon," Tess said.

"He may know something about Fern that I don't, but I doubt it."

Tess sighed in disappointment. Dahlia was silent as she ate a few bites of salad. Suddenly, she put down her fork. "Something's coming back to me. I do seem to recall that one of the parties thrown by Lana and her friends got out of hand—more so than usual, I mean. A lot of alcohol flowing, kids throwing up on lawns. The parents actually had a meeting to talk about it." She frowned and rubbed her temple. "It's all so hazy, but I think Fern was there. Yes, I'm almost sure of it. I remember being surprised when I heard that."

"Lana's mother probably made her invite Fern," Cinny said with a shake of her head that made her blonde hair swirl about her shoulders like fine silk strands.

"No doubt," Dahlia agreed. "Later, there was a rumor that even Fern got a little tipsy." She was thoughtful for a long moment. "I do recall that Fern's mother was madder than hops at that parents' meeting. Typical adolescent excess, I suppose. Hardly blackmail material."

"No, it isn't," Tess agreed. Getting drunk at a high-school party might embarrass a minister's wife if it got out, but she wouldn't commit murder to keep it quiet.

Cinny looked abstracted, as though her mind was sifting through possibilities. "What if Fern was so drunk she doesn't remember what happened?" She tucked her hair behind her ear again. "And Lana told her she did something really disgraceful and used that to blackmail her?"

"What could possibly be that disgraceful?" Tess asked. "We're talking about a shy, inhibited teenage girl here."

Evidently Cinny couldn't think of anything. "It was only an idea."

"Where would Fern get money to pay blackmail, anyway? No, it won't wash," Dahlia concluded.

They seem to have exhausted Dahlia's memories of Fern and Lana's high-school days. After finishing her sandwich, Tess reached for her purse and pulled out the index cards she'd taken from Lana's room. "These were in Lana's handbag. Maybe you can tell me what they mean, Aunt Dahlia."

Dahlia took the cards, scanned the first one, and nodded. "They're Lana's notes for the conference session she conducted on symptoms and treatments of common iris diseases." She tapped the first card. "Bacterial soft rot. Leaf spot. Gray mold. Oh, my, I've had problems with that one. It turns the leaf tips yellow and then brown and causes mold at the fan base. Three commercially available sprays are listed here, but I have always found carbendazim to be the most effective."

This was all very interesting—to iris aficionados, Tess supposed—but it didn't provide any clues to the identity of Lana's murderer. The notes were exactly what Tess had thought they were, but she'd wanted to make sure.

Dahlia was scanning the second card now. "More iris ailments. Ink disease and mosaic virus."

"I had no idea irises were subject to so many diseases," Tess said. "I thought they were very hardy."

"They are, as flowers go, dear," Dahlia said. "Extremely easy to grow. But like any other living thing, they can get sick and die, if they don't receive proper treatment." She shifted the third card to the top. "What's this?"

Cinny leaned over her mother's shoulder and read, " 'Malignant hyperthermia.' Never heard of it."

"Could it be another iris disease?" Tess asked doubtfully.

Dahlia frowned. "It does sound like a disease, but it's not one that affects irises."

"I thought the entire conference was on irises," Tess said. "Did Lana talk about other flowers in her session?"

"No," Dahlia replied. "I was there." She handed the cards back to Tess. "I wonder why she had that with her lecture notes."

"Maybe it was to remind her of something she wanted to ask someone at the conference," Cinny suggested.

"Could be," Tess said as she dropped the cards into her purse.

"Darn," Cinny sighed. "I was hoping Mother knew something really scandalous about Fern Willis. That woman is so self-righteous." She looked a little sheepish. "I guess you can tell she's not high on my popularity list, Tess."

"Hmmm," Tess murmured. "Well, maybe I'm wrong about what's worrying Fern."

Cinny brightened up. "I have an idea. I'll talk to Myrtle Ponder. She comes in the shop all the time." For Tess's benefit, she added, "She was teaching at the high school when Lana and Fern were there. Retired years ago. She's as old as God, but spry. Still runs errands on her bicycle."

"Myrtle knows everything that went on in this town

when she was teaching," Dahlia added, "but she isn't one to gossip."

"Leave it to me," Cinny told her mother. "I'll be very subtle."

That, Tess thought, *I would like to see.* At any rate, she doubted that Myrtle Ponder would know anything that Dahlia didn't.

As they finished lunch, Tess asked, "How long will it take you to make a list of books for me, Cinny?"

"Only a few minutes. I'm going to the shop from here, so I'll do it right away. We'll probably have most of the books on the shelf. We sell a lot of genre fiction, so we keep those sections well-stocked. I have an excellent idea. Why don't you come by the shop when you leave here, Tess. If I can place the order for the out-of-stock books today, you should have them sometime next week."

Tess could spare another hour, and she was eager to improve the Iris House library. Weeks ago, she'd thought of serving tea in the tower on Sunday afternoons as a way of introducing her guests to the library, but she'd had to store the thought away while she concentrated on more immediate concerns. The idea still appealed to her, though, and she could implement it as soon as the library was well-stocked.

"If Aunt Dahlia doesn't mind the detour," Tess said.

"Mind?" Dahlia asked in surprise. "Fern Willis is chairing a conference session called 'Putting on an Iris Show' at two. I'm not sure I could face her at the moment, considering what we've discussed. If we go by the bookshop, I may manage to miss all of her session."

Cinny cocked her head. "And you'll tell Fern that Tess and I caused you to be late."

Dahlia smiled. "Of course."

Chapter 16

The Queen Street Bookshop was a cozy oasis of walnut paneling, floor-to-ceiling shelves of books, and conveniently placed chairs and benches for customers who wanted to tarry for a bit.

When they entered, the woman who worked mornings at the shop was looking cross.

"You're late again," she said to Cinny.

"Oh, really?" Cinny managed to sound like the offended party.

The woman rolled her eyes and left, saying she was late for a doctor's appointment.

"My watch must be slow," Cinny said to no one in particular. "Besides, how was *I* to know she had an appointment?"

Tess and Cinny soon removed two dozen books from the shelves to be added to Tess's library, and stacked them beside the cash register.

While Cinny waited on a customer, Tess and Dahlia sat in a pleasant conversation area, which tempted browsers to linger for a cup of herbal tea. An urn of hot water and a selection of tea bags sat on a low table nearby.

Cinny rang up the customer's purchases and, as soon as the man left the shop, she bent over the big *Oxford Dictionary* which rested on an oak book stand in a corner near the reference-book section.

Dahlia was jotting down titles of several romantic novels she had read lately and enjoyed. She wanted to recommend them for the Iris

House library, she'd said. Tess was leafing through recent publishers' catalogs.

Cinny looked up from the dictionary. "What was that strange phrase again, Tess?"

Tess put a finger in a catalog to hold her place. "What phrase?"

"The one Lana wrote on that index card. Malignant something. I can't get it out of my mind, so I'm looking it up."

"I'm sure I don't see how it could have anything to do with Lana's murder," Dahlia said.

"I don't, either," Cinny agreed, "but it's going to drive me crazy until I know what it means."

"Just a minute." Tess fished the card out of her purse. "Here it is. Malignant hyperthermia."

"Spell it," Cinny said. Tess did.

Cinny turned more pages, frowning. "I can't believe it. This dictionary has never failed me before, but that's not in here." Disappointed, she ran her finger down the page before her. "Just 'malignant' which is defined as 'Showing great malevolence; actively evil in nature. Highly injurious. Threatening to life.' There's more in the same vein." She glanced up. "Sounds pretty murderous to me."

"Look up 'hyperthermia,' " Dahlia suggested.

Cinny turned more pages. "It says, 'Unusually high fever.' "

"What doesn't make sense about an extremely high fever that's life threatening? It couldn't have anything to do with flowers, unless it means something entirely different when you put the two words together." Disheartened, she closed the big dictionary with a thud.

Now that Cinny had brought it up again, Tess would have liked to know what the words meant, too, when they were used together as Lana had written them. Why *had* she had that card in her purse? If it wasn't some kind of plant disease, why would Lana have taken the card to the conference?

"Do you have a reference book on flower diseases in the shop?" Tess asked.

"If we haven't sold it." Cinny walked over to a bank of shelves against the south wall of the shop. "It should be in our horticulture section." She scanned titles and, after a few moments, took down a large hardback volume. She turned to the index at the back of the volume. "Not here, either." She closed the book and returned it to the shelf, frustration etching itself deeper between her elegant eyebrows.

"I've done a lot of reading about plant diseases," Dahlia said musingly, "and that just doesn't sound like one."

Wasn't "malignant" a term used to refer to cancerous tumors? "Sounds more like a human disease," Tess said.

"Ah ha," Cinny said, and moved away from the horticulture section. "Tess, there's a thick red book right there beside where you're sitting. I think it's on the bottom shelf." She watched Tess run her fingers along book spines. "There. That's it."

Tess pulled the book off the bottom shelf and straightened up. The title *Everybody's Medical Encyclopedia* was written in bold white letters on the book jacket. She turned to the index at the back of the book. And there it was. Malignant hyperthermia. Page 268.

"I found it," Tess said. "Listen to this. 'Malignant hyperthermia occurs in one out of twenty thousand surgical procedures involving muscle relaxants and general anesthetics. Muscular rigidity is often the first sign of the disorder; other symptoms include rapid or erratic heartbeat, rising temperature, and shock. This rapidly progressive reaction, which results from an inherited trait, is often fatal. Susceptible family members can be identified by blood tests and muscle biopsy. If a susceptible person needs an operation, it should be done under local anesthesia.' "

"What on earth . . ." Dahlia trailed off and the three women looked at each other wonderingly.

"Do you suppose Lana had this malignant hyperthermia?" Tess mused.

Cinny shrugged. "Could be, I guess."

"Was she planning to have surgery?"

"Not that I know of."

"We should be able to find out," Cinny said. "Lana used our family doctor, didn't she, Mother?"

Dahlia, who had become lost in thought during the exchange between Cinny and Tess, gazed at Cinny blankly. "What, dear?"

"If Lana had that disease, Dr. Brady should know about it."

"Yes, I suppose . . ." Dahlia's mind still seemed elsewhere.

"Could you ask him?"

"Why—oh, yes, dear. I'll call him this afternoon. It's confidential information between patient and physician, of course, but since Lana's dead, there may no longer be an ethical problem in Dr. Brady's mind."

"Even if he says Lana had the disease, I can't see how it will help us," Tess said.

"Neither can I," Dahlia agreed as she rose to her feet. She seemed restless all at once. She picked up her purse, walked to the front of the shop, and looked out.

"What's wrong, Aunt Dahlia?" Tess asked.

"What? Oh. I just remembered something I have to do."

"Let me pay for these books." Tess moved to the cash register and took out a credit card. Why was Dahlia so distracted suddenly?

She opened the door. The bell jangled.

"I'll wait for you in the car," Dahlia said and left.

"What got into her?" Tess asked.

"I was wondering the same thing." Cinny shook her head and began ringing up Tess's purchases.

"She said something strange the other day, when we

found Lana's body," Tess ventured. "I can't remember her exact words, but I got the definite impression that she and Lana had had some kind of run-in in the past."

Cinny began sacking up the books. "Oh, that. It was just Mother coming to the aid of her little girl."

"Oh?"

Cinny nodded. "A couple of years ago, I was dating an older man. He was wealthy, and very nice, and Mother thought he would make the perfect husband for me. Settle me down, you know." Cinny laughed. "I didn't agree and, anyway, Lana moved in on him about then and he followed after her like a little puppy. Oh, I admit my pride was hurt. But Mother was furious. She and Lana had words at the country club in front of about twenty people. I was never able to convince Mother that Lana hadn't stolen the love of my life."

"But wasn't Lana still married two years ago?"

"Yes, but I think she could already see the handwriting on the wall."

"What happened to the older man?"

"He got a good look at the mercenary side of Lana while she was getting her divorce," Cinny said, sounding a little smug, "and had second thoughts. He left town—and Lana—a few days after the divorce was final. Mother considered it poetic justice."

As Tess exited the shop with her purchases, she wondered if Cinny's losing a man to Lana would really have made Dahlia despise her so much. She decided that it probably would have.

After several miscarriages early in their marriage, Dahlia and Maurice had been told that it was unlikely Dahlia could ever carry a child to term. They had accepted the doctor's verdict and were considering adoption, when Dahlia unexpectedly became pregnant again. By staying in bed for six months, Dahlia managed to carry Cinny for eight months. Though born a month prematurely, Cinny had been a surprisingly robust baby.

To Dahlia and Maurice, however, Cinny's survival

was nothing short of a miracle. Of course, they doted on her and spoiled her unconscionably.

Yes, Tess could believe that Dahlia's hatred would be kindled by anyone who hurt her beloved Cinny. Could Dahlia's hatred get so out of control that she would murder the culprit two years after the fact?

No, Tess simply could not believe that.

Dahlia was unusually quiet on the drive to Iris House, apparently lost in contemplation of whatever it was that had made her suddenly want to leave the bookshop. Tess thought back over what had been said before Dahlia became so anxious to leave. Could it have something to do with malignant hyperthermia? They had then discussed whether Lana might have been facing surgery. Could that have upset Dahlia?

No, because Cinny had suggested that Dahlia try to find out from Lana's doctor, and Dahlia had agreed.

Tess didn't see how any of that could have thrown Dahlia into her present abstracted state, and she remained baffled by it.

She glanced over at Dahlia, wondering if Dahlia would tell her what was bothering her if she asked. She decided Dahlia probably wouldn't. Dahlia had barely responded to Tess's few attempts at conversation during the drive. She would let it go for now.

When Dahlia dropped her off at Iris House, Tess asked, "Are you all right, Aunt Dahlia?"

"Perfectly fine, dear," Dahlia said, and drove away with barely a glance at Tess.

Alexis and Harley Dinwitty met Tess in the foyer. Although perfectly groomed as usual, Alexis was pale beneath her makeup. Rather than adding color to her skin, her red silk dress made it appear ghostlike, as though she were recovering from an illness.

"We must talk to you, Tess," Alexis said without preamble.

"Come into my apartment," Tess invited, and led the way.

Primrose, who had been napping in a blue armchair, lifted her head and gave the Dinwittys an enigmatic yellow-eyed stare.

"Sit down," Tess said, indicating the sofa, "while I get rid of these books."

Tess dropped the sack of books in her office, then returned to the sitting room. Primrose gave her a haughty you're-disturbing-my-nap look, twitched her fluffy tail, and jumped to the floor. She then slitted her eyes in displeasure and streaked out of the room.

The Dinwittys sat side by side on the floral chintz sofa. "Would you like something to drink?" Tess asked.

"This isn't a social call. Sit down," Harley said, sounding too much like Desmond Butts for Tess's taste. Harley was a big man, over six feet tall, and had thickened with the years. Even his expertly tailored suits could no longer hide his bulk.

Alexis planted her red high-heeled shoes on the carpet, the sides touching, and pulled her dress down over her knees. Then she clasped her hands tightly in her lap. After a glance at her husband, Alexis said, "You're the last person I would have suspected of stabbing me in the back, Tess. I—" She halted as she evidently realized that she'd chosen an unfortunate figure of speech. Color crept up her neck.

"I did no such thing," Tess protested.

Harley heaved himself forward on the sofa cushion. "Exactly what," he demanded, "did you tell Chief Butts about me and Lana Morrison?"

"I didn't mention your name to the chief, Harley, except to say that I had *not* seen you with Lana night before last."

It was clear that Harley thought she was hedging. "Then where did he get the idea that I was having a flaming affair with the woman?"

Thinking that she owed no loyalty to Chester now,

Tess said, "Chester Leeds met with the chief this morning, and reported a *private* conversation I had with my cook and housekeeper which he'd eavesdropped on. Furthermore, he probably embellished it to make it sound more damning than it actually was."

Surprise registered in Alexis's eyes, then changed to acceptance. She touched her husband's coat sleeve. "I should have been suspicious when Chester came to me with that long face and a tale about Tess seeing you and Lana together, Harley. He said I should know for my own good. Now I see it was his way of getting back at me for winning the Club presidency."

Harley ignored her. He had not taken his eyes off Tess. She could imagine him looking at an unsatisfactory employee in exactly that way immediately before he fired him. "Am I to understand that you gossiped about me and Lana with your help?"

Tess squirmed in her chair. "It wasn't like that." But it was, in a way, which made her feel a little guilty. "I mentioned that I'd seen Lana going through the back hedge at one A.M. We did wonder aloud if she had been heading for your house. Unfortunately, Chester had slipped up on us and was taking in every word."

Alexis clenched and unclenched her linked hands. "I'm still disappointed in you, Tess." She had a this-too-shall-pass tone, but the look in her eyes was a mixture of hurt and disappointment. "I thought you were my friend."

"I'm sorry, Alexis." What else was there to say?

"For the record," Harley clipped out, not the least bit mollified, "Lana Morrison was a pathetic middle-aged woman who needed a man to give her self-esteem." *And financial support,* Tess thought, but did not say it. "Lana did ring my back doorbell that night and woke me from a sound sleep. I sent her straight back here. *I was not having an affair with Lana Morrison.* Pass that along to your cook and housekeeper and remind them that slander is a legally actionable offense. Do I make myself clear?"

As Harley talked, Alexis leaned back against the sofa and watched him in a detached sort of way that made Tess think she was not convinced Harley was telling the whole truth.

"Perfectly," Tess retorted sharply. "I'll speak to Gertie and Nedra, but I should think threatening Chester with a lawsuit would be more to the point."

"I'll take care of Chester," Harley snapped, and Tess believed him.

Alexis shifted her gaze from Harley to Tess. Then she looked at her hands which were gripping her knees as if they were the supports that kept her upright. "I don't mind telling you I'm scared. Chief Butts actually accused me of murdering Lana in a jealous rage."

"Don't feel he's picking on you in particular," Tess advised. "He accused me of the murder earlier today. He will probably accuse everyone who's staying at Iris House before he's through."

Alexis took this in and, somewhat relieved, glanced at the closed door between Tess's sitting room and the main foyer. "He has Randall and Reva in there right now. Do you think he's accusing them of the murder, too?"

"I wouldn't be surprised," Tess said. Evidently Chester, dutiful citizen that he was, had also detailed Randall's and Lana's flirtatious behavior yesterday at breakfast. She wondered if Butts knew that Reva believed it was Randall, not Harley, who had been having an affair with Lana. If he didn't now, he probably would find out if he questioned Fern Willis again.

Harley got to his feet with a grunt. "I've said what I came to say." He glanced down at his wife, appearing uncertain for the first time. "Are you going back with me?"

"Certainly not." Alexis stood. "I'm going over to the hotel. I wouldn't give that little wimp Chester Leeds the satisfaction of knowing his petty tattling sent me home with my tail between my legs."

Harley hesitated before he said, "Suit yourself."

Alexis brushed past him and went to the door.

"I truly am sorry about this, Alexis," Tess said.

"Not nearly as sorry as I am," she retorted as she let herself out.

Harley stood there with a troubled expression and watched her go. Things would be tense for a while around the Dinwitty house, Tess thought. As soon as Alexis shut the door leading into the foyer, Harley took a deep breath and reached for the knob.

"Wait a minute, Harley," Tess said. He dropped his hand and turned back to rake her with cold eyes. Tess rose from her chair, since sitting made her feel even more at a disadvantage with this hard-edged man. Harley Dinwitty hadn't become a multimillionaire by being merciful to people who got in his way.

Tess swallowed hard. "Did Chief Butts accept your story about sending Lana straight home the other night?"

His thick eyebrows shot up. "My *story!* Dammit, I thought I made it perfectly clear that I will not tolerate slander and innuendo concerning me and Lana Morrison."

"As I understand it," Tess went on with great effort, "slander is telling *lies* about someone, not truths they prefer to sweep under the rug."

Harley glared at her, his big hands balling at his sides. "What in hell are you talking about?"

"Evidently the chief doesn't know that at least half an hour passed between the time Lana left this house for yours and when she returned." Which meant that Chester hadn't heard that part of her conversation with Gertie and Nedra. No way would he have left that juicy tidbit out of his dutiful conversation with the chief, had he known. "If you turned her away at the door, where did she go?"

"How would I know?" he blustered. "She wasn't exactly happy to be rebuffed. Frankly, I think it shocked the hell out of her. She wasn't used to getting turned down. Maybe she went for a walk to cool off."

"In her nightgown?"

His face got red, his shoulders bunched up around his ears, and he thrust his square chin out threateningly. It was definitely a heads-are-going-to-roll look, and Tess's was the only head around. She trembled but stood her ground and refused to look away. After several moments, his shoulders dropped and his clenched hands relaxed. He was studying her as he must study an opponent in a business deal, looking for weaknesses.

Abruptly, he shrugged. "All right. I let her come in for a drink, and if you tell my wife *or* Butts, you will regret it. Believe that, Tess. I do not make idle threats."

Tess believed it, all right, and she suddenly wanted something solid between her and Harley Dinwitty. Looking as casual as she could, she walked around the chair in which she'd been sitting and planted her hands on its high back. She knew instinctively that if he realized he'd intimidated her, he would use it against her.

She looked him square in the eye and hoped he couldn't tell she was gripping the back of the chair to keep her hands steady. "So you *were* having an affair with Lana."

"No!"

"That's a bit hard to swallow, given that you've already admitted to inviting her in."

It would be even harder for Alexis to swallow if she learned that he'd had a woman in a nightgown in his house in the middle of the night.

He glared at her another instant, and then he seemed to sag all over. "You don't understand what a boost to a man's ego it is to have a beautiful woman throw herself at him. Especially a man of my age." What had happened to the pathetic middle-aged woman? That must have been for Alexis's benefit.

"I think I do, Harley. But how could you treat Alexis so shabbily?"

"I *said* there was no affair. I admit flirting with Lana was fun. It made me feel young again. But Lana flirted with everybody. I didn't think it meant anything. When she showed up at my door in her nightgown, I couldn't believe it." He ran a hand through thick iron-gray hair. "She was inside before I knew what had happened."

Tess looked at him askance.

"Okay, hell, I invited her in and fixed us both a drink. I couldn't help thinking about bedding her." He shrugged dispiritedly. "After all, there she was in that revealing nightgown and there I was in my pajamas. I knew my main attraction for her was money. I'm not a fool. Still, I was tempted, but in the end, I couldn't do it. I told her that and when she finished her drink, I sent her home. I love my wife, Tess. It would kill her to know that I even entertained the idea of letting Lana stay."

"Yes, it would," Tess murmured.

He looked at her for another long moment. "Just remember that I can be a formidable enemy." With that parting salvo, he spun on his heel and left the room.

When he was gone, Tess sank into the armchair. She put her head back, closed her eyes, and took several deep, bracing breaths. Was Harley telling the truth? She wanted to believe him, for Alexis's sake. If she told the police that Lana had been in the Dinwitty house for a period of time, the story would come out. Alexis would not believe that, after all was said and done, Harley had remained faithful to her. Nobody would believe it. All Tess would get out of it would be Harley for an enemy, something she surely didn't need. She shivered, remembering his final threat, but she could not let that keep her from doing the right thing. Would not.

She sighed and opened her eyes. Primrose appeared in the open doorway between the sitting room and hall, and looked around. Seeing that the invaders of her turf were no longer in evidence, she trotted over to Tess and rubbed against her leg.

Tess lifted the cat into her lap to stroke her. "So, you've decided you will put up with me, have you?"

Primrose's eyes drifted closed in contentment.

"What should I do, sweetie?" Tess asked the cat.

Primrose's only response was to stretch and yawn and push her head hard against Tess's fingers.

Tess resumed stroking and thinking aloud. "After all, Chief Butts didn't specifically ask me how long Lana was out of Iris House."

Primrose opened one eye to gauge whether Tess was about to stop stroking.

"I know, Primrose." Tess smiled and buried her fingers in the thick fur behind the cat's ears in a massaging motion. "As long as these human problems don't affect your comfort, what are they to you?"

Primrose yawned.

"I have decided," she told the cat finally, "to take Harley's word for it. For now, at least. I don't want Alexis to be hurt any more than she already has been unless it's absolutely necessary."

Primrose leaned heavily against Tess, purring loudly. Tess took it as a sign of approval for her decision.

Chapter 17

Half an hour later, Chief Butts left Iris House, slamming the front door behind him. Tess, who was still in her quarters, tensed when she heard the stained-glass panes rattle. *If he's broken a pane, I'll send a bill to the police department,* she fumed.

She stepped into the foyer, almost afraid to look at the door but, thank goodness, the colorful—and expensive—panes were intact.

Butts, whom she could see through a leaded triangle of yellow glass, was getting in his car at the curb in high dudgeon. Probably, Tess surmised, he was irate because nobody in Iris House had confessed to the murder so he could wrap up the investigation and get back to corralling tourists.

As she turned to go back to her apartment, Randall and Reva came out of the parlor. Randall's Western shirt was wet beneath the arms, and he was wiping his forehead with his handkerchief as he stepped into the foyer. He looked like a man who'd run a gauntlet and was stunned to have emerged alive. Reva, on the other hand, appeared merely cross.

Reva took in Tess and said snippily, "I suppose you heard every word that was said in the parlor."

Tess stiffened. "Not a single one. I was in my quarters until I heard Chief Butts leaving." She rested her hands on her hips and continued. "I have too much to do to spend my time eavesdropping on all the conversations that go on in this house." She didn't add, of course, that she would nevertheless love to know what had been said.

Randall wiped his brow again and stuffed his damp handkerchief into his shirt pocket. "I have a good notion to call my lawyer. You can't go around accusing people of crimes without a shred of evidence, even if you are the chief of police."

"You don't need a lawyer," Reva snapped. She gave her husband a contemptuous look over her shoulder. "Not yet, anyway."

"Thanks for the vote of confidence, Reva," Randall snapped back.

"It may make you feel better to know that Butts has accused several people of Lana's murder, including me," Tess told them. "Apparently it's part of his investigative technique."

"You?" Randall was clearly taken aback by Tess's words. He also began to look less worried. On the other hand, Reva's irritability with her husband didn't appear to abate.

"Yes," Tess replied to Randall's question. "I expect him to spread more accusations around before he's through." She sighed. "I guess he's frustrated because his investigation seems to be going nowhere."

Reva started up the stairs. "Well, I'm going somewhere. To the conference as soon as I change."

Randall ran up the stairs after her. "Are you sure you're feeling up to it, sugar?" Suddenly, he was back in his solicitous-husband mode.

Tess could not understand Reva's reply, but the tone was curtly dismissive. It would seem that the worm had turned, permanently.

She went to the kitchen to check on Gertie, who was pulling on her cardigan sweater, preparing to go home.

"Nedra left a little while ago," she told Tess, "and I'm dead on my feet."

She looks it, Tess thought. "Maybe we'll both sleep better tonight. Did Chief Butts talk to you again?"

"No, and it's a good thing. I'm so tired I might have confessed to anything to get him to leave me alone. I guess he's got bigger fish to fry—or more suspicious ones."

Tess nodded. "Alexis told me he accused her of the murder and I gather his approach to Randall was the same."

"Oh, he threw in Harley Dinwitty and Reva, too." Gertie buttoned her sweater and went into the utility room to retrieve her purse. Coming out, she added, "Hinted at it, anyway. I heard that much, but I don't think his heart was really in it with those two."

"Apparently Alexis, Randall, and I are at the top of his suspect list at the moment," Tess observed a bit worriedly.

Gertie looked sympathetic. "The man's a moron."

Tess wished she could agree, but she somehow thought that Butts was shrewder than he appeared.

Covering a yawn, Gertie muttered, "I better go before I stretch out for a nap right here on the floor."

Gertie left by the back door and Tess returned to her quarters to place a call to her father's home. She got her stepmother, Zelda, who said that Tess's father was in an evening meeting outside the embassy. Disappointed, Tess asked after the family and left word for her father to call her when he got home.

Having forgotten that she'd invited Luke to dinner that evening, Tess found herself standing in her kitchen at six o'clock wondering why on earth she'd suggested it. She had too many far more urgent things on her mind to plan a menu and prepare a meal for anyone. She'd probably have to make a trip to the grocery store, too, and Luke was due in an hour.

She rummaged through her pantry and refrigerator, hoping to find all the ingredients for *something* already on the premises. Her freezer contained a brisket, which there wasn't time to cook, and several packages of ground beef, chicken breasts, frozen vegetables, and half a praline cheesecake.

Dessert, at least, would be no problem. She set the cheesecake out to thaw.

One crisper contained spinach and other fresh salad vegetables, the other, red and green seedless grapes and a couple of apples. If her guest were another woman, she could get by with salad, a cheese-and-fruit tray, and desert. Unfortunately, Luke was a hearty eater.

Sighing, she closed the refrigerator and sank into a kitchen chair. She could thaw some chicken breasts in the microwave, add a can of mushroom soup, and . . .

No. She simply couldn't cope with it tonight. Carry-out food was invented for days like this. She went to the phone and ordered generous portions of rice, cashew chicken, and Luke's favorite, sweet-and-sour pork. With the main course taken care of, she put to-gether a spinach salad, set it in the refrigerator, and headed for the shower.

Over dinner, to which Luke had contributed a bottle of exquisite Chianti, Tess filled him in on the day's de-velopments in the murder investigation—Butts's *and* hers.

"You've had a busy day," Luke observed when she had finished. He got up to pour coffee and place two slices of cheesecake on dessert plates.

He set the coffee and dessert on the table, then put both hands on Tess's shoulders and massaged gently. Tess closed her eyes with a big sigh. But she couldn't close her mind to the nagging questions.

Didn't she have enough to do with running Iris House? Did she really think she could do a better job of tracking down Lana's killer than the police? Why didn't she stay out of it?

She knew that she would feel differently tomorrow, but tonight she was bone-tired. Briefly, she wanted nothing more than to crawl into her bed and let sleep shut out everything else. Primrose, showing more common sense than her mistress, had done exactly that as soon as Luke arrived. He had tried to coax the cat to join him and Tess in the kitchen, but Primrose had opened one eye, flicked her tail at him, and refused to budge from her wicker basket in Tess's bedroom. She would have preferred her favorite chair in the sitting room, but not when there was a turf-invader on the premises.

"Better?" Luke asked.

She reached up and patted his hand. "Much," she murmured.

He sat down, his face determined. "If I can't talk you into staying out of the investigation, I'll just have to help you."

Tess gave him a grateful, if weary, smile. It was sweet of Luke to offer. "I only wish you could."

"At least I can be there to protect you."

Luke's voicing her innermost fear—that she needed protection—triggered a stubborn resistance in Tess. "I'm not in any danger."

"Oh, no. You merely have a cold-blooded murderer running around this house, not to mention the fact that you have been accused of the murder yourself."

"Me and half a dozen other people."

Luke looked grave as he ate a bite of cheesecake and took a swallow of coffee. "Don't take Butts's accusations lightly, Tess. Go to him and tell him all you know."

"I *have* told him."

"Not exactly. You just said you withheld the information that on the night before she died Lana was inside the Dinwitty house with Harley for an undetermined period of time. You keep saying Lana was a black-mailer. Well, maybe Harley Dinwitty was her victim. After all, who would have been better able to pay her off handsomely to keep her quiet?"

"About what? Harley swears he wasn't having an affair with Lana."

"What would you expect him to say, dear heart?"

The endearment made a smile tug at Tess's mouth. "I wish you'd make up your mind, Luke. You're the one who told me the whole idea of Harley and Lana having an affair was preposterous."

Luke continued to look grave as he finished off his cheesecake. Was he trying to frighten her so that she'd stop snooping around? Of course he was.

"I have been wrong before," he said seriously.

"That's hard to believe," Tess responded with a twinkle in her brown eyes.

Her teasing didn't melt his troubled expression. He put his hands behind his head and stared up at the ceiling. Then he said gently, "If you tell the police all you know, then there will be no reason for anybody to harm you to keep you quiet." He dropped his hands and picked up his coffee cup.

He was still talking about Harley, of course. He really had begun to suspect that Lana and Harley had been having an affair and that Lana had been using that to blackmail Harley. Tess shook her curly head adamantly. "I refuse to let that man intimidate me! Oh, he made me so mad! Throwing out warnings and threats as though he had every right to tell other people what to do."

Luke plunked down his coffee cup. "What threats?"

Too late, Tess remembered that, in relating what had happened since last they'd talked, she had conveniently omitted that part. Well, the cat was out of the bag now, so she repeated what Harley had said.

He scowled fiercely. "There is good reason to be intimidated by Harley, love. The man takes no prisoners."

"I'll be careful."

"Well, I intend to have a talk with Mr. Dinwitty, anyway."

Tess waved this away. "Don't bother. He was trying

to scare me." And succeeding quite well, by the way. "Besides, I halfway believed him when he said nothing was going on between him and Lana." She got up to pour them both more coffee. "The trouble is, I half-believe all of them when they say they didn't kill Lana. Am I simply gullible, or what?"

"You want to think the best of people, sweetheart," Luke said, softening. He reached for the cup Tess had refilled.

"Let's take our coffee into the sitting room where it's more comfortable," Tess suggested.

When they were settled on the sofa with Luke's arm around her and Tess's head resting on his shoulder, she murmured, "Maybe I do want to think the best of people, but I can usually tell when somebody is hiding something, and Fern Willis definitely is." She lifted her head to take a sip of coffee, then set the cup on the table beside the sofa. "Unfortunately, if Dad can't tell me something damning about Fern, something Lana might have been blackmailing her about, I don't know where else to look. Some detective I am, huh? I've run out of leads already."

Luke was silent for a minute, thinking. Then he straightened up, removing his arm from Tess's shoulders. "Not totally," he said, and the determination was back in his voice. "Where's that partial phone number you said you copied down from Lana's house?"

"In the top right-hand cubbyhole of the secretary."

Luke got up and retrieved the piece of paper from the small cherry-wood secretary near the entryway. "This is a Chicago exchange."

"Really? I didn't recognize it." She frowned at him. "I wonder who Lana knew in Chicago?"

"Let's find out."

"How? I didn't get the last number."

"It's one of only ten possibilities, pet." Luke thought for a moment, then went back to the secretary where a mauve telephone rested. He pulled out a chair and sat down. "Leave this to me." Tess suppressed a smile. Luke's reluctance to get involved in her investigation was an act he put on from time to time because he worried about her.

He took a newly sharpened pencil from a cubbyhole and listed the ten possible phone numbers, beginning with 312-555-6740 and ending with 312-555-6749. Then he dialed the first number.

"Hello," he said brightly. "This is Luke Frederik and I'm trying to locate an old friend of mine, Lana Morrison." He grinned at Tess, who pantomined applauding. "I was told she might be at this number." He paused. "Thanks for your time, anyway." He hung up. "He never heard of her," he told Tess, and made a notation beside the first number.

The second number turned out to be a hospital, and Luke crossed it off the list. With the others, he used the approach he had used on the first number. Three calls went unanswered. The others connected him to people who all said they didn't know Lana Morrison and that he'd dialed a wrong number. While Luke was thus occupied, Tess curled up on the sofa and tried to fight off drowsiness.

Luke dropped the pencil and lounged in his chair. "Dead end. Sorry, hon."

Tess shrugged and covered a yawn. "I didn't really expect the number to turn up anything relevant, anyway. It's odd, though. If none of those people knew Lana, why did she phone one of them?"

He glanced at the list of numbers. "There are three that weren't answered. Maybe it was one of them." He folded the paper on which he had written and tucked it back in the cubbyhole.

"They could be businesses that are only open during the day," Tess suggested. "I'll try them tomorrow."

He came over to the sofa and pulled her into his arms. She nestled her head in the hollow of his shoulder.

"I keep wondering," she murmured, "why Chester took it upon himself to spill his guts to the police. Was it just to make trouble for the others?"

He ran his hands down her back. "If so, it's pretty childish behavior for a respected bank president." He rested his chin on the top of Tess's head. "Maybe he's throwing the spotlight on everybody else to keep it off himself."

His words jerked Tess momentarily out of the soft drowsiness in which she'd been floating. She lifted her head. "Which would mean he has something to hide. Could Lana have been blackmailing *Chester?*"

"It's hard to imagine anything Chester would be that desperate to hide. He leads a very mundane life."

"But we shouldn't leave a stone unturned. While I'm trying to dig up Fern's dark secrets, why don't you do the same with Chester?"

"I'll look into it." He brushed a curl off her forehead. "Enough detecting for tonight. Agreed?"

"Agreed."

He kissed her and she felt weightless in his arms. After some moments, he clasped her shoulders and peered down at her drooping eyelids. "You're really beat, aren't you?"

"I am," she admitted. "I'm sorry, Luke, but I've had it."

He dropped a kiss on the tip of her nose. "There will be other nights," he promised.

After Luke left, Tess slipped on a nightgown. She was getting in bed when Cinny phoned.

"Myrtle Ponder was in the shop late this afternoon."

"Myrtle Ponder?" Tess's sleepy brain wasn't up to guessing games.

"The retired teacher I told you about. The one who taught Fern and Lana in high school." Cinny sounded disgruntled.

"Oh, yes. I gather she didn't know of any deep, dark secrets Fern could have."

"She knows something, all right," Cinny said, "but all she would say was that I should let sleeping scandals lie."

Tess was too exhausted to think about this now. "Thanks for trying, anyway, Cinny."

Hanging up, Tess got into bed. Sleep began to wash over her as soon as her eyes drifted closed. She would worry about sleeping scandals tomorrow.

Chapter 18

The sound came to Tess from far away. A shrill
ringing that went on and on. She struggled up
from sleep as though surfacing from the bottom
of a sludge pit.

Now the ringing was in the room with her.
She dragged her eyes open and turned toward the
sound. The offending noise took the form of the
telephone on her bedside table.

Muttering an oath, she snatched the receiver
from its cradle. "He-hello."

"Tess?" The voice came through a crackle of
static.

She cleared her throat and raked tousled curls
out of sleep-glazed eyes. "Dad?"

"Did I wake you?"

"It's all right."

"I'm sorry, honey, but Zelda said you wanted
me to call as soon as I could. If I hadn't called
before I left for work, I didn't know when I'd get
to it."

Tess squirmed into a sitting position and tried
to get her bearings. "I'm glad you called. How
are you, Dad?"

"Working like a slave, but I love it. What's going on there? Have you opened the bed and
breakfast yet?"

"Just this week."

"Ah. Things must be pretty hectic."

"True, and judging from the advance reserva-
tions, Iris House is going to be a huge success.

163

Providing—" A piercing noise on the line sounded like chalk on a chalkboard. She winced and held the receiver away from her ear.

After a moment, she heard her father say, "—great, sweetheart."

Tess waited for another explosion of static to abate before she said, "Dad, something terrible has happened here."

"What?" His voice rose with a sudden injection of worry. "You aren't hurt—or sick, are you?"

"I'm fine, Dad. But one of my guests has been—" Static drowned her out. Muttering in frustration, she waited for the noise to die.

"This is a rotten connection," he grumbled. "Shall I hang up and call you back?"

"No!" Another transatlantic call might be delayed and, now that she was awake, Tess wanted to hear what her father remembered about Fern Willis.

"What were you saying, Tess?"

"One of my guests has been murdered." All at once, the line was free of static, and her words echoed ominously in the silence.

"Did you say murdered?"

"Yes, Dad. The officers of the local garden club are staying here during an iris growers' conference, and Lana Morrison was stabbed with Grandmother Darcy's cake knife."

"My God! That's not Lana Benchley, the girl I went to high school with, is it?"

Tess had a vague memory of having heard Lana's maiden name once before. "I'm afraid so."

"Oh, no. Spunky little Lana Benchley. She was always looking for a good time. Why, I took her to my senior prom when she was a sophomore. I can't believe it. How did it happen? Who did it?"

"The police don't know who did it, but they think it's somebody in Iris House." She named her other guests, all of whom he knew, at least by name.

"I don't like this, honey." The worry in his voice was stronger now. "If the police are right, all the rest of you could be in danger."

"Oh, I don't think—"

He overrode her protest. "You should close down Iris House until they catch the murderer."

Another rolling crackle of static gave Tess time to frame a reply. When she could be heard, she said, "I can't do that, Dad. It would set my business back for weeks if I shut down. I simply can't afford it."

"It's only money, Tess!"

All the money she had in the world, as it happened, Tess thought.

"If necessary," her father was saying, "I can send you something to tide you over."

Tess had not taken money from her father since she left college and she had no intention of doing so now. "Thanks, Dad, but no, thanks." She hastened to change the subject before he could press her further. "Listen, what I really called for was to ask you about Lana's cousin, Fern Willis." She went on to explain her blackmail theory. "Aunt Dahlia mentioned a high-school party where everybody got drunk. I gather it created quite a stir around town."

"You lost me, honey. I don't see the connection to Lana as a potential blackmailer."

"Maybe there isn't any," Tess admitted.

"Wait a minute—"

"What?"

"I remember that party. I think it was the summer between my sophomore and junior years of college. I'm afraid I overindulged. When I got home, my father stood me, fully clothed, under a cold shower until I begged for mercy." He chuckled softly. "Good Lord, I hadn't thought about that night in years."

"Can you recall if Fern was there?" Tess yelled above a fresh burst of static.

"Let me think." Static drowned out his next words. "—spiked the punch."

"Sorry, I didn't catch all that."

"I said Fern was there," he yelled before he realized that the line was again quiet. He lowered his voice. "Sat in a corner by herself most of the evening. The party was at Lana's house, and her parents were out of town. Apparently, Lana's mother had ordered her to invite Fern and find some parents to chaperone. Well, she invited Fern but there were no chaperones. Anyway, a couple of boys thought it would be hilarious to get Fern drunk, so they spiked the punch, then kept refilling her cup."

"Big joke," Tess muttered.

"The poor girl got loop-legged. Everybody did, frankly. It got completely out of control."

"So Fern got drunk," Tess sighed, "but it happened once, years ago, and it wasn't even her fault. She wouldn't pay blackmail to keep that quiet."

There was a long silence on the other end of the line. "Dad, are you still there?"

"I'm here. Just thinking. There *was* something else. My memory of the whole night is pretty foggy, but I do recall that Fern disappeared for a while."

"She was probably in the bathroom being sick."

"No— Remember, Tess, I'd had too much to drink, so I couldn't swear to any of this. But at some point, I became aware that a few of the boys were going in and out of Lana's parents' bedroom, and somebody said Fern was in there, and . . . Well, that's all I know, really, because I went home about then. Except—well, there was a lot of whispering and giggling going on in the hall outside that bedroom."

"Dad! Are you saying those boys raped Fern?"

Static prevented his answering right away. Finally, he said slowly, "A lot of rumors went around that more than one of them—well, you know—but the story went that Fern was willing. As I said, I can't swear to any of it."

"Willing, my foot! They got the girl drunk and raped her. What boys were involved?"

"I wouldn't want to mention any names, Tess, because I really don't know for a fact which of them it was. Besides, none of them has lived in Victoria Springs for years."

"I hope they have nightmares about it every night," Tess fumed, her hand tightening on the telephone receiver. She was outraged and angry with the unnamed boys and saddened for the shy seventeen-year-old virgin Fern had been—until that night.

"I trust you not to repeat any of this, honey," her father was saying. "It was a long time ago. Don't dig it up now. You'll only cause Fern more pain."

"But what if Lana was threatening to tell Fern's husband about that night?"

"Let the police handle it, Tess." He sounded like Luke. Tess thought they were both overreacting. The murderer had wanted Lana out of the way because she was threatening him. There was no reason for him to be a danger to anyone else.

She mumbled something that her father could take as agreement, if he chose to.

He seemed satisfied. "I'll let you get back to sleep now. I have a call on another line. I love you, sweetheart."

"I love you, too, Dad."

Tess hung up and lay for a long time, staring at the swaying shadows of tree branches on her bedroom wall and thinking about what her father had told her.

How had Fern lived with this knowledge all these years? None of it was her fault; no one could blame her. Yet it wasn't uncommon for rape victims to feel somehow at fault. Fern must have suffered agonies of mortification and shame when it happened, but she'd gone off to college, met Richard Willis, married, and

returned to Victoria Springs. Eventually, it must have
seemed that it happened to some other girl, long, long
ago. In another lifetime. Would she kill Lana to keep it
safely buried in the past?

It didn't ring true to Tess. Fern was an adult now
with a son older than she had been when she was violated by one or more drunken classmates. To have it all
come out now might be mortifying but, after all these
years, Fern must realize that she wasn't to blame for
what happened. She hadn't even known the punch was
spiked.

If Fern was the murderer, Tess reasoned, there had to
be something else that Lana had threatened to expose.
What could it possibly be?

Tess was beginning to feel drowsy again as she
thought about Fern's present life, looking for hints to an
even darker secret. And then, as she reviewed Fern's in-
terests and activities, it came to her. To most women, it
wouldn't be a motive for murder, but Fern Willis was
not most women.

When an ominous growling of thunder awakened
Tess the next morning, she was in the same curled position she had taken after her father's phone call.

She had been dreaming that she was fleeing down a
long tunnel and being chased by people armed with
cake knives. Throwing a terrified look over her shoulder, she recognized the lead pursuer as Fern Willis, her
lips drawn back from her teeth in a rictus of rage.

Chester Leeds, in black tie and tails, watched her
from a distance as she raced past, his arms folded
across his narrow chest. He had a smug smile on his
face, as though he'd concluded she was getting what
she deserved.

The end of the tunnel and freedom beckoned, and she
put on a burst of speed. Suddenly, a gigantic form
loomed in the opening, shutting out the light. It was
Harley Dinwitty in a military uniform.

"This is war!" Harley shouted.

Just before the thunder jarred her awake, she saw Alexis standing behind Harley, looking very small and sad. Alexis was saying something that Tess couldn't understand.

Tess groaned, rubbed her eyes, and rolled over. Her heart pounded rapidly in her ears. The dream had left a sense of urgency which she shook off with difficulty.

Reaching out, she lifted a lace curtain away from the window. Rivulets of rain streaked down the pane, and the gloomy sky was the color of slate. She hadn't known rain was in the forecast, but then she hadn't had time to read a newspaper or turn on the TV set for three days.

Yawning, she fumbled for the alarm clock, only to find that it had already been turned off. She must have done it in her sleep.

Sitting, she picked up the clock and brought it closer to read the dial. Seven forty-five. Good grief. Her guests would begin coming down for breakfast in fifteen minutes.

No time for her usual morning shower and shampoo. Tess made do with washing her face, brushing her teeth and hair, and slapping on a dash of makeup. After donning the first suitable garment that came to hand—a blue chambray dress, with a Southwestern design in apricot and navy banding the hem—she left her apartment.

Scents of fresh-brewed coffee, bacon, and baked bread tantalized Tess as she stepped quietly to the parlor doorway to survey the dining room.

They were all there, except for Fern. Unnoticed, Tess stepped back and glanced up the staircase. Was Fern taking breakfast in her room again this morning?

Tess ran up the stairs and knocked on the door of the Arctic Fancy Room. After knocking several times, she called, "Fern, it's Tess." If Fern was inside, she wasn't answering. Tess pressed an ear to the door but heard nothing.

Tess looked back up the hall, her gaze sliding past closed doors, then caught on one, which gapped open a few inches. It was the door to the Cliffs of Dover Room. She hadn't noticed it as she'd passed.

Retracing her steps, she stopped at the partially open door, pushed it wider, and stepped inside. Nedra was seated in a red-and-white chintz chair, her bucket of cleaning supplies on the floor beside her. Her head rested against the chair's high back and her eyes were closed. Hearing Tess, she lifted her head and blinked.

Tess had been reluctant to assign the room to a new guest; it seemed somehow disrespectful to Lana's memory. But she had it reserved for next week, after Lana's funeral.

"I thought you'd already cleaned this room, Nedra," Tess said.

"Yep." Heaving a sigh and planting her work-worn hands on the chair arms, Nedra pushed herself to her feet.

"Are you all right?"

"Yep. Had a notion."

"A notion?"

She shrugged and picked up her bucket. "Ever see that psychic on TV?"

The out-of-left-field question did not particularly surprise Tess. Much of Nedra's conversation came from that direction. "Can't say that I have."

Nedra stared hard at the last bed Lana Morrison had slept in before her death. "Laid me down right there—closed my eyes." She shrugged again. "Nothing. Tried the chair. Nothing."

Tess was getting a glimmer of what Nedra was driving at. "Did you expect to get some vibes from Lana's spirit?"

"She said they linger sometimes."

She, meaning the TV psychic, and they, meaning spirits of the dead, Tess surmised.

"Don't think she's here, though," Nedra said. "Bunch of foolishness, probably. Me, I got work to do." She pulled the master key on its chain from the pocket of her cotton shirt and trudged off. Then Tess heard her opening a door farther down the hall.

Tess looked around the red-and-white room with its shiny brass accents. Lingering spirits, she thought. If only it were true, and Lana could tell them who had murdered her. But if spirits lingered, surely they would prefer gloomy places with shadowy corners.

She walked over to the table next to the bed where a small notepad and pen lay beside the creamy white telephone.

Smiling to herself, she murmured, "If you're here, Lana, pick up that pen and write the name." Nothing happened. Tess sighed and touched the telephone, idly fingering the redial button.

She was turning away before the number that appeared on the phone's digital panel finally registered. She looked again. The area code was 312, the same area code of the number that had printed out when she punched the redial button on Lana's home phone. It was a Chicago exchange.

Catching her breath, Tess read the complete number. Three-one-two-five-five-five-six-seven-four-one. Wasn't that one of the numbers Luke had dialed from her apartment last night?

She'd soon find out.

Repeating the number to herself, she hurried from the room, ran downstairs, and let herself back into her apartment. She pulled Luke's list of numbers from a cubbyhole of the cherry secretary. Three-one-two-five-five-five-six-seven-four-one was the second number on the list. Luke had written *hospital* beside it and drawn a line through the number.

She stared at the number for a full minute.

What did it mean?

The answer did not come to her.

Chapter 19

The pall hanging over the dining room matched the sky outside. Alexis, Marisa, Chester, and the Isleys were seated around the table.

Alexis wore a black cotton skirt and a high-necked white blouse with a cameo brooch pinned at the neck. No diamonds or bright colors for her today. Alexis, it seemed, did not want to call attention to herself. Her thick, shining black hair was twisted into a severe bun and pulled so tight in front that her eyes had a startled look which emphasized the circles beneath them.

Marisa looked more rested this morning, very young and springlike in a yellow dimity dress with narrow white lace trimming the collar and cuffs. Judging from Marisa's more relaxed demeanor, Fern must have let up on the girl. No doubt Fern was too busy worrying about the possibility of a written record of her secret, the same record she had been searching for in Lana's house.

Had Fern found the damning evidence? Tess wondered.

Chester, in a pale-gray suit, his thin hair slicked straight back, looked about as gray as his jacket this morning. Tess wished she could believe that Chester looked drawn because he regretted carrying tales to the police. Unfortunately, she couldn't.

Randall was wearing a green Western shirt, and Reva had on a pink silk blouse and the color was back in her cheeks. They appeared more at ease with each other than they had the day before, as if they'd patched up their differences. Or at least decided to present a united front to the world.

Fern had not come down while Tess was in her apartment. Was she avoiding the others for fear of giving away her guilt? But if Fern was guilty, what was she guilty of? Murder? The unfortunate secret that Tess had been so sure of the night before? Both?

Remembering last night's flash of insight, Tess felt far less certain about it now. Like most things that were quite real in the middle of the night, it seemed less substantial in daylight. Even after seeing that hospital number on the phone in the Cliffs of Dover Room. Besides, no hospital was going to give out information on former patients to unauthorized inquirers.

As Tess was telling herself the only way she was going to confirm her suspicion was to pull it out of Fern, the woman herself appeared and mumbled a greeting, studiously avoiding Tess's gaze. So, Fern *had* been in her room when Tess knocked. She hadn't wanted to talk to Tess alone. Tess decided her leap of logic in the middle of the night wasn't so farfetched after all.

In a severely tailored brown dress and a minimum of makeup, Fern looked older than her years.

Gertie, who stuck her head out of the kitchen only long enough to give Tess a grave look, had spread an old-fashioned country breakfast buffet on the sideboard: scrambled eggs, hash-brown potatoes, gravy, link sausages, bacon, fresh-squeezed orange juice, a medley of fresh fruit, coffee cake, biscuits, butter, jams and jellies.

Tess followed Fern down the buffet, helping herself to eggs, bacon, and coffee from the sideboard, then took the empty chair between Alexis and Marisa. Fern sat at the end of the table, facing Chester across its generous length.

"Good morning, all," Tess greeted the somber group.

"What's good about it?" Alexis mumbled, looking out the window.

"Come on, everybody," Tess coaxed. "This gloomy weather won't last. See, the sun is starting to break through the clouds already. Let's try to put the tragedy behind us and look ahead."

"Ahead doesn't appear any too comforting." Reva pushed a folded newspaper across the table to Tess. "Evidently you haven't seen the local rag this morning."

Tess opened the weekly *Victoria Springs Gazette* to the front page. Emblazoned across the top was the headline

ARREST IN MORRISON MURDER IMMINENT, SAYS POLICE CHIEF.

Tess's heart beat faster as she read aloud the accompanying article:

"Police Chief Desmond Butts, in an exclusive interview with the *Gazette* yesterday, said, 'We're checking out several suspects in the [Morrison murder] case and expect to make an arrest soon.'

The body of Lana Morrison, 48, a local woman actively involved in several Victoria Springs social and civic organizations, was found Monday afternoon outside Iris House, a new bed and breakfast owned by Tess Darcy. The victim had been stabbed.

Ms. Morrison was a guest at the bed and breakfast. A tour of the Iris House gardens was in progress at the time the body was discovered. About forty people with the tour group were questioned and released by the police. Employees and guests of Iris House, all local residents, were also questioned.

'This wasn't a random thing,' Chief Butts

said. 'It was premeditated, and Lana Morrison knew and trusted her killer.'

Asked if suspects in the investigation were guests of the bed and breakfast at the time of the murder, Butts replied, 'No comment,' but went on to say, 'We're pretty sure we know who did it, and we're gathering sufficient evidence for an arrest warrant now.' "

Tess tossed the newspaper aside. "This is great," she seethed. "Terrific publicity for Iris House."

"Forgive me if I can't spare a worry for your precious bed and breakfast," Alexis snarled. "That says they know who did it."

"If they knew," Randall muttered, "they'd make an arrest."

"The article says Butts *is* about to arrest somebody." Alexis glanced around the table. "Somebody in this house."

Marisa looked startled as she rested her elbows on the table, cradling her coffee cup in both hands. "The article doesn't say it's one of us."

Was she really that naive? Tess thought.

"It might as well," Alexis snapped back. "Everybody in town will know that's what 'No comment' means."

"Butts is bluffing, I tell you," Randall insisted, clearly making an effort to believe his own words. "Why would any of us want to kill Lana?"

Chester stared hard at Alexis, then shifted his focus and gave Randall a long, narrow look. "Don't be stupid, Isley."

Randall dropped his fork and knife. "What's that supposed to mean?"

"It means that every one of you, with the possible exceptions of Tess and Marisa, had reason to want Lana dead."

"Don't you mean every one of *us?* You can't exclude yourself," Alexis said.

Chester bridled, grabbed his fork, and stuffed a strawberry into his mouth.

"Yes, Chester," Reva put in. "People who live in glass houses ought not to throw stones. They can get cut up pretty badly that way."

Chester reached for half a buttered biscuit and took a bite. "Unlike the rest of you, I have been cooperating with the police." The words were hard-edged with self-righteousness. "Would I do that if I were the murderer?"

"Of course you would!" Alexis snapped. "It's a clever ploy to take suspicion off yourself."

Chester stared at her. "Why have you turned on me? What have I ever done to you, Alexis?"

Alexis merely shrugged. "I'm only saying I wouldn't feel too smug if I were you. The police aren't dumb."

"Don't count on it," Randall muttered.

"*I* have no motive," Chester said gravely, replying to Alexis.

"Oh, please." Reva rolled her eyes. "You've had it in for Lana ever since the last Club election."

"I myself heard you threaten to get even with her," Fern added.

Chester looked down the table at Fern as he shrugged off her words. "The police will hardly consider a little club election a motive for murder."

While the others talked, Marisa got up for another biscuit and more coffee. Returning to the table, she split the biscuit and added butter. She didn't look at the others, clearly wanting no part of the bickering.

Nobody had responded to Chester's last statement. He forced a chuckle. "Does anyone really imagine the police will believe I'd kill over a silly club election?"

Chester must feel pretty sure of himself to force the issue like this, Tess thought.

"If they knew you—" Reva began.

Tess interrupted their childish squabbling. "I don't think the murder had anything to do with the Club election."

Chester seemed surprised and acknowledged Tess's support with a nod of his head. "Thank you, Tess."

"It makes as much sense as anything else about the murder," Alexis insisted.

Tess shook her head. "I think whoever killed Lana did it because she was blackmailing him—or her." She caught a flash of fear in Fern's eyes before Fern managed to hide it.

Tess's words got everybody's attention, even Marisa's. Alexis's expression was particularly tense. She started to speak, but Tess interrupted to say casually, "Fern, I'd like to discuss something with you before you leave the house."

"Sorry, I have an early appointment at the funeral home, to make arrangements for the burial. There seems to be no one else to do it." She didn't sound happy about it but, Tess assumed, she preferred the unwanted task to talking to Tess in private.

"I knew you were stressed out about something," Alexis said to Fern.

Fern smiled tiredly. "I wouldn't say I'm exactly stressed. It's just one more item to add to my busy schedule."

On the contrary, Tess mused, stressed was exactly what she was, and it wasn't only the funeral arrangements. The main stressor was Fern's secret. A new thought occurred to Tess. Maybe the words written on that card in Lana's purse had something to do with Fern. If so, Fern could also be worried about her health.

Tess watched Fern as she queried, "Have any of you ever heard of malignant hyperthermia?" But Fern's face gave away nothing this time.

"What's that?" Alexis asked.

"It's a condition caused by an inherited trait. Evidently, you can have the susceptibility all your life without knowing it. From what little I've read, the symptoms don't appear until you have surgery. General anesthesia can be fatal to someone with the trait."

A table full of blank, mildly interested faces met Tess's sweeping perusal, but she asked anyway, "Are any of you contemplating surgery?"

Heads shook in denial.

"What are you getting at, Tess?" Alexis asked irritably. "You can't drop blackmail into the conversation, then go off on something else entirely."

"Right, Tess," Reva agreed. "Let's get back to blackmail. Do you know something we don't?"

Were they too eager to divert the conversation from a discussion of malignant hyperthermia? Tess looked around the table, wishing she could fathom what was going on behind the perplexed stares. "From what I've heard, Lana was financially strapped. She was desperate enough to do almost anything for money."

"Including trying to steal other women's husbands," Reva murmured, exchanging a guarded look with Alexis.

"That may have been her long-range plan," Tess said, "but she needed something to tide her over in the meantime."

"How do you know all this?" Marisa asked curiously.

Tess was embarrassed to admit that she'd looked at the balance in Lana's checkbook. Instead, she opted to say mysteriously, "I'm not at liberty to reveal that."

After a pregnant silence, Chester said, "Well, if it was blackmail, that lets me out. My life is an open book."

Randall threw back his head and laughed, startling everybody. "An open book, Chet? With a few X-rated chapters, right? For example, those little jaunts to Kansas City."

Chester's face went from gray to white to a mottled red. "On occasion, I conduct business in Kansas City." He was obviously struggling to stay in control of himself. "That's hardly blackmail material."

Randall leaned back comfortably in his chair and looked at Chester with an amused smile. "Business, huh?

Well, that's one way of putting it. But there's more than one kind of business, isn't there, Chet old man?"

Chester's face was as stiff as a stone. "I have no idea what you're talking about."

"I'll be happy to spell it out for you—"

Chester made a noise low in his throat and erupted out of his chair. Even Randall was taken off guard, but he recovered quickly and shot to his feet. Tess had the impression Randall welcomed the confrontation.

"Go ahead, you little pipsqueak," Randall challenged. "Take your best shot."

Tess jumped up. "Gentlemen!" Since she was closer to Chester, she stepped around Marisa's chair and grabbed his arm, which was as rigid as a piece of wood. An angry red flush suffused his face, and he tried to shake off Tess's hand.

"Let go of me, Tess." His voice had become shrill. "I've had about all I can take. He's a despicable piece of filth. I tell you he's—" With a violent jerk, he freed his arm from Tess's grasp and lunged forward. Randall was prepared. Stiff-armed, he brought his hand up, planted it firmly on Chester's chest, and shoved. "Don't make me hurt you, little man."

Chester stumbled back, swaying and scrabbling to keep his feet under him. He reminded Tess of a puppet whose strings were all being pulled at once. Finally, he managed to get his balance, but for another moment he wavered, his eyes blazing. Then he lurched past Tess and out of the room.

In the silence that followed Chester's departure, Alexis said wonderingly, "What was *that* all about?"

Reva looked at Tess with a shrug. "Sorry, Tess. Randall should learn to keep his mouth shut."

Randall dropped into his chair. "I get sick of his pompous posturing. He's such a sorry excuse for a man he has to convince himself he's not queer by buying sex."

A little gasp escaped Marisa. Fern was staring at

Randall. Alexis's eyes narrowed, as though a conjecture had been confirmed.

It was a second before Randall's meaning struck Tess. So *that's* what Chester did in Kansas City. Well. No wonder Chester had gone into orbit. If this became common knowledge, Chester's sterling reputation as the trusted, conservative banker, holder of the community's purse strings, would be tarnished. It wouldn't matter that one thing had no necessary effect on the other.

If Randall knew Chester's secret, then Lana may have known, too. Probably had, in fact. "Did you tell Lana this, Randall?" Tess asked.

Randall ducked his head and mumbled, "What if I did?"—confirming Tess's suspicion.

"If Lana *was* blackmailing somebody, sounds to me like it might have been Chester," Alexis said. "I wonder if the police know about Chester's trips to Kansas City."

They all looked at Randall, who said defensively, "They were trying to pin the murder on me. What did you expect me to do? I told them they ought to take a closer look at a few other people. Like Chester. Lana may have taunted him about those trips, and we all know Chester can't take a joke."

"She was blackmailing him," Alexis said eagerly, as though it was a relief to know that other people had motives for murder, too.

"I wouldn't put it past her to have been blackmailing several people," Reva said.

"Lana had the gall for it, that's for sure," Alexis agreed.

Marisa gave the two women a wide-eyed look. "I thought you were all friends of Lana's. Why, you didn't even like her."

"Are you trying to tell us you did?" Reva retorted with sarcasm.

"Yes, I did," Marisa said defiantly. "When I moved here, I didn't know anyone. Lana went out of her way to befriend me. Several times, she invited me to lunch.

My best friend died shortly before I came here. The doctors removed a ruptured appendix but they couldn't save her. Lana was a great comfort to me."

"I didn't know that," Tess said. "About your friend, I mean."

Marisa bit her bottom lip and blinked back tears. "Her name was Janet Forsythe, and we were as close as sisters." She shook her head as though to dispel the memory. "Anyway, I thought Lana was *nice.*"

Alexis's lips quirked. "Believe me, when Lana befriended anyone she had her own private agenda. I found out the hard way. She was up to no good with all those lunches, Marisa. She expected to get something in return."

"You're wrong. Lana never asked me for anything."

Reva brushed this off with a wave of her hand. "Flatout asking wasn't usually Lana's way. She was too devious for that."

Fern was studying Marisa with a displeased look, but she said nothing.

"Well, I liked her," Marisa insisted, "and I don't think it's right to criticize a person when they're not around to defend themselves."

Tess interjected a change of subject before the conversation escalated to another argument. "How is the conference going? I haven't had a chance to attend any of the sessions."

"It's hard to keep our minds on irises when we're all being accused of murder," Alexis said. "But I've heard nothing but compliments from the out-of-town registrants."

"I hope to be able to attend a session or two this afternoon," Tess said. "This morning, I'm going to start reorganizing the library."

Fern glanced at her watch, then hurriedly finished her coffee. "Excuse me, everybody. I'm due at the funeral home in thirty minutes."

Chapter 20

Tess gave Fern a minute, then followed her upstairs. She tapped on Fern's door and said quietly, "Let me in, Fern. We have to talk."

There was a furtive movement on the other side of the door, then Fern hissed, "Leave me alone!" It sounded as if her mouth was pressed against the crack between the door and facing.

"I can't do that."

"I won't let you in!"

"Then you force me to go to the police." Resorting to a little blackmail of her own did not make Tess feel good about herself, but she had to get at the truth.

More time passed, and then there was the sound of the bolt being pulled back, and the door opened. Fern looked furious enough to strike Tess and, for a moment, she actually seemed to consider it. Then she stepped back and let Tess enter.

Fern closed the door and crossed her arms. "This is outrageous." Her voice shook. "You'll soon have nothing but vacant rooms if you insist on invading your guests' privacy like this. What do you want?"

Tess felt sorry for her, but she knew of no other way to find out what Fern was so frightened of. "I think you know what I want."

Fern neither moved nor spoke. She merely waited.

"The other day when we were at Lana's house, you weren't searching for her will."

"Oh, really?"

Tess shook her head. "Lana was blackmailing you, and you think she kept a written record. Did you find it?"

"I don't know what you're talking about."

"Then I'll explain. It happened when you were seventeen."

Fern gasped and held up both hands, as if to block Tess's words.

Tess said gently, "Some of your classmates spiked the party punch and, like all the others, you got drunk. Then they raped you."

Fern's head moved back and forth in adamant denial. "No—" She walked to the window, turning her back on Tess. "No." Softer this time. After a pause, she murmured in a low voice, "Even if what you say happened, it wasn't my fault."

"I know that."

She turned around. "Then why are you torturing me like this?"

"Because it's time we—all of us—laid our cards on the table."

"If you think I'd kill Lana to keep her quiet about a violent attack in which I was an innocent victim, then you don't know me at all."

"That's not what she was blackmailing you with." Tess wondered briefly if she had it all wrong. But Lana *was* blackmailing Fern, and it was the one thing that Reverend Willis's wife, leader of the local antiabortion movement, would go to any lengths to keep quiet.

Tess played her trump card. "You were the innocent victim, yes. You were horribly violated that night, and I imagine, if you even remembered later what happened, you tried to put it out of your mind. But you couldn't. Because you were pregnant."

Fern's lips quivered.

"You must have been beside yourself, Fern. Evidently you didn't feel you could go to your parents, so you had a secret abortion. You must have turned to Lana for help, and that's how she knew about it."

Fern didn't look controlling or self-righteous now. Instead, Tess thought of an animal, frozen in fear, blinded by a car's headlights. Not knowing which way to go.

At length, Fern chose a direction. "All those years, she never mentioned it. Until she needed money. I told her we didn't have extra cash lying around, but she said we could take a second mortgage on our house." Tears spilled down her pale cheeks. "How was I supposed to explain that to Richard?" She wiped away tears with the back of her hand.

Tess felt terrible. She would never have forced the issue if there had been any other way to find out if what she suspected was true. She put an arm around Fern. "You were only seventeen, Fern. You were in a panic. You had to confide in someone."

"I didn't even know who the father was. I—I didn't know what to do. At first, I wanted to kill myself, but I just couldn't do it. I couldn't go to a doctor in Victoria Springs, either. Sooner or later, my parents would have found out about it. And Lana was so much more—worldly than I."

Tess patted her shoulder comfortingly.

"You thought Lana could tell you what to do."

She nodded dully. "She knew of an abortionist who would do it in his office for two hundred dollars. Between us, we came up with the money. I thought, for once in my life, that I could trust her." She wiped away more tears. "I had to trust somebody, didn't I?"

Tess patted her again. "Of course you did. You were desperate. I'm sure you felt the same overwhelming desperation when Lana tried to blackmail you. No jury in the world will convict you of first-degree murder. You may only get a suspended sentence."

Fern's tear-glazed eyes widened in horror. "I didn't *kill* her!"

"Fern, I heard you threaten her. She was going to destroy your life. Who knows how many of us would have reacted violently in those circumstances."

She jerked away from Tess. "No! I mean, yes, I threatened her. But I couldn't really have killed her. Oh, I know what you're thinking. If I could kill my own child—"

"That's not what I'm thinking at all."

"I've said it to myself many times."

"Fern, you've suffered enough. You have to quit laying this guilt trip on yourself."

She blinked back tears. "Tell that to my husband and the pro-lifers in my church." She looked grim. "Oh, I hated Lana for what she was doing to me, but I didn't kill her. I was going to go to her when I cooled off and plead with her. On bended knee, if I had to. If that didn't work, I would have had to tell Richard. But before I could do anything, she—died . . ." She buried her face in her hands and sobbed.

Tess bit her lip. "I'm sorry, Fern. I know this is painful for you."

"Are you going to tell the police?" she mumbled from behind her hands.

"Not right now," Tess sighed. "Maybe—" If it turned out that Fern was telling the whole truth. "Maybe I won't have to, ever."

Fern lifted her head. "Thank you, Tess," she whispered.

"Don't thank me yet."

Fern stared at her.

"Do you have any knowledge that Lana was blackmailing other people, too?"

She shook her head, but said hopefully, "Chester, maybe. You saw how he reacted to Randall. Or Harley Dinwitty."

"Harley?"

"Since the last time we talked, I've learned that Lana was definitely after him, and I don't know many men who ever turned her down. Even if they weren't having an affair, Lana may have threatened to tell Alexis they were if Harley didn't pay up. Lord knows, he could afford to give her a bundle without even missing it."

But Harley Dinwitty was a realist. He knew that paying blackmail would not end it.

"I gather you didn't find a written record in Lana's things," Tess said.

"No, nothing, and I searched everywhere." She drew in a shaky breath. "I'm going to be late for my appointment at the funeral home."

Tess had forgotten the appointment. She went to the door but, as she started to open it, something else occurred to her. "Fern, you said you had the abortion in a doctor's office."

"Yes."

"In Chicago?"

"Chicago! Heavens, I could never have gone so far without my parents knowing. It was hard enough to slip away to Joplin."

Tess shook her head in puzzlement and left the Arctic Fancy Room.

Why had Lana been calling a hospital in Chicago?

The phone was ringing as Tess entered her apartment. It was Luke.

"I called those numbers on your list, the ones we couldn't reach last night," he said. "None of them knew Lana Morrison."

Tess sighed.

"I made a few local calls, too," Luke went on, "but I can't dig up any dirt on Chester Leeds."

"Then you didn't dig in the right places." Tess told him what had happened at breakfast.

Luke made a "tsk-tsk" sound and moved on. "Looks like Chester is getting hit from all directions. One of my sources told me that Harley Dinwitty transferred all his accounts out of Chester's bank yesterday. Chester will have a tough time explaining that to his board of directors."

Lordy, Lordy, there was poetic justice in the world, after all.

And that's what Chester had meant at breakfast when he said Alexis had turned on him. But Tess was sure Alexis had had nothing to do with it. Harley had vowed to "take care of Chester," and he'd done it in the way that would hurt the most. Tess almost felt sorry for Chester.

Tess opened the floor-to-ceiling draperies. Sunlight sliced between rapidly dissipating clouds and flooded the tower room. It looked as though the rain was gone for good. The circular staircase leading to the tower needed additional light, too, but it would take more than opening draperies. She hadn't been up to the tower in weeks and had forgotten how poorly illuminated the stairs were.

She made a mental note to have a new light fixture installed over the staircase, one that could accommodate several light bulbs. Until then, she would place a floor lamp beside the staircase. She didn't want somebody missing a step and injuring himself.

Standing in the center of the room, she surveyed the full bookshelves that curved around the inside half of the tower. Many of the volumes were old and faded. Aunt Iris must have kept every book and magazine she ever owned. One shelf contained old schoolbooks, from first-grade primers to high-school biology and algebra texts. An entire section was occupied by stacks of old *National Geographic*s and gardening magazines.

The magazines seemed a good place to start, and Tess began lifting stacks from the shelves and setting them on the floor in front of the big windows. Perhaps the town library or some charitable organization would want them.

During trips across the room, laden with magazines,

she had a bird's-eye view of the front yard and street. White and purple irises looked more vibrant than ever after this morning's rain. Raindrops still clinging to blades of grass glittered like diamonds.

Tess saw Fern walk, alone, across the yard, get into her car at the curb, and drive away.

Randall came out and headed for the lot beyond the hedge, where the Isleys' car was parked.

A few minutes later, Chester appeared hesitantly on the front walk, looked in both directions—probably checking to see that Randall was gone—then set off briskly on foot in the direction of the hotel.

Perhaps ten minutes after Chester disappeared, Marisa, Alexis, and Reva strolled away from Iris House, following the route Chester had taken, but at a more leisurely pace.

Removed from them, watching from the lofty height of the tower and basking in the bright warmth of the spring sunlight, Tess felt suspended in an unreal world, as though the events of the past few days had been merely a bad dream from which she was, at last, awaking. It seemed hardly possible that one of the people leaving Iris House on this rain-washed April morning was a murderer.

After removing all the magazines, she dusted the empty shelves, using the cloth and spray can of wood cleaner she'd brought up with her. Then she went through Aunt Iris's books and pulled out the school textbooks, plus additional tomes that were tattered and worn or dealt with esoteric subject matter not likely to be of interest to Iris House guests. Like *Life Cycle of the Snail Darter* and *Benefits of Earthworm Cultivation.* Aunt Iris had had eclectic tastes in reading material.

When she was finished, several stacks of books had joined the discarded magazines lined up in front of the windows and covering the wicker sofa, chair, and coffee table.

She arranged the remaining books, along with the

new ones she'd bought at Cinny's shop, in the four floor-to-ceiling sections—one section for nonfiction, one for general fiction, one for mysteries, and one for science fiction and romance combined. She placed the books within each section in alphabetical order by author. She was pleased to see that there was now plenty of empty shelf space for the additional books she wanted to buy.

Engrossed in her work, Tess managed to forget about the murder. She hummed softly to herself as she worked, and the morning passed quickly. When someone called to her from the bottom of the circular staircase, Tess was amazed to realize that it was almost one o'clock.

"Tess?" It was Dahlia.

Tess opened the door and peered down through the shadows at her aunt, who was standing at the bottom of the stairs.

"Oh, there you are," Dahlia said.

"Hello, Aunt Dahlia." Blowing a curl out of her eyes, Tess noticed a streak of dirt down her right arm, and her hands were grimy. "I'm organizing the library."

"I'll come and help you," Dahlia said, starting up the stairs.

Taking in Dahlia's white skirt, lemon-yellow shirt, and matching yellow sandals, Tess suppressed a smile. If Dahlia got started on the library, her clothes would be ruined. Not to mention her manicure.

"No, I'm coming down for lunch," Tess said.

Dahlia was already two-thirds of the way up the winding stairs. At which point she came to an abrupt halt, swaying slightly forward, then back. She grabbed hold of the banister. "What on earth?"

Tess squinted down at her aunt, relieved that Dahlia seemed to have steadied herself. Why hadn't she made sure the staircase was well-lit before now? "Aunt Dahlia, be careful."

"Well, I never! Turn on some more lights, Tess, for heaven's sake!"

"There aren't any more lights until I have a new fixture installed." Tess started down the stairs. "What is it?"

"Stop!" Dahlia ordered shrilly. "Don't take another step, Tess. There may be more."

Tess halted. "More what?"

Dahlia's hand moved across the space in front of her. From Tess's vantage point, it appeared to move in a straight line through thin air. "It's a string, Tess, tied across the staircase. Twine, actually."

"I'm coming down." Tess descended slowly to meet Dahlia, sweeping both hands in front of her in case there was another obstruction. There was none.

Because the stairs were so dim, she couldn't see the twine until she was upon it, even though she knew it was there.

If she'd been coming down the stairs unaware . . .

The sturdy twine had been pulled taut across the stairs, at just below knee level to someone coming down, and tied to the posts on both sides. It hit Dahlia, who was standing one stair down, across the thighs.

"Thank goodness you saw it in time," Tess said.

"I didn't see it until I ran into it," Dahlia told her. "Fortunately, I was moving slowly." She tugged on the twine, then bent over the post where one end was knotted. "It's higher up on someone ascending, so you're not as likely to lose your balance." She lifted her head to peer at Tess. "If you'd come down those stairs before I got here . . ." She finished the thought with a shake of her head.

A shudder ran through Tess. She'd have taken a nasty fall, for sure. She could have broken an arm or a leg, or, even worse, hit her head. She could have been killed!

"It wasn't there when I went up," Tess said shakily.

"Obviously," Dahlia said. "What time was that?"

"I went back to my apartment after breakfast. But I was there less than half an hour. It must have been nine or nine-thirty when I came up the stairs."

Dahlia began picking at the knot with her fingernails again. "Somebody waited until you were in the library, then set this trap for you. Did you hear anything?"

"Nothing."

Dahlia nodded. "Naturally, they were taking care not to be heard."

"But who was it?" Tess demanded, aghast. "And why?"

Dahlia finally loosed one end of the twine and started on the other side. "I can't say why," she replied grimly, "but this little surprise was arranged by one of your guests. Do you know which of them were still in the house when you went up?"

"All of them." Tess's eyes skimmed the puddled shadows on the landing and the visible portion of the second-floor hall below them. The dimness was more than merely inconvenient now, it was positively sinister.

"I saw every one of them leave the house while I was in the library. And they all knew I'd be up there this morning, too, because I mentioned it at breakfast."

Dahlia released the final knot and wound the twine loosely until it fit in the palm of her hand. "Why don't you go down to your apartment. I'll see if Gertie or Nedra saw or heard anything, and then I'll join you."

Chapter 21

Showered and shampooed, Tess wore a white terry-cloth robe and scuffs. She was in her kitchen making a sandwich when Dahlia tapped at the sitting-room door, then came in without waiting for an answer.

Dahlia's dark eyes swept Tess with concern. "You should keep your doors locked, Tess."

"I left it open because I knew you were coming. Did you talk to Nedra and Gertie?"

Dahlia sighed. "Yes. I had hoped that Nedra, at least, might have seen somebody on the tower stairs, but no such luck. Gertie was no help, either."

Suddenly aware of the difference in her own appearance and her aunt's, Tess attempted to smooth down her damp, tangled curls. Not a hair on Dahlia's head was out of place, she noted, and wondered how Dahlia did it. Did she sleep sitting up?

Tess poured her aunt a cup of blackberry tea from the pot still steeping on the kitchen counter, and Dahlia settled into a chair at the kitchen table.

"Aunt Dahlia, do you go to the beauty shop every day or what?" Tess didn't quite manage to keep the envy out of her voice.

Dahlia touched a finger to a wispy curve of bangs. "I only go once a week, dear. You know that."

"But how do you sleep and still keep your hair looking like that?"

192

Dahlia leaned toward Tess as though about to reveal a carefully guarded secret. "Satin pillowcases."

It was worth a try, Tess thought, making a mental note to pick up a pair of satin cases the next time she was in town.

"Would you like a sandwich?"

"No, dear. I've already eaten." Dahlia studied Tess, a frown appearing between elegantly plucked brows. "I know what you're doing, Tess. You're avoiding the subject. How are you feeling?"

"Still a little shaky," Tess admitted. "To think that somebody in this house tried to hurt me . . ."

"You must have some idea who it was. Have you made one of them angry—argued over a bill or something?"

"I've been thinking about it," Tess said, "and I believe something I said frightened Lana's killer."

"*What* on earth did you say, Tess?"

"It could be one of several things, actually." She ignored Dahlia's censorious look. "At breakfast, I said I thought Lana was killed by somebody she was blackmailing. They were all present when I said it, and the killer could think I'm getting too close to the truth." She swallowed hard and went on, "Then there was that private conversation I had with Fern after breakfast." She told Dahlia what had transpired in Fern's room that morning.

Dahlia looked stunned. "What a traumatic experience for a seventeen-year-old girl. Dear, dear. And years later, when Fern thought she'd put it all behind her long ago, that traitorous woman threatened to tell the world." Dahlia made a clucking sound. "Lana Morrison had absolutely no conscience."

Tess couldn't disagree. She picked up her sandwich, realized she wasn't hungry, grimaced, and put it down again.

Dahlia was watching her closely. "You must be very careful, Tess. Whoever it was might try again."

Tess had already thought of that. In fact, she'd thought of little else since Dahlia had discovered the trap set for her. "I think my best course is to go on as if nothing happened. I'll tell Nedra and Gertie to keep quiet about the twine on the stairs."

"I did that already."

"Good."

"But you must tell the police that somebody's trying to kill you."

"I will. Later. After all the guests come back to Iris House. One of them is going to be surprised to see me unharmed. Maybe his face will give him away."

"I don't like this, Tess."

"If I tell the police now, Chief Butts will be here to meet them at the door and throw around wholesale accusations. The element of surprise will be gone."

"Be careful," Dahlia reiterated, clearly unhappy about the delay in telling the police. She squeezed a lemon wedge over her teacup and stirred in sugar.

After taking a sip, she set her cup down and said, "After what's happened, my news doesn't seem nearly as interesting as I thought."

Upon discovering that somebody in the house wanted to harm her, it hadn't occurred to Tess until now to wonder why her aunt had come to Iris House while the conference was going on. "What news?"

"I finally got in to see Dr. Brady this morning."

Tess looked at her blankly. Dr. Brady was the Darcy family's physician, and . . . "Oh. I'd forgotten. You were going to ask him if Lana was susceptible to malignant hyperthermia."

"And I did. Of course, he blustered on for a bit about confidentiality, and I reminded him that Lana was dead. Finally, he said that if she had the trait, he was not aware of it. And, as far as he knew, Lana had no plans for surgery."

"I'm beginning to think it had nothing to do with Lana's murder, anyway. I mentioned it at breakfast, too, but nobody seemed to have heard of malignant hyperthermia before. I can't imagine why Lana wrote the words on a card and put it in her purse."

"Nor can I, Tess. Here's the curious thing. The other day, when you and I and Cinny were talking about it, I had the feeling I'd heard those words before. But I couldn't pin it down. All the way home, I tried to remember in what context I'd heard of malignant hyperthermia, but it simply wouldn't come." It certainly explained Dahlia's self-absorption when she drove Tess to Iris House from the bookshop that day. "This morning," Dahlia went on, "as soon as I sat down in Dr. Brady's waiting room, it came to me. Just like that." She snapped her manicured fingers. "Amazing how the mind works, isn't it?"

"Amazing," Tess agreed, wishing Dahlia would get on with whatever it was she was trying to say.

"When I spoke to Dr. Brady, he confirmed it. Because, of course, *she's* dead, too."

"Who?"

"Margaret Stackpole."

"Stackpole, as in Marisa?"

"Margaret was Marisa's grandmother, wife of that old hidebound skinflint, William. Do you know he disowned his only child? But back to Margaret. She died during routine surgery for the removal of her gallbladder. They found out on autopsy that she had the gene or whatever it is that makes you go into malignant hyperthermia when you're given anesthesia." Dahlia looked pleased with herself for a moment, then her eyes narrowed. "Of course, that doesn't tell us why Lana had that card in her purse. It couldn't have had anything to do with Margaret Stackpole. She's been dead for at least twenty years."

"Marisa could have inherited the trait," Tess mused. "Apparently, she isn't even aware that her grandmother had it, though. Marisa did say something about how Lana had befriended her when she was new in town.

Maybe Lana had remembered very recently what killed Marisa's grandmother and meant to tell Marisa, but she never got around to it."

Dahlia nodded. "Lana probably wrote it down so she wouldn't forget."

"I'll make a point of telling Marisa myself before she leaves Iris House. There may be a test she can take to see if she inherited the trait."

"Mmm," muttered Dahlia. "You know, I remember wondering at the time why Lana was going out of her way to be friendly to a girl young enough to be her daughter. Do you suppose she simply liked Marisa?"

"Evidently. It seems she was concerned enough about her to find out what killed Marisa's grandmother, and she wanted to make sure Marisa understood the trait could be inherited."

"Maybe she had some real human feelings, after all," Dahlia mused doubtfully.

As she dressed and brushed her hair, Tess tried to arrange the seemingly unconnected pieces of information she'd gathered into some logical pattern. She was fully dressed before she realized that she'd put on a pink blouse with a red skirt, but she didn't bother changing. Instead, she convinced herself the combination didn't look all that bad.

She sat down at the secretary in the sitting room and began to make notes as she thought it through.

Lana had been blackmailing Fern.

Fern was probably not Lana's only victim. There was plenty of blackmail material to go around.

Harley Dinwitty would go to great lengths to save his marriage.

As would Alexis.

And Chester Leeds, to protect his reputation.

Randall Isley. How far would a man go to avenge himself against a woman who'd scorned and humiliated him?

Reva Isley. She had good reason to loathe Lana.

Did the cause of Margaret Stackpole's death figure in Lana's murder somehow? Tess kept coming back to that odd tidbit which didn't seem to fit into the puzzle anywhere.

Tess read her notes through again, frowning in concentration.

Tess was watching out the sitting-room window for her guests' return. She saw Chester first, walking up the street from the hotel. A few yards behind Chester were Reva and Alexis, with Fern and Marisa bringing up the rear.

Tess stepped into the foyer as Chester opened the front door.

He blinked at her, startled. Was it because he expected her to be injured from a fall down the tower stairs? Or simply that he hadn't expected to find anyone in the foyer?

"Oh, hello, Tess. Going out?"

"No, just passing through."

"Oh," he said again, and went up the stairs.

Tess closed the front door and waited for the others. By the time Reva and Alexis had reached Iris House, Fern and Marisa had caught up with them. The door opened and Alexis led the way in. She was looking back at the others, saying, "That lunch today was awful. The roast was dry and the vegetables were overcooked."

"I heard the head cook was out sick," Fern said.

"Well, I'm going to speak to the hotel manager. It reflects on The Club since we're sponsoring the conference and— Oh, good Lord, Tess! I didn't see you there." Alexis came to a dead stop and clutched her throat.

Fern, who was right behind her, bumped into Alexis. "Oops, sorry."

"So am I, Alexis," Tess said. "Didn't mean to startle you."

Alexis stepped aside with a nervous laugh and Marisa and Reva followed Fern in.

Tess was trying to watch all of their faces at once. Alexis was definitely surprised to see her, but she'd been looking over her shoulder and would have been surprised to see anyone. Fern looked vaguely disgruntled. Marisa's expression was a little tense, but then she'd just spent several hours with Fern. Reva looked a bit tired, but nothing more. She and Marisa excused themselves and went upstairs.

Tess chatted with Fern and Alexis for a few moments before returning to her apartment.

Well, that little plan had failed miserably. Chester and Alexis had been surprised to see her, but not inordinately so, under the circumstances.

Alexis's startled cry had given the others enough advance warning of Tess's presence in the foyer for them to hide any shock they might be feeling.

Tess sank into the chair beside the secretary and read through the notes she'd made earlier, pondering again the scraps of information that seemed unconnected to the rest. Lana had been interested in malignant hyperthermia. Margaret Stackpole had died of malignant hyperthermia. Margaret Stackpole's granddaughter was a guest at Iris House.

The three things could be related. But how?

Tess told herself she still must see that Marisa was aware of the danger of inheriting the potentially lethal gene from her grandmother, but there was time enough for that. Marisa had no plans to undergo surgery.

Tess frowned and tried to catch hold of a flicker of memory. She'd recently heard of *someone* who'd had surgery—someone besides Margaret Stackpole—but she couldn't for the moment remember who or where she'd heard it.

Wait. Now she remembered.

Tess gasped as an incredible notion flooded her mind.

Now, Tess, she told herself. *Don't go off half-cocked.* It was impossible. But was it?

She rose to pace the apartment.

"Why didn't you tell me about the attempt on your life?" Luke thundered.

Primrose, who was napping in her favorite chair, leaped down and streaked from the room.

Luke had arrived at Tess's door at three-thirty, after Dahlia had phoned him with the news. It seemed that Dahlia, after leaving Iris House, had gone back to the conference but had continued to fret about Tess's refusal to report the incident to the police right away. She must have decided Luke was the next best thing and called him from the hotel.

"I would have told you eventually," Tess said.

"Eventually? *Eventually!*" Luke paced across the sitting room and back, exactly as Tess had been doing before he arrived. "What does that mean?" he demanded. "A week? A month?"

Luke's imperious tone was the surest way to get Tess's back up. Temper lifted her chin. "When I felt the time was right. I had a plan to catch the killer first."

Blond brows shot up and he stopped pacing. "A plan to catch the killer? I believe Dahlia mentioned that. Something about surprising the murderer when he returned to Iris House, expecting to find you dead—or at least maimed."

"The plan didn't work." Tess's voice sagged with disappointment. "I was in the foyer to meet everyone who returned from the conference. Nobody seemed excessively surprised to see me. If the murderer is one of them, he's very good at hiding his feelings."

"He's very good at murder, too," Luke said grimly. "It was sheer luck that Dahlia found that twine before you fell over it."

"I know. There's still Randall," Tess mused. "He hasn't been back to Iris House since this morning . . ."

"It's time to call the police, Tess," Luke said, stepping to the secretary.

"Not yet!" Tess grabbed his hand from the telephone. "I've spent the last two hours thinking. Here." She snatched up the sheet of paper containing the list she'd made after Dahlia left and handed it to Luke. "I started this the other night at dinner, remember? But I've gathered more information since then."

Luke rapidly read what she'd written:

SUSPECTS & POSSIBLE MOTIVES

Alexis Dinwitty—Thought Lana was having an affair with Harley.

Harley Dinwitty—Lana blackmailing him. Threatening to tell Alexis they were having an affair.

Fern Willis—Lana blackmailing her. Threatening to tell Fern's husband and her antiabortion friends that Fern had an abortion when she was seventeen.

Chester Leeds—Lana blackmailing him. Threatening to reveal the real reason for his trips to Kansas City.

Randall Isley—Lana rebuffed his advances, humiliated him. Lana possibly blackmailing him, too. Threatening to tell Reva they were having an affair.

Reva Isley—Thought Lana was having an affair with Randall.

Marisa Stackpole—Something to do with the fact that Marisa's grandmother died on the operating table of malignant hyperthermia and Marisa may have inherited the trait???

Luke looked up. "How did you learn all this?" There was a touch of admiration in the question.

Tess felt a flush of pride. "By asking questions."

"Fern Willis really had an abortion when she was seventeen?" he asked wonderingly.

"Indeed she did. Fern told me so herself, and she admitted that Lana was using it to blackmail her. She denied killing Lana, though."

"You didn't expect her to admit to murder, did you?"

"I believed her, Luke," Tess said firmly. His blue eyes narrowed doubtfully. "I guess you had to be there," she added.

He merely cocked his head as he read what she'd written about Chester and moved on. "Do you have any evidence that Harley Dinwitty and Lana were having an affair?"

"No, but it doesn't matter."

"How do you figure that?"

"Lana could have been threatening to tell Alexis they were involved, even if they weren't," Tess said urgently. "Chester had already tattled to Alexis that Lana paid a visit to Harley in the middle of the night. But Harley didn't *know* she knew that until after Lana's murder. So he might have killed Lana to keep her quiet."

"If this is all you have to go on, any one of them could have done it. Except Marisa Stackpole." He looked at Tess's notes again and frowned. "What does this malignant hyperthermia have to do with anything?"

"Maybe nothing," Tess admitted, "but before you arrived the wildest idea struck me."

Luke shook his head. "Why does that not surprise me?" he drawled.

Tess pretended not to notice the drawl. "First I called that Chicago hospital—that's one of the numbers you called last night—and found out it's in Cook County." She told him the complicated train of thought that had led to her brainstorm.

"Since we know the county, the Bureau of Vital Statistics in Illinois could confirm or deny my theory," Tess finished, "but it might take a week to get the information by mail, and I doubt they'll give it out over the phone."

Luke's eyes darted to the telephone. "It's worth a try."

"Somebody would have to search their files."

"Leave it to me," Luke said, and reached for the phone. "I investigate businesses I'm considering investing in all the time. I'm very good at coaxing information out of people who have no intention of giving it to me."

Tess knew that, having seen him in action the night before.

"Be my guest," she said.

When Luke hung up the phone, he turned to Tess. "You were right." Did he have to sound so surprised?

Tess sank into a chair. No wonder Luke was surprised. Down deep, she herself hadn't really believed her wild idea could be true. Now that the cooperative clerk in the Illinois Bureau of Vital Statistics had confirmed it, though, everything fell into place.

What a series of risks the murderer had taken!

"So," Luke said, "what do we do now?"

"I have an idea," Tess told him.

"Naturally," Luke said.

Chapter 22

Tess passed around a tray of cookies while Gertie served coffee and tea. Setting the tray on a low table, Tess surveyed the subdued assemblage in the parlor. Most of them would have preferred being anywhere else she was sure, but had been afraid to decline Tess's invitation, which had been phrased to sound as if the gathering was at the request of the chief of police.

Desmond Butts stood with his back to the empty hearth, his arms crossed, his beefy face set in disgruntlement. Tess had refused to tell him the reason for the meeting, suggesting only that he might learn something that would lead to a quick arrest.

Luke stood alertly beside him. He determinedly did not look toward the spot where a certain person sat.

Fern's blunt hands nervously pleated a lace-edged handkerchief. Despite the fearful inner turmoil she must be experiencing, she sat proudly erect and met Tess's gaze without flinching.

Alexis sat slumped between Marisa and Nedra on the sofa. She'd given Marisa one dismayed look when she sat down, then huddled on the sofa, her eyes downcast. Marisa leaned toward her to whisper something, but Alexis merely shook her head in negation. Every so often, Marisa looked at Alexis worriedly, then glanced curiously at Butts.

Nedra stared at the scuffed toe of her loafer as

she tapped her foot impatiently. She had been leaving for the day when Tess called her back, mentioning the redial button on the phone in the Cliffs of Dover Room and hinting that Lana may have left them a clue to her killer after all. Nedra's shirt and cotton slacks were limp and wrinkled after the day's work, her straw-colored hair stood out in several directions, and there was a faint dirt smudge on her cheek. But her eyes were bright and darting inquisitively from face to face around the room, her thoughts clearly racing at breakneck speed, as usual. For an instant, her glance locked with Tess's in mutual anticipation.

Gertie smiled at Tess from the footstool. She had removed her apron, and her tent dress flowed to the floor, hiding the footstool. Gertie's gingery hair had been brushed into a semblance of order.

Reva and Randall, both having changed into jeans, T-shirts and white Nikes, again occupied the velvet love seat. Tess noticed that Reva was not pretending one minute that Randall wasn't there and the next that his mere existence irritated her, as she had during the previous gathering in the parlor. Nor did she seem to mind that his arm lay loosely across her shoulders. It would seem that Randall was being given one more chance.

Chester, in the gray suit he'd worn all day, sat stiffly in a chair in one corner of the room, looking totally out of sorts. He must be extremely worried about his bank's loss of the Dinwitty accounts. He took a small appointment book from his coat pocket and began looking through it, as though reviewing appointments for the next few days.

Harley Dinwitty was not present. Tess had tried to reach him to invite him to the meeting and learned he was out of town. Dahlia was absent also. Tess had decided not to call her, as Dahlia had an alibi that removed her from the suspect list. Of course, Dahlia was going to have a fit when she learned she'd been excluded, but Tess was prepared for that.

Butts cleared his throat portentously and glared at Tess.

Tess hastily stepped forward from the doorway leading to the foyer. "Thank you all for coming. As I've already told you, new information in the murder investigation has surfaced and I—we," she amended hastily, smiling at the scowling Butts, "thought that if we got together and shared what we know, we could solve Lana's murder."

Fern gave a soft gasp. "You didn't say anything about solving the murder."

"What did you think this gathering was for?" Butts snorted. "A tea party?"

Alexis took a sudden, intense interest in her wedding ring, twisting it round and round on her finger. Then she flashed a brief, troubled glance at Tess.

Gertie gave Tess a rallying smile and Nedra nodded encouragingly.

Marisa sat forward on the sofa, her eyes brightly interested.

Luke made a thumbs-up sign.

"Now, Miss Darcy, let's get on with it," Butts ordered.

"With your permission, Chief," Tess said sweetly, and Butts gave a peremptory nod.

Tess looked around the parlor. "Lana Morrison's murderer is in this room."

"Which is what I said from the beginning," Butts reminded her.

The air throbbed with a collective holding of breaths.

"You did say that," Tess replied. "The problem all along, Chief, has been that you've had to deal with an abundance of motives. Am I correct?"

Butts muttered an agreement.

"Lana was a self-centered, manipulative woman who did not hesitate to use others to her advantage," Tess went on as she sent another inclusive glance around the room. "Even the people closest to her were not exempt."

"You, Miz Dinwitty, for example," Butts put in. "On the very day of the murder, you learned that your friend Lana Morrison had betrayed you by making an aggressive play for your husband. You had a darned good reason to want her out of the way."

Alexis blanched and opened her mouth.

Before she could launch into a defense, Tess jumped into the gap. "Whatever you may have wanted to do to Lana, Alexis, I think you were too distraught that afternoon to leave your room until you heard the ambulance. At which point Lana was already dead. I further believe that Harley did not accept Lana's sexual advances."

Butts frowned at her, but waited for her to explain herself.

"Here is what I think really happened last Sunday night," Tess said. "Lana, wearing her nightgown, slipped out of Iris House at one A.M., squeezed through the back hedge, and went to the Dinwitty house, rousing Harley from sleep. Though stunned to find Lana on his doorstep in her nightgown, Harley was nevertheless flattered by the attention, and invited her in for a drink. But a drink is all they shared, and after that Harley told her she would have to leave. Lana, seeing that she was unable to steal Harley from under Alexis's nose, resorted to blackmail. She threatened to tell Alexis that she and Harley had been intimate unless Harley paid hush money."

Butts sent a smirk in Alexis's direction, as if an opinion had been confirmed.

Alexis's head jerked up and her eyes blazed, but she said nothing.

Tess nodded sadly. "I'm sure that's what happened. I'm also sure, knowing Harley, that he adamantly refused to pay blackmail. He may have been certain that Alexis would believe him when he denied Lana's allegations. Or he may have killed Lana to prevent her going to Alexis. Harley didn't know that Alexis had already heard about that middle-of-the-night meeting between Lana and Harley before Lana was killed."

Alexis jumped to her feet.

"Sit down, Miz Dinwitty!" Butts thundered. "If I'm going to spend my valuable time listening to this, so can you."

Alexis sank back in her seat.

"I wasn't finished, Alexis," Tess hastened to say. "Harley wanted to prevent Lana's going to you with her lies, but I don't think he killed her. The type of man Harley Dinwitty is argues against it. In his business dealings, he must have coped with unpleasant people and unfair situations many times, and—" She exchanged a smile with Luke. "—from what Luke tells me, he does so calmly and intelligently. When he doesn't come out on top, he makes the best of a bad situation and goes on to something else. It's only logical to believe he would deal with personal problems in the same way."

Tess surveyed her audience, settling for a moment on Fern. "Harley wasn't Lana's only blackmail victim. Lana had threatened to reveal a secret she had known about Fern since they were teenagers if Fern didn't take out a second mortgage on the Willis house and give the money to Lana."

"You said you wouldn't tell," Fern whispered.

Butts gave Fern a hard look. "This is a murder investigation, Miz Willis."

"I made no promises, Fern," Tess corrected, "but no purpose would be served by disclosing your secret here. Suffice it to say that Fern and her family would have suffered had Lana carried out her threat."

Fern stared at the hands clasped tightly in her lap, her face suffused with color.

"Like all of us, Fern has her faults, but a propensity to violence is not one of them. Furthermore, she has a sacred regard for human life. It is my opinion that Fern Willis is incapable of premeditated murder."

Fern lifted her head, gratitude flooding her face.

Butts continued to scowl at Fern, still trying to make up his mind about Tess's conclusion.

"Chester had a secret of his own," Tess said, "and I suspect Lana had dug it out and was also blackmailing him."

Chester's appointment book snapped shut. When he looked at Tess, his eyes were as hard as marbles, and if looks could kill Tess would have dropped where she stood.

"I have no trouble believing that Chester can be vengeful. But frankly I don't think murder is the way he would choose."

"Miss Darcy," Butts trumpeted, "you and I are going to have a little talk later about all these secrets you haven't seen fit to share with the police."

"If you wish," Tess said agreeably. She was counting on Butts's being so happy about making an arrest that he would overlook her withholding of evidence. That is, if her conclusions were correct.

"As for the Isleys," Tess said, turning toward the velvet love seat, "Randall flirted outrageously with Lana on the day of her death, and Reva knew it."

"Now, see here—" Randall sputtered.

"Shut up, Isley!" Butts ordered, and Tess threw him an appreciative look.

"It is common knowledge that Randall likes the ladies. His blatant flirtation with Lana Morrison may have been the final indignity as far as Reva was concerned. But with Randall's past history, Reva couldn't have blamed his latest indiscretion completely on Lana. No, for Reva, divorce would be a far simpler solution."

Reva's brows lifted, but she accepted Tess's conclusions without comment.

"As for Randall," Tess went on, "it's possible that during the last day of Lana's life, his attentions became so persistent that Lana turned on him. Scorned him. Humiliated him. There are men who would kill such a woman in a burst of rage. But Lana was not killed on a moment's impulse. The murderer had to arrange to meet Lana in the side yard and take the knife from the gazebo to kill her with. In other words, it was premeditated."

"That was obvious from the start," said Butts.

Tess acknowledged this with a look. "Something happened the afternoon of Lana's murder that made me think Lana had told Randall to leave her alone. Marisa ran through the backyard, obviously upset, with Randall following her. As I recall, Randall said something like, 'I was only being friendly,' which made me think he'd turned his attentions away from Lana and made a pass at Marisa."

Randall gave an exasperated snort. "That's a load of crap. All I said to her was hello."

Luke frowned at Randall but Tess ignored him. "We are all aware that Marisa and Johnny Willis have been seeing a great deal of each other and Marisa very much wants Fern's approval. What would Fern do if she knew that Randall was making a play for Marisa? She might tell Johnny that Marisa had encouraged Randall. Hence, my conclusion as to why Marisa was upset."

Randall's eyebrows had risen a good two inches. "You couldn't honestly have believed that."

"Oh, but I did." Tess looked at Marisa, who was shaking her head in distress.

Tess turned away abruptly. "Let's see. Who else was here that day? Oh, yes, my aunt Dahlia. But she was leading a tour through the gardens, in full view of forty people when the murder occurred. That leaves Gertie, Nedra, and me, but none of us had a motive for the murder.

"Which brings us to today. The murderer rigged a trap for me on the tower stairs while I was in the library this morning. He or she tied a stout piece of twine across the stairs, which aren't very well lit, by the way. I advise all of you to avoid them. If Aunt Dahlia hadn't arrived and discovered the twine before I came down, I could have been seriously injured."

She certainly had everyone's attention now.

"Upon reflection," Tess said, "I realized that something I said at breakfast had been interpreted by the murderer as a serious threat. So he or she decided to remove the threat. Eventually, I came to the conclusion that what set the murderer off was my mention of the words I found on a card in Lana's purse. Malignant hyperthermia. Later I learned that Margaret Stackpole, Marisa's grandmother, died of it during a routine surgical procedure. Since the trait that causes it is inherited, that meant that Marisa could be susceptible as well. I concluded that Lana had intended to warn Marisa of the possibility. Nothing suspicious in that."

Butts had been restlessly shuffling his feet for several moments and now exploded. "I've listened to enough of this nonsense. Miss Darcy, you started by saying that the murderer is in the room, then stood there and went through everybody here and tried to convince me that none of them could have done it."

"Not quite, Chief Butts," Tess said sternly. "It's true that nobody I named committed the murder."

"Then what in tarnation is the purpose of this meeting?" Butts demanded. "To pull the wool over my eyes? Well, it won't work. One of you is the murderer! Who else could it possibly be?"

A circle of puzzled faces looked up at Tess, but nobody answered Butts's question.

"Shall we," Tess suggested quietly, turning toward the sofa, "ask Janet Forsythe?"

Chapter 23

Marisa—or rather Janet—froze. So did everybody else as their gazes followed Tess's until they were all fixed on Marisa, who, after a few moments of stunned silence, managed to pull herself together. A mask of perplexed innocence came down over her face. Oh, yes, Tess thought. She was very good at hiding her feelings, at playacting. She had, after all, been acting a part for months. But this time her hands gave her away by grabbing her knees in a death grip.

"Why are you looking at me, Tess? My friend Janet Forsythe is dead."

"It was Marisa Stackpole who died," Tess said.

Janet's mask slipped a little. "That's—that's laughable." But she wasn't laughing.

"I don't know how Lana found out, but she did. Perhaps you talked too much during those lunches you and Lana shared. I believe something you said early on made her suspicious, and that's why she kept inviting you to lunch. To glean information that she could follow up on and prove her theory. I believe you mentioned that your friend died during emergency surgery. Lana must have known that Marisa's grandmother, Margaret Stackpole, had died during surgery of malignant hyperthermia and that it was caused by an inherited trait. Lana just put two and two together."

Janet sat forward on the sofa, darting a look toward the doorway leading to the dining room and from there to the kitchen and the back door. It was the only exit still open. Reading her thoughts, Luke crossed the room and planted himself in the doorway.

"There's no way out for you, Janet," Tess said quietly. "Earlier today Luke talked to a man in the Illinois Vital Statistics Bureau. The man searched their Cook County death-certificate records and reported that Marisa Stackpole died in a Chicago hospital during an emergency appendectomy operation less than a month before you arrived in Victoria Springs, posing as your friend. She died of malignant hyperthermia, the same thing that killed her grandmother. I've already mailed the bureau a check and requested that they send the death certificate to Chief Butts."

"Wait a minute," Alexis said incredulously. "Marisa got here before her grandfather died. Surely he would have known if she was an imposter."

"I don't think William Stackpole ever saw his granddaughter. He and his son were estranged before Marisa was born."

Butts lumbered to the center of the room. "Miss Darcy, are you sure about all this? William Stackpole was a shrewd old codger."

"He was dying," Tess said, "and he knew it. He probably sent for Marisa, and Janet decided to take her place. They were about the same age, and William desperately wanted to believe his granddaughter cared enough to visit him in his last days. Perhaps he also wanted, before he died, to warn her that she might carry the gene that had killed her grandmother." Something in the young woman's eyes convinced Tess she was right on that point. "Of course, Janet wasn't worried about the gene. She was interested in the Stackpole estate, which William had willed to his granddaughter."

The young woman they all knew as Marisa rose shakily to her feet. "This is insane. You've flipped out, Tess Darcy!"

"No," Tess said wearily. "I wish I was wrong, but I'm not. Lana was still calling the Chicago hospital where Marisa died when she arrived at Iris House. The hospital's number printed out when I touched the redial button on the phone in the Cliffs of Dover Room. When she was unable to get any information from the hospital, she, as Luke and I did later, thought of contacting the Vital Statistics Bureau. Since that's not the last number Lana called from Iris House, she must have phoned from the hotel."

"You can't prove—" Janet began.

Tess held up a hand. "When Lana returned from the conference that day, she had the proof she needed. She told you that afternoon, Janet, and demanded money. I strongly suspect the two of you were in the south side yard at the time. Then she went back to her room and Randall appeared, perhaps looking for Lana. You were understandably upset—not at anything Randall said, but because Lana knew your true identity. You ran from Randall, across the backyard. Thinking that he was somehow the cause of your flight, Randall followed. Later, you arranged to meet Lana in the side yard again, perhaps telling her you would deliver the blackmail payment. You armed yourself with the cake knife, and when she appeared, you killed her."

"No!" Janet wailed. Sweat filmed her face.

"It's no use denying it any longer," Tess said unhappily.

Janet stumbled against a table as she tried to dart around it. Butts, Luke, and Randall moved to block her way.

"Janet Forsythe," Butts intoned, "I am arresting you for the murder of Lana Morrison. I advise you to come quietly." He pulled out a pair of handcuffs.

The snap of the metal rings imprisoning Janet Forsythe's slender wrists was ominously loud in the hushed silence.

Butts pushed her ahead of him toward the front door. "You have the right to remain silent . . ."

* * *

"Did you ever see such a strutting banty rooster?" Alexis inquired after Butts had sauntered out of Iris House with his prisoner. He hadn't mentioned meeting with Tess again. As she'd hoped, the arrest made up for her transgressions.

Luke had come over and put an arm around her, and she'd sagged against him in relief when she saw the front door finally close behind Butts.

"The chief's picture will cover half the front page of the next *Gazette,*" Randall surmised. "What do you bet he'll call them as soon as he's got Marisa—I mean Janet—behind bars."

"It's not fair," Gertie said. "Tess should get the credit for solving the case. I've a good mind to call that paper myself."

"Don't you dare." Tess looked up at Luke and laughed. "I'm more than willing for Chief Butts to bask in the limelight. I have a bed and breakfast to run."

"And plans for the evening," Luke murmured. "With me."

Fern was still staring at the doorway through which Butts and his prisoner had exited. "I've had serious doubts about that girl all along," she sniffed. "Thank goodness you unmasked her, Tess, before my Johnny got in any deeper."

"Johnny is already in pretty deep, if you ask me," Reva remarked. "It'll take some time for him to recover from the shock."

Fern frowned. "You're right, Reva. I'm going home this minute and tell him what's happened before he hears it from someone else." She left the room at a trot and ran upstairs for her purse. Once more, Fern was in control of her little corner of the world.

Chester cleared his throat self-importantly. "I'm still put out with you for what you said about me, Tess. I'm not really a vengeful person."

Randall smothered a laugh, which Chester ignored.

"However," he went on, "I'm big enough to overlook your misunderstanding of my character."

"Thank you, Chester," Tess said, managing to sound perfectly serious.

"How did you get on to that imposter in the first place?" Chester asked.

"That note in Lana's purse—malignant hyperthermia. I couldn't get it out of my mind. It was important or she wouldn't have bothered to write it down. I just couldn't make it fit with anything else I'd learned about Lana. Then, earlier this afternoon, Aunt Dahlia told me that Margaret Stackpole died of malignant hyperthermia, and I knew there was some connection between that note in Lana's purse and Margaret Stackpole's granddaughter, Marisa, but I didn't know what it was. Had Lana meant to warn Marisa that she might have inherited the trait from her grandmother? I wondered. I told myself I'd make sure Marisa knew the potential danger she was in; otherwise, she could die as her grandmother had. Later I realized Marisa—Janet, rather—already knew. But I digress . . . Finally, I thought of the possibility that Marisa was already dead and, once I'd thought of it, I couldn't think of anything else. That's when it occurred to me that that girl we knew as Marisa Stackpole was really somebody else. After that, it was only a matter of getting the information from the Illinois Bureau of Vital Statistics." Looking up at Luke, she added, "Which Luke did masterfully, I must say."

"I'm going to sleep well tonight for the first time since Lana's death," Reva said softly.

"Me, too." Alexis lifted her wrist to peer at her watch. "Gracious, the evening conference session starts in half an hour."

Chester shuffled his feet. "Alexis, may I have a word with you?" His tone was uncharacteristically humble.

"I know what's on your mind, Chester," Alexis said,

"and you'll have to take it up with Harley." She hurried from the room.

Chester followed, looking a little sick.

The others left the parlor one by one, Gertie and Nedra to go home, the others to get ready for the evening conference session. Within moments, Luke and Tess were alone in the room.

He turned her to him and dropped a kiss on her forehead. "Congratulations on solving the case, Detective Darcy. I do have one suggestion, however."

"What's that?"

"The next time you find a body on the premises, let the police handle it."

"I believe I've heard that one before."

"It's still good advice."

"Generally speaking, yes. But Butts might never have solved this case if we hadn't helped him," Tess protested.

"We got lucky. This time. But as you said, you have a business to run. You don't have time to conduct any more murder investigations. Right?"

She smiled. "Right, Luke." The point was moot, anyway. What were the chances of another murder victim ever turning up at Iris House?

He pulled her into his arms. "Now, about this evening."

She looked up at him, a soft smile on her face. "What did you have in mind?"

"Let's retire to the privacy of your apartment for this discussion," he suggested, grabbing her hand and leading the way. "It may take a while."